THE CASE

OF THE

Flashing

Fashion Queen

Dix Dodd Mysteries

THE CASE OF THE

A Dix Dodd Mystery

N.L. WILSON

(the writing team of Norah Wilson and Heather Doherty)

PUBLISHED BY:

SOMETHING SHINY
PRESS
Norah Wilson / Something Shiny Press
P.O. Box 30046, Fredericton, NB, E3B 0H8

Cover by The Killion Group, Inc.
Book Design by Hale Author Services

Note re Bonus Material

Please note that bonus material in the form of an excerpt from Family Jewels, A Dix Dodd Mystery by N.L. Wilson, appears at the end of this book. That bonus material will make this book appear several pages longer than it actually is. Bear that in mind as you approach the end and are anxiously trying to judge how much story is left!

Chapter 1

A LOT OF people specialize.

If you have a toothache you go to the dentist, not the doctor (unless he's a really hot doctor and then you go there first). If you need a new roof, call the roofer. Groceries? Call the grocer. You wouldn't go to a mechanic for your annual pap smear, nor have your OB-GYN under the hood of your … um … car. Okay, bad analogy. But you see where I'm going, right?

The point is, when you have a special job in mind, you call a specialist. And if you live in Marport City and need someone to get to the truth of a matter — and when the matter is private and dear to your heart — you call me.

You see, I'm a private detective. I'm not so new to the business itself, but new to being out on my own. Six months' new. I worked for years at a private detective company called Jones and Associates. The number one company in Marport City. All professional. All business. All men. And no matter how hard I worked there, how brilliantly I put things together (and that would be damn brilliantly, thank you very much), I was always the 'girl'. The one sent to do the coffee runs. The one who ordered office supplies and hunted down the lost files. I never had a real shot at advancing there, despite my many years of service and their many years of promises. So a few months before my fortieth birthday, I set out on my own. Hung up my own shingle.

The boys at Jones and Associates told me I'd never survive, that I'd be hauling my skirted butt back there within the year. Well, it's been six months, and I'm still hanging onto that shingle. Hanging on by my fingernails, mind you, but hanging on.

These days, I specialize in trailing men who cheat, or who are suspected of cheating. I trail them for wives who are wondering about girlfriends, and girlfriends wondering about wives. Overprotective moms, neurotic dads, and yeah, the occasional jealous ex-girlfriend who just has to know. I find out where, when, with whom and if you're really interested — how. I take pictures. I take notes. I check gas gauges, tire treads and odometers. I follow trails left by credit card receipts and miscellaneous bills. I check out alibis.

As you can imagine, it isn't always pretty. But it's always interesting. And some cases aren't always as they seem.

Take for example the case of Jennifer Weatherby, or as I like to call it, The Case of the Flashing Fashion Queen. Who would have known that one phone call, that one seemingly ordinary phone call, would turn into such a mess?

But then, death is always messy. Or rather, murder is messy. Especially when I'm caught smack-dab in the middle of it.

"Hey, Dix. Jennifer Weatherby just phoned to double check our address. I'm guessing her ETA is about two minutes."

Oh, thank God! I glanced up at my assistant. "Thanks, Dylan," I said, as though I'd never doubted she'd show.

Jennifer Weatherby had called me two days ago, on May 30. Called, in fact, just as I was writing out the rent cheque for the landlord, and wincing at how pitifully few dollars remained in my account.

Five thousand dollars. That's what she'd offered me. I'd just about dropped the phone. But Mrs. Weatherby had been clear: five large for a week's worth of work.

But here's the thing — sometimes these hot new clients don't show. Sometimes they call in a fit of anger or jealousy, but when they calm down, they decide they don't need a private detective after all. And often they're too embarrassed to call and cancel. So, yeah, I was more than happy when Dylan told me she was en route.

His message delivered, I expected him to turn and leave. Well, kind of. Dylan Foreman rarely did what was expected.

Good thing he was the best assistant I'd ever had.

Okay, the *only* assistant I'd ever had. And strictly speaking, he wasn't really an assistant. He was an apprentice. All aspiring private investigators have to complete a period of apprenticeship. I'd done mine with Jones and Associates. When Dylan Foreman knocked on my door just a month after I opened for business and laid his story on the table, I couldn't refuse him.

The man had a law degree, on top of a degree in communications and another in criminology. After passing the bar, he was scooped up by one of the top firms in the city and had been well on his way to making a name for himself in criminal law. But all that changed one day when he got a call from a scared kid.

The kid had been abducted by his father, a client of the law firm and a suspected child abuser. Bastard had picked the boy up at school and driven him five hundred miles to another city. Police were searching for him frantically. Dylan had been working late that night when the call came in from the missing child. The kid had hit re-dial on the phone while his father had left him alone to go out for beer. Scared and crying, he'd told Dylan the things his father had been doing to him.

So Dylan called the police, gave them the number that had come up on the call display and they'd had the kid within the half hour. Found the little boy alone and scared, battered and bruised.

Dylan knew what he'd done. The minute he'd picked up the phone to call the cops, he knew his career was effectively over before it ever really got started. But all he could think about was the fact that the client had called earlier in the day and the senior lawyers had done squat to protect that kid.

Needless to say, he got flack. Then he got fired. Eventually, he got disbarred.

"If you had it to do over, would you do the same thing?" I'd asked him.

"In a fucking heartbeat."

I'd hired him on the spot. He worked hard; and thankfully, he worked cheap.

And omigod, he was handsome! And young — all of twenty-eight. Okay, yeah, I had sort of a crush on him, but nothing serious. Nothing that kept me up at night. He was just ... nice to look at.

He was pretty good on the computers, too, up to and including some minor hacking when the situation demanded. He also made a mean cup of coffee (and I liked my coffee mean), and he didn't mind getting his hands dirty when it came to that. Plus, holy hell, my clients *loved* him. If I had a dollar for every time I'd come out of my office to find a dejected damsel crying on his broad shoulders, the male strippers at The Nuts and Bolts next door would be some happy young men. Except the Canadian mint stopped making dollar bills years ago, and it's damned hard to make a loonie stay inside a G-string unless you tuck it ... Well, you get the picture.

Where was I? Ah, yes, Dylan Foreman, and why I tolerated his idiosyncrasies.

Simply put, we were well matched. What I lacked in compassion, Dylan more than made up for. I could deliver the bad-tasting medicine, but it was Dylan who had the bedside manner. He had a sympathetic ear, a compassionate nature, and a way of really listening to women that few men possessed. While I told the women their men were cheating, he told them they deserved so much better than the dogs who cheated on them. They left my office feeling low, and his desk feeling relieved.

"We're in perfect proportion, Dix," he told me once, when I'd remarked on this.

Dylan was handsome in that I'm-not-trying way — chocolate brown eyes, shoulder length brown hair begging to have fingers ran through it. He was built like a basketball player, long, lean and muscular.

And all six foot four of him now stood in my doorway.

Perfect proportion indeed.

"Was there something else you wanted, Dylan?" I fought down the fluster that I was really too old for. Knowing, dammit, that I could always blame it on a hot flash, if need be.

"I was thinking about the business cards." Dylan entered my office and closed the door behind him.

"Oh, no, not again." I leaned back in my chair, coffee cup in hand, and clunked my feet up onto my desk. We'd been making do with those print-it-yourself, perforated thingies, but the time had come to order some real business cards. It was kind of fun, but also kind of becoming a pain in the ass getting them perfect. "I told you, nothing fancy on the cards. Just plain simple: *Dix Dodd, Private Detective.* Address and phone number."

He frowned. "Boring. We need something people will remember. Something that'll make you stand out. You know … something with flair."

"Such as?"

"Dix Dodd, Private Detective. Call me if you think you're getting screwed, or know you're not."

I groaned.

"Come on, Dix! It's perfect. To the point. Unforgettable."

I shook my head. "And completely not going to happen."

We both heard the footsteps in the hallway and our conversation halted. The door to the outer office opened to admit a female. I could see her silhouette through the frosted glass window of my office as she stood beside Dylan's desk. She tipped a hand to her hair, then back down again. She raised a cigarette to her lips, lit a lighter, but pulled both away before she lit the smoke, and before I needed to run out to remind her of the building's no-smoking policy.

"Don't worry," Dylan said, heading for the door. "I'll think of something else for the business cards."

"Thanks, I just want something —"

Without benefit of a knock, my door flew open. Dylan stepped aside before the doorknob caught him in a place that could do damage. My feet thumped to the floor; my chair tipped forward as I sat up straight.

"Dix Dodd?"

"Yes."

"I'm Jennifer Weatherby."

Beside me, Dylan stood dumbstruck. A first, in my experience.

Of course, I didn't acquit myself much better. I pride myself on my unflappable self-control. Pride myself on my smoothness in dealing with all kinds of clientele. I didn't fidget. I didn't blush. And I didn't stutter out of nervousness. But I have to admit I was a little stunned by Mrs. Weatherby's appearance. It's nothing for women to come into the office a bit overdressed to hide from prying eyes. After all, as much as I may not like to admit it, paranoia often plays a large role in the lives of the women who called upon my services. But this chick had gone just a tad overboard. Like, jumped-off-a-cruise-ship-in-the-middle-of-the-Pacific overboard.

Jennifer Weatherby stood just a few inches short of six feet tall in her modest heels. Modest *height*, that is. Nothing else about those violet velvet puppies could be called modest. The hem of the purple dress she wore stopped just above the knee. She wore a wide black belt cinched at the waist, and broad shoulder pads that would have made Darth Vader envious. While the neckline of the dress didn't exactly plunge, it didn't need to. The lady was well endowed. If Mr. Weatherby was cheating, he certainly wasn't a boob man. Mrs. Weatherby tipped a well-manicured index finger to the rim of her wide glasses, pushing them back up on the bridge of her nose. Her blond hair was piled high in a feat of engineering that must have required a ton of product. I braced for the reek of hair spray, but all that wafted toward me was perfume. *Lavender* perfume, of course.

Dylan recovered before I did from this first encounter with the

Flashing Fashion Queen.

"Mrs. Weatherby," he said. "Can I get you a coffee?"

I held my own cup protectively close.

"No, thank you," she said. "I ... I don't tolerate caffeine well. Makes me jumpy." The last thing I wanted to see was this lady jumping.

"Perhaps a juice, Mrs. Weatherby?" I offered.

"No ... thank you," she said shakily. "Nothing for me."

On this cue, Dylan left, closing the door behind him. He'd give us time. Enough time for me to get to the heart of the matter: enough time for an S.O.B. fest, but not enough for a sob fest.

"Please have a seat Mrs. Weatherby."

I could tell she was nervous. She moved to cross her left leg over her right as she sat, then her right over her left. She finally settled on pressing her knees so tightly together I just knew they'd have those little round, red circle things on the inside if and when she ever relaxed them again.

She cleared her throat hoarsely. Man, she must have been crying for days.

"I don't know where to begin."

That was my cue to cut to the chase. "Why do you believe your husband is cheating, Mrs. Weatherby?"

"Jennifer ... please call me Jennifer."

I nodded. "Okay, Jennifer. Why do you believe your husband's cheating?"

"Oh, I don't *believe* my Ned's cheating." She pressed her hands to her impressive chest as she drew a deep breath. "I *know* he's cheating."

I opened my desk drawer and pulled out the pad and paper. I'd long ago learned that clients do not like tape recorders on the best of days, and I didn't bother suggesting one to Jennifer Weatherby. The Weatherby name was well known in Marport City. Ned Weatherby had positioned himself to make a fortune on personal computer safety before anyone even suspected there was a need for such things. But when the viruses and spyware started to hit, he launched his product to the panicking masses just in time to save the businesses that had become so technology-dependent. He'd been a shrewd businessman, buying out his partners just months before he'd patented and launched the product — convincing them cleverly that the company was doomed. Some said Ned Weatherby had unleashed the viruses himself, but nothing was ever proven. Whatever the cause, the effect remained — the Weatherbys were loaded. And in Marport City, loaded meant life in the proverbial fish bowl. Mrs. Weatherby would want her privacy.

"Tell me about the cheating, Mrs. Weather ... I'm sorry, Jennifer." I looked down at my notepad, as always placed upon my lap so the client couldn't see what I was writing. Some people talked more with the eye contact, needing the comforting encouragement to go on. Others, I'd found, talked more without it, needing the smallest pretense of detachment and privacy as they spilled their stories.

"Ned and I have been married for a long time. Almost twenty years. And I ... I thought it was a good marriage. I thought he was happy. I know I was. Who wouldn't be happy with a man like my Neddy?"

Good. She was an eyes-averted talker. As long as she kept talking, I'd keep my gaze lowered.

"But you don't think so anymore?"

I heard her pull a tissue from the box strategically placed on my desk.

"He has a mistress. I'm one hundred percent sure he does."

"You've seen her?"

"Oh, yes. Many times." Her words were muffled through the Kleenex she held to her face, but in my job you get used to tissue-speak.

I was beginning to think Jennifer Weatherby needed a divorce lawyer more than she needed a private dick. The vision of the five thousand dollars growing wings and flying away popped into my head. If she was that sure her Ned was cheating, why did she need me to gather the proof? "Do you have a name?"

She looked up at me startled. "Er, I told you, Jennifer Weatherby."

"No, I mean, do you have a name of the other woman."

She sat up straight. "No, no name. But I've seen her many times. She drives by the house all hours of the day and night. Once when I was out in the front garden having my tea, she slowed her car down, and stared back at me."

I was beginning to have real doubts about this client. "That really doesn't mean —"

"And I've seen them coming out of a motel together. The Underhill Motel."

"The Underhill?"

She nodded, anxiously. "Yes, I was out shopping one day and saw Ned leaving there with this ... this floozy."

'Floozy'. That word always struck me funny and I bit down on my lip to kill the giggle. I always pictured an intoxicated duck whenever I heard it.

I knew the place. The Underhill Motel was one of the older motels in the city, known for its cheap rooms and its hourly rates. A lot of the call girls work out of it. I made a mental note to check with some of my contacts. But it struck me that whatever Ned Weatherby was up to, and whomever he was up to it with, he apparently wasn't out to impress them — not at the Underhill.

"Is it possible," I asked, "that your husband was employing a prostitute? Maybe this was just a one-time thing? Not a mistress but a —"

"No! Absolutely not! I'm sure she's more than just a prostitute. She loves Ned. She *has* to love Ned. I mean, who wouldn't love my Neddy-bear."

I looked down on the doodles on the legal pad — tight circles usually grouped in two, and ladders going to nowhere. Something that looked like demonic chicken tracks. No, wait ... those were webbed feet. Duck tracks, then, wending crazily around the bottom corner of the page. And one big, block lettered word — NOTACHANCE.

Well, now it was a word.

I had serious doubts about this case. Usually clients wanted proof and confirmations of suspicions. Mrs. Weatherby appeared to have both. The other angle, I knew, would be that she wanted blackmail material. And, okay, though it wasn't my favorite thing to participate in, it did up the ante a bit more. "What is it you're looking for from me then, Mrs. Weatherby? I mean, if you're sure Ned is cheating, what can I do to help you out?"

"I want you to follow Ned for a week. I want his every move documented. His whereabouts recorded.

"Here's what you need." The Flashing Fashion Queen snapped open her purse and dumped its contents onto my desk. *Holy Hannah.* I could not believe what this woman toted around. Six paper-wrapped tampons (in different sizes, no less), four different shiny tubes of lipstick, foundation, blush ... There were packages of bobby pins and even a small can of hair spray. The woman was a walking feminine first-aid kit. Of course, among the jumble was an envelope marked for Dix Dodd. This she handed to me as she began piling the rest back into her purse.

"I've enclosed Ned's itinerary for this week. Or rather what he says he'll be doing this week. And I need you to photograph him everywhere."

"When he's with another woman?"

"Even when he's not."

I looked at her skeptically. Now the winged five thou was flying above my head twittering, 'Catch me if you can!'

"I know my husband, Ms. Dodd. And I love him desperately."

"But if he's —"

She handed me the second envelope — this one pulled from a deep pocket of her purple dress. "That's five thousand dollars. And there'll be five thousand more at the end of the week. That's ten grand for one week's work, Ms. Dodd. Surely, that's worth a few extra rolls of film. And a few less questions."

Surely it was. I picked up the package.

"I just have one question, Jennifer. What does this woman ... this other woman, look like?"

She swallowed hard, and wet her lips. "She's ... she's about your height. Slender. Blond hair, hazel eyes."

Hazel eyes? How close of a look had Jennifer Weatherby gotten?

"Oh, I forgot to tell you, she's threatened me. Several times she's called the house telling me she wanted me out of the way."

I blinked, then stared at her. "This might be a matter for the police then, Jennifer."

"No, it's a matter for you, Dix. I have faith in you.

Chapter 2

To say I did the happy dance when Jennifer Weatherby left my office would be the understatement of the year. I did the cookie-dough-right-out-of-the-package two step, the I-got-the-pool-to-myself cha cha cha.

Ten thousand dollars in cold, hard cash for a single week's work! And five of it already warming my pocket.

This would be my biggest payday ever. And all I had to do was follow one of Marport City's most successful citizens around for a week. From what I knew of Ned Weatherby, I really didn't think I'd be digging up all that much dirt, but what the heck? Despite his reputation for being a bastard in business, he didn't have one for being a bastard with the ladies. But it was Jennifer's money. And for ten large, I'd give the lady what she wanted. Lots and lots of pictures. Documentation. Proof was in the pudding, as they say. I just wasn't so very sure the pudding was going to be licked off any interesting body parts.

According to the itinerary she'd left me, Jennifer Weatherby wanted me to start checking out her husband that very night. That gave me just hours to get my digital camera ready, the voice recorder charged. We only had two other cases on the go, and I left them in Dylan's capable hands. I even managed to sneak in a few hours' sleep before I started what I assumed would be a long, boring case. A long, boring week.

For the most part, it was just that. When Ned was home with Jennifer, I dozed in vehicles (the various cars and vans I borrowed from those who owed me favors, or those to whom I was now indebted), always parking nearby so that when Mr. Weatherby left, Dix Dodd was on his tail. I lived on greasy fast food and coffee so mean it spit back.

Thanks to a listening device Mrs. Weatherby volunteered to plant on the phone in her husband's den (the legality of which was questionable, strictly speaking), I recorded conversations between Ned Weatherby and his mother (loved the flowers dear but you really shouldn't have), Ned and his old army buddies (did men never outgrow toilet humor?), his lawyer Jeremy Poole, whom I'd heard of, his accountant Tucker Flaherty, whom I'd never heard of, and three conversations with an unfortunate caterer — a Mr. Kenny Kent — who just couldn't seem to get it right. And I recorded endless conversations between Ned and his secretary Luanne Laney.

On hands and knees, I snuck through the bushes on the golf course as I followed Ned Weatherby around. I trailed my mark into his church when he went for choir practice, slinging on a gown and auditioning myself when the pastor — a serious young fellow by the name of Pastor Fitz Ravenspire — found me lurking in the pews. (I must say, for a man of the cloth, he sure didn't mince words when it came to my singing talents.) I waited outside the men's room at so many ball games, the beer-and-nuts guy thought I was trying to pick him up. Boring few days. Yep, exactly what I expected. And when Ned Weatherby's lights went out at night, I lay down exhausted in the car seat and drifted off with the smell of vinyl and ass drifting up my nostrils. Drifted into complacency. Boring. Boring. BORING!

So anyway, did I mention I'm an idiot?

Because boring lasted all of five days, then went out with a bang.

Every evening, Dylan met with me. Between six and eight, when Ned Weatherby headed home and I followed at a discreet distance in whatever vehicle I could wangle, I would call my assistant. As soon as Ned turned down Ashfield Drive with its row of humongous houses, I'd hit #1 on my autodial. Dylan would meet me down the block from the Weatherby home — close enough that we could see the driveway, far enough away so that we appeared to be visiting elsewhere. And of course, always parked in a slightly different location.

Dylan would slide into the passenger seat and the two of us would go over what was happening at the office. A quick study, he knew not to bring the overdue bills along, not even the ones where the friendly reminders had turned considerably more hostile. Those would be taken care of soon enough anyway. Mostly he would fill me in on our other two cases that were on the board.

Why not do that whole thing over the phone, you're thinking, rather than arranging this nightly tête-à-tête? Because I'd have starved to death. Mrs. Weatherby had insisted I conduct the entire surveillance personally, and given how much money she was paying me, I wasn't about to quibble. So to keep continuity, I was reliant on Dylan to bring me enough stakeout food to get me through the night. When this case was over, I never wanted to see another wrapped burger or oversized shake as long as I lived.

Each evening as we met up, Dylan left his window down a little lower, and pushed up against the passenger door a little closer. By this fifth night, he was practically hanging his head out the window. "Gee, Dix," he said, exaggerating a gag and waving a hand in front of his nose. "Wonder why you're alone on a Friday night."

Did I mention I desperately needed a shower?

It was just after seven and my mark was home. It had been a busy day for Ned, but I'd known that going into it. Jennifer had inked it in on the now grease-stained and worn itinerary she'd provided. *Friday: meet with J. Poole 9am his offices, 11:30 lunch meeting with potential clients from Toronto — expected to go into the afternoon, 4:15 massage at gym/meet for racquetball if time permits.*

Dylan picked up the wrinkled itinerary and looked it over. "Did you follow him into the massage?"

"Hardly!"

"Dix, I'm surprised at you," he said. "And frankly, a little disappointed."

I sighed. "It's a restricted gym. Men only. Even the staff are men."

He waited.

I opened the glove compartment and pulled out my fake mustache. "Good thing I can pass for a guy when I have to." Which of course, is really quite easy — memorize a random fact about some big-boobed starlet, tell a good flatulence joke (and under pain of death, never use the word flatulence), and say, "How 'bout them Blue Jays/Leafs/Raptors?". And of course, pray you don't have to go for a pee.

Dylan lifted an eyebrow. "Tell me you didn't give him the massage."

"Hell, no. But I was the bungling incompetent trainee who delivered the towels to the room."

He nodded. "Now, that's the Dix Dodd I know and respect. And did our Mr. Weatherby behave?"

"Model customer. Just what you'd expect from a choirboy. He even kept his t-shirt on."

"You're kidding!"

"I'm not."

This had surprised me. In fact, a lot of things I found out about Ned Weatherby this week had surprised me. The stories around Marport City always painted him as not just a shrewd businessman, but a bit of a prick about it. Before trailing him, I could have easily pictured this guy elbowing little old ladies aside if he spied a quarter in the middle of the street, or cheerfully drowning puppies if puppy-killing paid. But I'd witnessed no such bad conduct. If anything, Ned Weatherby was too good to be true. Literally. Because I'd seen too much to believe *too good to be true* could be true.

I watched as Dylan — a good six feet with a few inches to spare — attempted to get comfortable in the passenger seat of the vehicle-du-jour, a subcompact Hyundai. He put his left ankle on his right knee then down again. With one foot on the floor, he attempted to hike the other up on the dashboard, but that wasn't about to happen. Finally, he just gave up and let his feet stay flat in the nut-crushing confines of the car.

Good. Served him right for so indelicately pointing out that I stank. It sort of leveled the playing field, seeing him sitting there with his folded knees nearly touching his chin. My satisfaction was short-lived, however, because he found the lever on the side of his seat and reclined it.

Oh, yikes!

In this half-reclining, totally sexy pose, he sipped his own super-sized drink and rattled the ice in the cup. "You'll be pleased to know things are under control at the office."

The office. Right. I paused to sip my drink. "The McGarvie case?"

"You nailed it. The guy was cheating with her best friend." Dylan said. "Lori Lee McGarvie won't be marrying that dog. She's moving on and not looking back."

"Your words?"

He beamed with pride. "Hers."

"What about Roberta Street?"

"Hitting the road."

Ha ha. I poked the ice in my drink with my straw. "Without her cheating boyfriend, I hope."

"Actually, with Lori Lee McGarvie."

"Excuse me?"

I blinked wide as Dylan flashed a sugar-eating grin. He locked his hands behind his head. "I have a sense about these things. And I just love happy endings."

He did. Believe in happy endings, that is. Of course, if he stayed in this business long enough, he'd wise up.

Dylan nodded toward the house where Ned Weatherby had yet to enter. The millionaire was outside still, wandering around the gardens in the early evening light. He picked at the flowers and examined the shrubs. He pulled the rare weed that the gardener had missed.

"Why doesn't he go in?"

"He does this every night," I said, sticking my cold drink in the cup holder and wiping my condensation-dampened fingers on my jeans. "Fiddles around outside for a while. He'll stay out there until the sheers pull back and Jennifer knocks on the window."

"Regular green thumb, is he?"

"He's a lot of things." I hauled out the photographs from the week and handed them to him. Most of them were taken with a very sharp telephoto lens that would have given any paparazzi an orgasm. Ned in meetings with his staff looking annoyed at times, perplexed at others, never quite happy about the discussions on the table. Ned with his lawyer having a business lunch at Chez Lenore, and heading to the racquetball court after. Ned at the dentist, the jewelry store. But never at the Underhill Motel. And the closest he got to a blond babe all week was his ready-to-retire secretary Luanne Laney, and she was more silver than blond.

There was one photograph that was out of place. A hellishly angry one that I'd shuffled to the bottom of the pile before handing the pics to Dylan. I watched his eyes as he riffled through them and came to this picture.

"This guy . . ." Dylan pointed to an older gentleman standing beside Weatherby in the photo. "This guy I've seen before." The two were standing beside Ned's BMW. And even from the still shot, the anger of the stranger was evident. His hands were fisted, his face red.

"That's Billy Star," I said.

"Did you get an audio on this exchange?"

"No. Wasn't close enough. And he's obviously no blond chick so I don't think Jennifer would be too concerned with that."

Dylan flipped once more through the pictures. "Here," he said, pointing to the one of the boardroom gathering. It had taken some roof climbing, fancy angling and a fifty-dollar bribe to get that shot through the window, but I was nothing if not resourceful. "That's the same guy sitting to the left of Weatherby."

"Good eye." I smiled like a mama cat watching her kitten nab its first mouse.

No, not a *mama* cat. Definitely feline, though. Hell, as I sat there with Dylan, I could almost hear myself purring.

"Man, he even looks angry here in the boardroom," Dylan said. "Controlled but pissed-off. That guy's got some serious attitude with ol' Ned."

"Billy Star works at Weatherby Industries. Top floor. His office is right next door to Ned's."

"Not after this, I take it." Dylan flipped again to the picture of an angry Star giving Ned the one finger salute.

"That's what I would have thought too. But this gentlemanly exchange happened yesterday, Thursday. And I saw Billy strolling back in to Weatherby Industries again this morning."

"Wonder what they were fighting about?" Dylan mused, echoing my very thoughts.

I was curious, too. Damn curious. Mentally I began building scenarios and checking off possibilities. Were they fighting about business? Old money? New money? Maybe the blond bombshell Mrs. Weatherby suspected her husband of boinking was playing honey in the middle — hottie in the middle? — with these two. But then I thought Mrs. Weatherby was being paranoid, didn't I? *Didn't I?* The only way I'd know for sure would be to check it out. The winged money Jennifer Weatherby had given me, coupled with that she had promised, tweeted their chastisement as they flew above my head.

"We'll never know what they're fighting about, because that's not what we're being paid to find out."

"Yeah, but doesn't it drive you nuts, Dix? The not knowing stuff like this. Isn't that why you got into the business in the first place?"

I got into this business because after twenty years of working in an office with chauvinistic men, they still treated me like the new kid on the block. No, the new *girl* on the block. I got into the business because I was tired of watching newbies come in and get promoted over me just because they had dicks. I'd had enough of not being taken seriously because of the way I looked. I knew I could do better. Damn right well knew it.

I shrugged the tension from my shoulders. "Yeah, a little. It comes with the territory — insatiable curiosity. The need to know more than you need to know."

"What's your intuition saying about this Billy Star guy? How do you read him?"

That's another thing I liked about Dylan, he didn't laugh off female intuition the way some guys did. I let my head roll back into the seat and closed my eyes, not just because they were tired, but sitting this close to Dylan ... sometimes I just needed the pretense of privacy myself.

"He's a hothead. That I'll give him, but ..."

As I pondered how best to sum up my feelings about Billy Star, Dylan must have figured I'd drifted off, because the next think I knew, I felt his hand on my arm and his low-voiced whisper in my ear.

"Dix? You asleep?"

The tingle that went down my spine crawled around me, gripped me. I felt my nipples tighten under my t-shirt.

Holy frig!

It had been a long time since the touch of a man had made me react like that. And that had ended badly. In heartache and anger and many nights cursing myself as much as I cursed him. And damn it, as much as I hated to admit it, a night or two wondering where he'd gotten to. I was the one who always searched the faces at the airports, and glanced back over my shoulder at the movies when I heard a certain laugh. And, I reminded myself, the one who'd sworn never again.

"I'm awake." I sat up straight.

"Ned Weatherby just went inside."

"Did he pick a rose from the garden?"

"Yeah, but Jennifer didn't knock on the window. Ned just —"

Dylan's words were cut off by the panic-stricken scream of Ned Weatherby, "Help! Somebody help!"

My eyes saucered as I looked at Ned Weatherby running down his neat stone-paved driveway. His face was contorted with shock. Blood reddened his shirt. He still held the rose in his hands — the thorns cutting into it, his blood dripping down from it.

"My wife ... somebody's killed my wife. Somebody help!"

Even as we jumped from the car and ran, I was on my cell dialing 911.

"77 Ashfield Drive. Yes, Ashfield Drive, and hurry. I think there's been a murder."

I hung up quickly before the emergency dispatcher could ask me a million questions I didn't have the answers to. Yet.

Yes, I'd be speaking to the police. I had no doubt about that. I had to tell them what I knew, about Jennifer's visit to my office a few short days ago. But for now, I had to get into that house before they did. See for myself. And it was more than insatiable curiosity; this was personal. This was my client.

Dylan and I ran up the driveway together, but he reached Ned first. Reading my intent, he turned Ned around so that his back was to me as I dashed into the house through the open front door.

The Weatherby home was impressive. Even in my heart-thumping state, I couldn't help but take in that fact. Great high ceilings, marble flooring in the foyer. The house was huge, and from where I stood, there must have been four or five different doorways or hallways before me. It was like a maze. But I didn't need a map to tell me which way to find Jennifer Weatherby, I just followed the trail of blood. The trail that started right at my feet.

Already I could hear the sirens, and from just outside the door, the sounds of Dylan gently grilling Ned about what he'd seen.

Quickly I followed along the foyer and through a set of open double doors.

And oh shit, there she was. Jennifer Weatherby lay face down on the floor of what appeared to be a study. A fire burned in the fireplace, incongruously cheery. Two glasses of wine — one full, the other half full — sat on an occasional table between two tall wingback chairs. The plain white pantsuit she wore was soaked through with blood — two dark bullet holes torn in the fabric. One tan sandal remained on her foot, while the other lay askew on the hardwood floor.

I rushed to her and bent to check for a pulse. But before my fingers even touched her neck, I knew what I'd find. No pulse. No life. Just the cold feel of death on my hands. And Jennifer's blood.

"Oh Jennifer," I whispered. I knew I'd get no response, but I had to say it. "I'm so sorry."

Her words rang in my ears. The words I'd so easily dismissed as she'd said them when leaving my office. *"Oh, I forgot to tell you, she's threatened me. Several times she's called the house telling me she wants me out of the way."*

Guilt lumped itself into an indigestible ball in my stomach. Dammit, I should have done something.

Oh, sure, I'd warned her it sounded like a matter for the police, but when she shrugged it off, I hadn't pressed it. Mainly because I was convinced Jennifer Weatherby was just being paranoid. And now she lay dead before me. All because I hadn't taken her seriously.

I stood up, a new determination burning in my gut. I would find that mysterious blond mistress no matter how long I had to tail Ned Weatherby. No matter what it took. Because Jennifer's other words rang through my mind also.

"It's a matter for you, Dix. I have faith in you."

Chapter 3

Yes, I'm cynical. I'll be the first to admit it. And I have a chip on my shoulder when it comes to some men. Okay, most men. But for good reason. Some days just go from bad to worse to argh!, and when they do, damned if there isn't always a man smack in the middle of it.

Detective Richard Head was one such man. To say that he'd been a thorn in my side from time to time would be like saying Johnny Depp was just a little bit hot in that pirate costume.

You see, Richard Head and I had a history. No, not a romantic one. God forbid! I wasn't his type, and he sure as hell wasn't mine. Our history was one based on mutual dislike, and mutual distrust. We'd flipped each other the finger so often it had become automatic, a reflexive action.

Police Detective Head didn't like private detectives, and he liked female private detectives even less. And he absolutely loathed a certain female private detective who happened to catch him getting a little too close with the new dispatcher at the 10th precinct awhile back. Actually, Richard's ex, Glory, had been a client of Jones and Associates two years ago. Or rather had attempted to be a client. But when she couldn't pay the hefty retainer fee, I'd volunteered my services — off-hours and off the books. I know, I know, not very businesslike. But Glory was a sweetheart. She was only working part time and just didn't have the money. So I helped her out. And it worked out for both of us. She found out her suspicions of a cheating husband were true. And when I went out on my own, she sent a couple of her friends my way — she had been that impressed with my work.

But Detective Richard Head had not been impressed by my work. Glory had kicked him out on his ear when I handed over the incriminating evidence. Saddled with alimony payments, Richard had been forced to move in with his mother.

His *mother*. God, I'd almost forgotten that part. No wonder the man hated me.

But my point is, Richard Head never forgave me for doing my job and catching him red-handed (or ass-handed, if you prefer).

And I'd never wanted him to.

Did I mention I have a chip on my shoulder?

By now, you've no doubt figured out which police detective caught this call.

Yep.

By the time Detective Head arrived, the patrol response guys had been there probably five minutes. Ned Weatherby had gotten control of himself. Sorta. By that I mean he wasn't screaming now so much as crying softly (thank you, Dylan). The police had gotten him inside before too much commotion was caused. Ned kept shaking his head and asking, why, why, why would someone want to do this to his Jennifer? He looked bewildered, lost, his bottom lip quivering as he snuffed back the tears. At least he was acting that way. For all I knew, he and his mistress were jointly responsibly for Jennifer's demise.

I would find out. I sure as hell wouldn't leave it to Marport City's finest.

Of course, Detective Head looked about as thrilled to see me as I was to see him. When the first officer on the scene explained that I'd touched the victim to check for a pulse and that the bloody tracks on the floor were mine, Detective Head launched into a furious attack on me for contaminating his crime scene, compromising the evidence, etc. I fired back that if I hadn't checked for life signs, he'd be tearing my head off right now for failing to come to the aid of a victim whose life might have been saved by some timely first aid.

Midway through my counter-attack, I saw his expression change. The fury that twisted his features just moments ago was gone. And just like that, it clicked: he'd like nothing more than to pin this murder on me! Considering I was standing beside the dead body, the victim's blood on my hands, it's a wonder he wasn't standing there with a first-class woody.

Oh boy.

Minutes behind the many wailing police sirens (guess the boys in blue figured they could afford a few extra cars to a murder scene on Ashfield Drive), came the flashily painted media vans. They parked all along the street, contrasting startlingly with the BMWs and Hummers and Lexuses (Lexi?) of Ashfield Drive. Tanned reporters in their fresh-pressed suits and their gelled hair leapt from the vans before they'd barely rolled to a stop. They grilled the neighbors, who were now milling about, for details, staying off the Weatherby property, but precariously close to the yellow police tape. A few officers — the younger ones — strolled into camera range, trying to look appropriately serious and authoritative in the background. But hell, all they needed was a "Hi mom, it's me!" sign.

No one was admitted to the Weatherby house, of course, except for officials — cops, forensic specialists, ambulance crew, the ME from the Coroner's Office. Well, hardly anyone. I was still inside. From where Detective Head had parked me on the living room couch with a less-than-polite 'stay there', I watched the activity outside through the picture window, gazing through sheers that made everyone look ghostly.

Right behind the news crews, a brand-new Porsche pulled up and an anxious-looking Jeremy Poole leapt out. Gawd, he looked just like his media pictures. Did he ever take off his suit and tie? The lawyer approached one of the uniforms on crowd control, nervously running a hand though his hair as he did. From where I sat, I could hear the conversation between Poole and the young officer drifting in the front door, which still stood open.

"I'm Mr. Weatherby's lawyer. I demand to see my client."

In his grief-stricken state, Ned Weatherby had called his lawyer? Interesting.

"I'll need some identification, sir," the officer said.

"Oh, for heaven's sake." Obviously ticked that the officer hadn't recognized him, he reached into his back pocket for his wallet. He began fumbling through cards, dropping one after the other while the young officer waited, and the media zoomed in.

"It's all right, officer. I can vouch for Mr. Poole."

I glanced up to see Ned Weatherby framed in the open doorway. Apparently, I wasn't the only one who'd been watching Jeremy Poole's arrival. I flicked my gaze back to the scene outside in time to see every cameraman and reporter snap their heads in Ned's direction as though their necks were rigged together.

"Shut the fuckin' door!" Detective Head yelled.

But it was too late. At least a dozen photographs had been snapped and every newspaper in the province — hell, every newspaper in the country probably — would have a picture of a distraught Ned Weatherby admitting his lawyer into the house. Speculation would roll like a donut downhill.

"Oh, Jeremy, it's horrible!" Ned said, clutching his lawyer's arm and drawing him inside. "Someone's ... someone's killed Jennifer."

"There, there, Ned. I know," Poole said. "I'm ... I'm so very sorry."

"Who would want to do this to Jennifer?" Ned looked like a child asking if the boogeyman had really snuffed out Santa Claus — desperate for answers in the land of disbelief.

"Who's in charge here?" Even in trying to be commanding, the lawyer's voice sounded edged with panic.

Detective Head stepped forward. "I am."

"Your name, sir?"

"They call him Dick Head," I called from my assigned seat on the sofa.

If looks could kill, the medical examiner would have had another body to deal with, but I held my ground under the detective's glare. Okay, that probably was not the smartest thing for me to have done, but I wanted Detective Head to get the message loud and clear. I wasn't about to roll over and do tricks for him on this. I wasn't scared because I had nothing to be scared of. And I wasn't looking for an ally in him.

And I sure as hell wouldn't be intimidated.

"I'll deal with you later, Dodd," Head scowled at me before turning to Jeremy Poole. "I'm in charge, and the name's, *Richard* Head."

"Yes, very funny," Jeremy said, obviously thinking the name was a joke of some sort at his expense.

I snorted a laugh.

"Goddamn it —"

"Jeremy," Ned Weatherby interjected, "This is Detective Richard Head."

The lawyer paled. "Really?"

"Really."

"My apologies, Detective Head." Poole cleared his throat. "I'm Mr. Weatherby's lawyer. If you have any questions for my client, you'll ask them in my presence. We'll be in the kitchen."

"Why do you think Weatherby needs a lawyer?"

Good one. Damn, I hated giving that guy credit, even in my mind.

"Mr. Weatherby is not merely a client. He's also a personal friend." Poole laid a hand on Weatherby's shoulder. "Come on, Ned. I'll fix us some tea."

I guess Poole wanted Head to know where things stood also, because with that they turned their backs on the detective and headed toward the kitchen.

"Did you call Billy Star yet?" I heard Poole whisper as they passed me.

My ears perked up as I recalled an angry Billy Star from the pics I'd shown Dylan earlier.

Ned's shoulders sagged. "Oh, Christ, no, I haven't called anyone. I … I suppose I'd better call him. That's one call I sure as hell don't want to make. And … and I need to call Luanne too. I need to call her first."

The kitchen door swung closed slowly behind Ned and his lawyer, and all Head could do was watch it close him out.

He kicked the sofa. "Pansy. Did you see the shoes on that lawyer guy? He must spend on loafers what I spend on my whole fuckin' wardrobe."

"It's going to be a long night, isn't it, Detective?"

"Shut up, Dodd."

By the time midnight rolled around, every light in the Weatherby mansion blazed. Almost every inch of the house had been dusted for fingerprints. Detective Head had personally overseen the CSI's work as they swabbed my hands and seized my bloody-soled runners and neatly tagged and bagged the evidence. He looked on as they fingerprinted me, and smiled as they took a hair sample (more like a handful of it). If there had been a way he could have gotten away with it, I'm sure he would have ordered a cavity search.

"Let's go over it one more time, Dodd." Detective Head chewed on a toothpick like he was warming up for an Olympic sport. *Oh, geez, he must be trying to quit smoking again.*

Could this day get any worse?

"Shall I go slower this time, Detective?"

"Just keep it up." He glared at me. "You're in serious shit here, Dodd. And your smart mouth isn't doing you any favors today. But that's just fine with me. Just fine. I'd like nothing better than to throw you away for a good long time."

"You can't just —"

"I can do what I damn well please."

"Ah, there's this little thing called 'the law'. You might have heard of it."

Head leaned in close. Close enough so that no one else could hear him, and so that I could smell mint on his breath. Apparently, his tooth-picks were flavored. "I never liked you, Dodd," he said. "I don't like anyone who makes their living by being a rat."

Sure, blame the rat for nailing the snake.

He leaned closer still. "Which is why it's going to give me so much pleasure to personally see to it that you rot in jail for this crime."

"Even though I didn't do it, Detective?" I kept my voice calm; I didn't so much as twitch a muscle. My eyes were clear and steady. But on the inside, things were liquefying as fear spread. "We both know I didn't kill Jennifer."

He eased back, a tight smile on his face. "I know no such thing."

"I told you — several times, in fact — Jennifer Weatherby hired me to follow her husband."

"Yeah right! She hired you to trail her husband, because of some mysterious blond mistress that nobody else has ever seen or heard tell of. How do we know she exists? Maybe she's one of them ET types, huh? Straight from the planet Pleasesavemyass."

"You're an asshole, Head. And you look the part, too. It's a wonder your mother doesn't dress you better."

His fists clenched, but he was smart enough to unclench them. "You know what I think, Dodd? I think you've got a thing for Ned Weatherby yourself."

My jaw dropped. "You can't be serious."

"I don't think anyone hired you. I think you've got the hots for moneybags and that's why you've been stalking him. That's why you had the pictures and all those notes. Jesus, you followed him into the locker room! We got laws about stalking in Ontario. You might have heard of that."

I tried for calm. Fought for control. "You know you're reaching for straws, don't you, Dick?"

He glared at me.

"Jennifer Weatherby came into my office just this past Monday," I continued. "She was extremely upset. She was convinced her husband was cheating on her. And she wanted me to follow him for a week to see if her suspicions were correct. That's what I did. Thus, the pictures."

"How convenient. What did you do Dodd, sneak back here when Ned was in a meeting? Wait till he left for work then sneak in here and shoot Mrs. Weatherby? Get her out of the way so you could have her husband?"

I bit down on the other words — harsh, angry, four-letter words — that threatened to color the room. I was losing my patience. "Look," I said. "You can waste your time harassing me. You can diddle the night away because of some personal vendetta. So be it. But damn it, *Dick*, there is a murderer out there. She threatened Jennifer, and apparently has made good on those threats. So what are you going to do about it?"

The smile on his face slowly widened as he stared at me. He chuckled. Chuckled deeper. Then he laughed out loud.

Okay, when Richard Head laughs out loud, everyone hears him. Everyone turns and stares. And he knows it. He starts out putting his hands on his belly. He squares his shoulders. And he tosses his head back as if his thick, red neck were made of rubber. Then he bellows his ha-ha's. Red-face roars them. This theatrical-grade performance will go on for a good minute, while everyone within hearing distance — let's say about eight square miles — runs to see what's so damn funny.

And yes, every damn cop in the house came into the living room where he sat across from me.

He wiped the laugh-tears from his eyes. "Okay, then Dixieland, or whatever your name is . . ."

"My name is *Dix*."

"I don't really give a rat's ass what your name is. Listen to me very carefully, Dodd," he said. The room was so still and quiet his words couldn't be mistaken. Nor could their meaning. "Let me tell you a story . . . Let me tell you what I've got here. I've got one dead woman, to wit, Jennifer Weatherby. I also have one wealthy widower. And I look at a woman like you, alone and wanting a man. *Needing* a man — if you know what I mean. A woman like yourself would find Ned Weatherby quite appealing. Quite the catch for an old —"

"Now, wait a minute —"

"I'm not finished."

"Fine. What's your theory?" I sat back. "Go on then, Dickie."

He let the name slide. He was having too much fun. Everyone watched the exchange.

"So we have one dead woman. One wealthy man, and one stalking spinster."

The fucker was so baiting me.

"And what do we find in the possession of the obsessed stalker? Photos. Notes. Evidence that she's been going out of her way to follow a married man — one that she could only love from afar." He put the back of a hand to his forehead in a mock swoon. "Hell, Dodd, you've even been sleeping outside his house! How pathetic is that?"

Damn him! I'd offered up my notes and photos, figuring they'd prove

I was working for Mrs. Weatherby. Instead, Dickhead was twisting the evidence against me. Good thing I hadn't told him about bugging the phone. He'd have slapped the cuffs on and carted me off to jail already for that alone.

I took a deep breath, spoke slowly, deliberately. "I told you, Jennifer Weatherby hired me to follow her husband. She said he was cheating on her."

"Ned says they were happily married."

"Jennifer said they weren't."

"So that's why they were planning their 20th wedding anniversary party for tomorrow? That's why the invitations were sent out, and Kenny Kent, the caterer, booked? That's why Ned bought a $50,000 diamond ring?" He held up a receipt, one he'd apparently found in Jennifer's study. "And why she bought him a Rolex watch just last week? Because they weren't getting along?"

Holy shit.

"Holy shit."

"It was getting to you, wasn't it, Dix? It was getting to you to watch the man you secretly love so in love with his wife. That's why you killed her, wasn't it, Dodd?"

I waited for a sound. There wasn't one. No one would have breathed out loud at that moment. Especially not me.

"I was hired."

"Prove it."

"I will," I said. "Just as soon as I get out of here."

The toothpick broke between Detective Head's teeth.

"Look, I've cooperated with your investigation. Now, either charge me with something or let me go, Detective. I have work to do. I have a job to do. A job I'm damn good at, as you're well aware." Not to mention that I had to get my ass out of the fire. My grin ached, but it held. And I stared at Head just as hard as he stared at me.

"Get out of here, Dodd," he snarled. "But don't leave town."

A half dozen retorts jumped to mind, all ending in 'fuck you', but for once, I said nothing.

I grabbed my jacket, and crossed the room on legs of rubber from sitting too long. My ass had fallen asleep, and I hated that. My hand was on the doorknob, and I was almost out, when Detective Head had to toss one more piece of crap my way.

"I'll need the proof, Dodd. I'll need the paperwork."

I turned. "What do you mean?"

"You claim that Jennifer Weatherby hired you for ten thousand dollars, and that she already paid you half. I'll need to see something. Carbon of the receipt you gave her, the copy of the contract for services." He smiled. "I'm sure that won't be a problem for you."

"Of course it's not a problem!" I snapped back at him.

Big problem, big problem, big problem.

Often clients don't want any paper trail back to them. Jennifer was — had been, rather — one of those. Thus we had no contract, and she hadn't wanted a receipt. My mind whirled. I could still produce a receipt. I'd just started a new receipt book two weeks ago. I could re-copy the other receipts, then slide Jennifer Weatherby's in on the right date, in the event my receipt books were seized by the police. Of course, if the thought occurred to me, it would occur to Dickhead, too. No way he'd buy it, especially without a corresponding deposit record. He'd just go looking for the other people to whom I'd issued receipts and do a forensic comparison of the carbon with the original. I cursed myself for not depositing the cash the very next day. Instead, I'd pocketed five hundred, stashed the rest of it in the monstrosity of a fireproof filing cabinet at the office, and headed out to tail Ned Weatherby. Dylan had even offered to deposit it for me, but I told him to leave it there for a few more days. That way he could bring me more cash if I needed it, which he'd done when I'd had to come up with another hundred to buy access for that boardroom shot. Dammit all to hell.

"Good," Head said. "Because otherwise, I'd have to believe I was right about you, Dodd. That you had the hots for Ned Weatherby, and that's why you were stalking him. And that's why you murdered his wife."

Detective Head snapped another toothpick into his mouth.

I turned on my heel and left, imagining the shit-eating grin he was no doubt wearing.

Oh just smoke, *damn you!*

Chapter 4

EARLIER IN THE evening, after Dylan had been grilled by Detective Head, I'd told him to go home. By that time, it was already 10 p.m., and since we'd need to be sharp in the days ahead, I ordered him to get some rest.

"Home. Straight home. Do not pass go; do not collect two hundred dollars. Home, Mr. Foreman."

It was well after midnight before I got away myself. Of course, I had no intention of taking my own advice. I stopped by my place just long enough for a power shower (not to mention the first leisurely pee I'd had since I began this case) and a change of clothes before driving to the office.

When I pulled into the parking lot and saw a light shining from my office window. *Dylan.* I should have known he'd ignore my instructions.

Despite myself, I felt a little warm and fuzzy.

Then I caught the drift of my thoughts and got a grip. Oh, man, it must have been a harder night than I'd thought. Dix Dodd didn't do warm and fuzzy. I was cynical. Chippy. Tough as shoe leather.

To underscore my 'tude, I climbed out of my car and slammed the door. Then slammed it again because the freakin' thing never did close right.

I spat on the asphalt because that felt about right, squared my shoulders and marched across the moonlit parking lot towards the building. And I mean across the parking lot. I'd parked as far away from the building as I could, a practice I'd started in an effort to work some much-needed exercise into my day, but which had become habit.

It had rained and the asphalt shone black beneath my feet. The air was fresh, clean and damp. And appreciated. Really appreciated for the first time in … ever. Fear of jail can do that to a person — make them take notice of the finer things.

Yes, it was true. Dix Dodd, hard-assed PI, was scared this time. Not that I'd cop to it. Nosiree. I could hide it very well, thank you, under my smart mouth and fuck-you attitude. No one would be the wiser.

But, dammit, things didn't look good for me.

There was no paperwork from Jennifer Weatherby to prove that she'd hired me. And Richard Head would do whatever he could to prove my guilt.

I dashed moisture from my cheeks. Goddamn rain.

It was shortly after one in the morning when I let myself into the building and climbed the dimly lit stairway to my office.

"You look scared," were the first words out of Dylan's mouth.

I snorted a laugh. "Nah. That's just caffeine withdrawal."

He handed me a cup of coffee and perched himself on the edge of my desk. He half sat/half stood with one foot firmly planted on the ground and the other dangling lazily off the side of the desk. He looked tired. Tired and scruffy at this late hour. He'd not shaved in a day or two judging by the stubble that roughened his face. I suspected he was dying for a shower. He ran a hand through his hair, then across his face, making that uniquely masculine rasping sound. He crossed his arms easily over his chest. I swallowed, and out of ever-growing necessity, I crossed my arms over my chest too.

"How did it go with Head?" he asked.

"He's an asshole." I leaned back in my chair and rubbed the crick in my neck that just wouldn't give. I let my eyes drift shut, just for a second.

"I thought he was a dickhead?"

"He is." I nodded as if this were perfectly logical. Perfectly feasible. "He's both."

"That would give a whole new meaning to 'go fuck yourself', wouldn't it?"

My eyes shot open wide. "Okay, now that's funny."

"Good to see you smile, Dix."

So that's what that strange sensation in my cheekbones was. Hmm, go figure.

"Head's a lot of things, Dylan," I said. "But one thing he is *not* is stupid. This could be very bad for me. Head's been waiting for a long time to even the score."

"Yeah, but you and I both know he can't pin this murder on you."

"Really? Let's see what he's got — my fingerprints and footprints all over the crime scene, a connection to Jennifer Weatherby, opportunity, since I knew when she'd be home and Ned wouldn't, and let's not forget, a motive fabricated out of thin air by the man who probably hates me more than any other in Marport City. And that's a pretty long list to be at the top of."

"And don't forget the week's worth of trailing evidence they got from the car," Dylan added.

As if I could.

"Did they find the bug?"

"No."

"Well, that's a mercy."

"Yeah, a small one." I closed my eyes again. "Even if he can't pin the murder on me, he'll do his damnedest to put me out of business. I'm so humped on this one, Dylan."

The silence was uncomfortable. Hard and heavy.

The desk creaked as Dylan stood. He strode over to the filing cabinet and picked up a yellow legal pad. "I've been thinking on the business cards, Dix."

I opened one bleary eye. "You're kidding, right?"

"Why would I be kidding?"

"I don't really think this is the time for that."

He ignored me. "I've got a couple ideas." He cleared his throat. "How about this: *Dix Dodd, Private Investigation Service. If clues were shoes, we'd be wearing Prada.*"

I opened the other eye. "Ahhhhh ... no."

"If clues came in two's, then we'd tango for you-s."

"Big no."

"If clues were booze, we'd be drunk on your doorstep."

I groaned. No, I mean it, I really, really groaned. "That's awful, Dylan."

"Okay, well that was just my first three shots. I have more."

He stood taller, drawing himself up to his full six-four. Damn, the man looked good.

"What's your next shot?"

"Dix Dodd, private detective, keeping your man your man for over twenty years."

"I've only been in business solo for six months."

"Yeah, well, I'm thinking ahead."

Dylan looked at me, straight on. Steady and so sure of himself. So sure of me. It was the least I could do to be the same. Screw this feeling sorry for myself shit! Pity party over; there was work to be done.

I slammed down the last drink of coffee, then slammed the empty mug on my desk. "Okay, we need a plan."

"Right."

"We have to find this mistress Jennifer was so sure about. My money's on her. Now more than ever."

Dylan went to the large whiteboard that hung on the wall beside my desk. He erased all that was on it, signaling — whether consciously or unconsciously — that he too knew the severity of my situation. He drew a stick figure, putting a triangle skirt on her to mark her as female. "Okay, what do we know about this mysterious mistress of Ned Weatherby's?"

I just stared at him for a moment while he waited for my reply. "Thanks," I said. "About the business cards."

"You mean you liked my ideas?"

"Oh, hell, no. They were gawd-awful." I hesitated. "Thanks for your faith in me."

"Any time, Dix." I caught the flash in his eyes before he put up his own guard again. But for a moment those brown eyes had been softer, and if I'd let myself believe it, for a moment there was more there. He turned towards the whiteboard. "Any time at all."

We worked into the wee hours of the morning. I reprinted the digital pics that I'd emailed to the office. Detective Head had confiscated the originals of course. As he had with my notes, but I'd sent backup copies of the same to the office every day (thank you, digital technology). Dylan and I went over every little detail. We brainstormed theories. Charted possibilities. Had wild, passionate sex on my desk.

Okay, that last part was just in my mind. Again and again and again.

The sun was just coming up as Dylan grabbed his keys and with a, "Back in a few minutes," headed out the door.

Despite the adrenaline rush of the last few hours, despite the pounding headache, and the coffee I'd consumed, I soon realized if I was going to function at all, I needed some good old-fashioned sleep. Luckily, I'd installed a cot at the office for just that purpose, given the crazy hours I keep. It wasn't the comfiest thing in the world, but I'd been sleeping hunched up in cars for days, so if felt like the most decadent of pleasures just to lie prone and stretch out.

My body was ready for sleep, but unfortunately my mind just wouldn't cooperate. *Where would I find her, this mysterious mistress?* As my tired mind finally relented and began drifting from consciousness to sleep, I could almost see her turning the corner of it. Walking like a ghost along the streets as I pictured them. Dancing on the edge of my grasp and the edge of my vision.

"You're never going to find me!" Her voice was singsong, but not singsong-sweet. More that singsong mocking kind of thing, as she danced around me. Of course, I knew I was dreaming, but she still pissed me off.

"I wouldn't be too sure of that." I reached to grab her, catching only a wisp of her gown before it slipped through my fingers. I wanted to turn her around to face me. Wanted to push the flowing locks of hair back from her face to get a good look at her.

Somehow she knew this, and evaded me with ease.

"I'm too smart for you, Dix Dodd. I'm too smart for all of you."

"Don't count on it, Blondie." It's not that I'm prejudiced against blonds, and I never partake in the dumb blond jokes. Well, almost never. Hell, I'm a blond myself. But until I knew the mystery mistress's name — a detail Jennifer hadn't been able to supply — Blondie would have to do.

Blondie tittered. "Don't let the hair color fool you. I'm one smart cookie." She flounced away from me.

I woke up with my right hand swinging, and my butt on the floor.

And the smell of hotcakes and sausage drifting in from the outer office. I shook my head, rubbed my hands over my face. Then I got off my butt and followed the aroma.

Over breakfast Dylan and I formulated a plan of action.

"So where do we go from here, Dix?"

Dylan speared yet another sausage. He'd scored our breakfast from the shop around the corner, and already he'd put away twice as much of it as I had. Still, I knew he'd not put an ounce onto that lean frame.

"Objective remains the same as when the Flashing Fashion Queen hired us." I took a sip of the latte Dylan had brought. Heavenly. "We have to find Ned Weatherby's mistress."

"Our boy Ned was pretty clean this week, wasn't he? Kind of makes you wonder ..."

I swallowed a syrupy, buttery bite and refrained from licking my fork. Somehow, when someone else unwraps the fast food, it doesn't seem so bad. "I know what you mean. Ned was practically — no, he was *literally* — a choir boy this week. It was almost as if he knew he was being watched."

"You think Jennifer told him she'd hired us?"

"I doubt that very much." The logic behind a wife telling her husband he was being tailed was, well, non-existent. That would negate the whole purpose of the exercise. I couldn't see it happening, especially considering how much dough Jennifer Weatherby was paying me. "However, if I blew cover while I was trailing him, then Ned would certainly modify his behavior."

Even as I offered that possibility, I knew it wasn't very likely. I'd never been made by a mark before. At least, not to my knowledge. The one and only benefit of being so ordinary, so average, so nondescript, was that I could blend in practically anywhere. But what other explanation was there?

"Maybe Jennifer told someone she hired you," he offered. "And they told Ned. Women often have close friends they confide in."

"That's good." I nodded. "That's very good. Can you check on that?"

"I'm on it. I'll check with some of the neighbors. At times like these, neighbors are often ready to share what they know."

Certainly any female friends of Jennifer Weatherby would be more than willing to share some time and information with the young, handsome Dylan Foreman.

"While you're at it, ask if she belonged to any health clubs. Or charities or anything like that. Might find something out there."

"You bet."

Dylan stood, grabbed his jacket and headed for the door. He never dawdled, but the speed with which he wanted to attack this particular assignment moved me. I knew he was worried about me. I stood, tossed the plastic breakfast trays and utensils in the trash and grabbed my own jacket from the coat tree in the corner.

"Where are you off to?" Dylan shrugged into his leather jacket.

"The Underhill Motel."

He hesitated but knew better than to question me, or try to stop me. The Underhill was in a rough part of town, but we both knew I could handle myself.

We locked the office, and headed our respective ways. Whereas I always parked at the far end of the lot, Dylan parked his bike as close to the building as he could get it. He gave me a mock salute before starting the bike and roaring off.

I reminded myself to get him a set of motorcycle chaps for Christmas.

Surely that would be an acceptable employer-employee gift? Not too formal. Not too personal. Not too expensive. Not too cheap. And I could just picture them on him — protecting his legs should he fall on the pavement. Keeping him warm when he drove at night. Perfectly framing his denim-covered . . .

Gawd, I'd better knit him a sweater. Something loose fitting and long-sleeved.

I just hoped I wouldn't be sending it to him from a federal prison.

Chapter 5

B ELIEVE IT OR not, things got stranger.
A person learns a lot in this business — the kind of stuff that could never be found in any academic textbook. You won't find Lying Jerks 101 among the possible course selections at your local university; they offer no degree in Psychology of Cheaters. I've yet to come across anyone with a Masters in Bullshit Busting, or a PhD in Intuition. But all of these and more are available to your average PI, if you've got the knack for reading people and are prepared to study their behavior.

Curse or gift? Damned if I know. Maybe a bit of both.

For example, I've learned that insecure men often laugh a lot, especially if they're insecure businessmen, and they'll watch you the whole time you're laughing back to see if you really think that they're funny. People who say they want to be left alone, often really do just want to be left the hell alone. Men with small dogs in the park are looking to get laid, especially if they put a ribbon in the dog's hair. And oh, by the way, the pinker the ribbon, the hornier they are. (The men not the dogs). Yeah, if you watch closely you'll learn a hell of a lot about people, but you'll learn even more if you watch with sideways glances.

But here's the trick of it. Sometimes it's just as important to not let first impressions fool you. At least not when it comes to the way people look.

Because I've also learned that people come in all shapes and sizes, and in the long run, that means diddlysquat about their character. That is to say, we judge people by their external appearance at our peril. The most doe-eyed of women are often the strongest. The most macho seeming of men can be brought to their knees with a good solid kick to the ... whoops, I mean with the right words. Although that foot-to-gonads thing does come in handy sometimes. So, okay, though I may mentally dub a person on first sight (e.g., Jennifer Weatherby as the

Flashing Fashion Queen), I don't judge on first sight. Maybe that's why I'm rarely surprised.

Rarely, but Mrs. Jane Presley, the owner/caretaker of the Underhill was one of those people who managed to surprise me. Because on first sight — God, it was years ago now, when I was first running errands for Jones and Associates — I'd pegged her as a pushover. A sweet little old lady who probably had cookies baking out back and rescued kitties on the weekend.

Not.

To this point in my career, I'd probably been to the Underhill Motel a few dozen times. Posing as a hooker, running surveillance, chasing leads, following up on suspicions that so often proved true. That's where I learned a lot of what I wanted to know, and the one thing I didn't the first night I drove by here, so long ago. But hey, we all have our heartaches.

Where was I? Oh, yeah. I'd been to the Underhill so often Mrs. Presley was on my Christmas card list.

She was a tiny woman, all of four feet ten and maybe ninety pounds with a brick in each pocket. When you entered the Underhill, it was she you encountered — standing under a sign that read, "No I *don't* know Elvis". She always wore flower-patterned, short-sleeved blouses with a pencil-pen-pencil combination tucked into the front pocket. Her skirts flowed from her hips nearly to the floor. I'd never seen her don the glasses that hung from the chain around her neck, but their granny style fit her image perfectly. Her make-up was understated, and her smile was wide and genuine. Friendly. Easy. Geez, you just wanted to give her a hug.

Unless you pissed her off. Because despite first impressions, Mrs. Presley was as tough as freakin' nails.

She had a no-nonsense reputation, and her two hulking sons — Cal and Craig — each of them six feet tall, helped her keep the Underhill no-nonsense. She had rules and they were ironclad. Once you were barred from her place, you stayed barred. No exceptions. No second chances. A person could come to the Underhill Motel, take care of business and pleasure, but keep it clean. The cops knew it was a local hooker hangout, but as long as things didn't get out of hand, then they left it pretty much alone. Better to have things under one roof on the outskirts than under many near the 'better' parts of town. Plus, Mrs. Presley had been known to help the police out on occasion.

Oh yeah, and she always wore blue suede shoes. Really.

But like me, Mrs. Presley could read people with sideways glances.

And she used this instinct of hers to help keep the place out of trouble. It was somewhat unnerving to stand with someone who could read you as well as you could read them. I have often wondered what her first impression of me had been.

There was no doubt that Mrs. Presley's keen eye for detail helped keep things under control. No one wanted to bite the hand that housed them. But as I learned, the prostitutes actually appreciated Mrs. Presley's eagle eye. Once she saw a face, she never forgot it. She looked after 'her girls', too. She wasn't a madam, she once told me, but she was a mama. And it gave the girls who worked the Underhill a small sense of security to know that she was looking out the curtains with her binoculars when they checked in with their johns.

I'd packed a few photos. If Mrs. Presley knew anything, if she'd seen anything, she'd tell me.

This was the scenario I envisioned: I'd show Mrs. Presley the pictures of Ned Weatherby, she'd identify him as a client (a Mr. John Smith, no doubt), and if she knew who the mistress was, she'd tell me. Especially when I told her that murder was involved. Then I could prove to Detective Head once and for all that I wasn't lying. Prove that I didn't imagine the whole freakin' thing. That I wasn't totally stalking Ned Weatherby like some love-starved fool. I'd locate the mistress, get a confession and present the evidence to the police by noon.

Damn, I was good! In my own mind, I had it all sewn up. Supper at Donatta's on 33rd Street would be an appropriate celebration afterward. I'd order the grilled shrimp with a nice unoaked chardonnay.

Why, I was actually smiling when I walked into the Underhill.

But like I'd said, things got stranger.

"This guy?" Mrs. Presley paused. "You're sure it's this guy you're look-ing for?"

"Yes." My answer came out with more exasperation than I intended to show. My finger pressed into the first photo of Ned Weatherby — out-side his house, picking a rose from the garden.

When I'd first walked into the Underhill Motel, Mrs. Presley had been anxious to see my pics, and just as anxious to offer me a commen-tary of her thoughts on all of them. "Oh this guy looks angry. Look at the legs on that one, will you. I've seen chickens with more meat on their bones. Why the hell don't men wear hats anymore? Hats are classy, don't you think, Dix?"

"Excellent questions, Mrs. P, but right now, I just need to know if you've seen this guy."

"Ned Weatherby."

Great! She recognized him! I knew it. "Yes, Ned Weatherby!"

She pushed the photos back across the counter. "Never been here."

My jubilance evaporated. Of course. Mrs. P knew him from the local rag, the front page of which he made every other month in recent years. She didn't need my private eye pics to ID him. "You're sure about that?" I asked, maybe a little too pleadingly.

"Positive. Ned Weatherby has never been to the Underhill."

I'd been so sure she'd tell me Ned and his blond bimbo had been frequent guests. Damn.

"Could you please go over the photos just once more?"

"Don't see what good it'll do," she grumbled, but she pulled the photographs closer and studied them again.

"Ma," the distinctively male voice rose from the back room. "Ma, you got any of that spicy pepperoni left?"

"Don't you dare, Cal," she called back over her shoulder. "You know damn well that'll give you the heartburn."

"Ah, ma. Come on!"

"Forget it. I'm not going to be up rubbing your back again tonight, young man." She looked up at me. "Kids."

"How old are your sons?" I asked. "They're twins aren't they?"

"Yes, they're twins," Mrs. P answered. "And they'll be twenty-eight in November."

"Really?"

"Just babies, eh, Dix?"

Babies? Those hulking creatures? "Full grown, I'd say." I pushed towards Mrs. Presley the pictures from Ned's choir practice — the one of him sitting with the other choir members, the one of him talking to the serious-looking Pastor Ravenspire. They were deep in conversation in this one, and I had the feeling they were discussing more than *Amazing Grace*. The pastor looked concerned; Ned looked tired.

Mrs. Presley looked over the pictures quickly. No matter. I knew she wasn't missing a thing. She glanced up at me. "How old is that young fellow you got working for you, Dix? That good-looking one you had with you that time when you followed that deadbeat who was cheating on his pregnant wife."

I cleared my throat. "Twenty-eight."

"Yep, full grown man. But I don't have to tell you that." She winked.

Damn her and her sideways-glancing intuition!

I felt the color rising in my cheeks. "Mrs. Presley, if we could go back to the pictures. Let's go through them one at a time."

She slung out a dramatic sigh to emphasize what I already knew — she was losing patience. But I wasn't ready to give up yet. My intuition told me I was missing something. Something vital. Something I'd find here.

The picture I pointed to now was one of Ned and his lawyer leaving the gym. An easy, casual picture. Both held racquetball rackets held loosely at their sides. But that's where the similarity ended. Ned was tall, while Jeremy was shorter than average. Their legs stuck out under the white of their gym shorts, but while Ned's legs were hairy and dark, Jeremy's were nearly as white and smooth as his shorts. In the photo, he bent to scratch his ankle, his finger digging into the socks as he walked. He looked more like the bell-ringing Hunchback of Notre Dame than one of Marport City's finest young lawyers.

I directed Mrs. Presley's attention to the picture of Ned and a red-faced Billy Star angrily exchanging words in the parking lot, tapping my finger on Ned's image.

Mrs. Presley shook her head. She handed the pictures back to me and I let my breath out slowly.

"Ned Weatherby has never been here, Dix."

I resigned myself to defeat on this point. The motel was a dead end. Damn! I'd been so sure. "Thanks anyway, Mrs. Presley."

"You didn't have to bring the pics in, Dix. You could have just asked me if I'd seen that guy who's been all over the news."

I cringed. Ned Weatherby was indeed all over the news. And no staid head-and-shoulders file shots needed — every camera had flashed towards the house when he'd stood in the open doorway.

"It's on every channel. Here, I'll find it for you." Mrs. Presley picked up the remote control and aimed it at the small television that sat high and muted in the corner. No sound came over the speakers as the thin-faced, big-haired weather girl in the corner mouthed the latest weather report, while the caption gave all the information anyway.

"That's okay, Mrs. Presley," I said. "I'll catch the news later."

And I certainly would. I sighed. And I just hoped later in the day I wouldn't *be* the news. God, I hoped Dylan had had better luck. As it stood now, Detective Richard Head would be having me for breakfast.

"Dix, you look like hell all of a sudden. What's up?"

"It's nothing," I said. "I was just so sure that you'd recognize Ned from visiting the motel. But I've got other leads." I gathered the photos up again and tucked them back into the folio. "Thanks for the help."

"Any time."

I turned and headed towards the door.

"And Dix," Mrs. Presley called to my retreating form. "If you want me to tell you about the other person in those pictures — the one that used to come here all the time, just let me know."

"Other person?" I turned to face Mrs. Presley again. "What other person?"

"That one you *didn't* ask about. But you're the detective, Dix Dodd. I'm just the lady at the desk. You go on now. Have a nice day."

I'm an idiot. "I'm an idiot."

I should have just handed Mrs. Presley the pictures and let her fill in the blanks — all the blanks, any of the blanks. Instead, I'd told her what blank I wanted filled in and with whom. My intuition was right on track; my brain had simply derailed.

"What did I miss, Mrs. P?"

"Sit down, honey." She nodded towards the small sofa and coffee table in the small lounge. "I'll ask Cal to make us some lunch. We're gonna be here awhile."

My face dropped.

Mrs. P looked at me and grinned. "Ah, come on, don't look so sad. This isn't some kind of Heartbreak Hotel, you know."

Chapter 6

Now, I'm not saying Mrs. Presley is one to gloat. Oh, hell, who am I kidding? She sat there with a sandwich in one hand, a cup of tea in the other, and a self-satisfied smirk on her face. Yeah, yeah, I guess I asked for it. And man, did she make me suffer, talking about the weather and countless other trivialities before getting to what I was dying to hear.

Damn, I was blown away.

"You can close your mouth now, sweetie," she said when she'd finished dishing.

I closed my mouth. "Sorry, Mrs. Presley." Like any well-chastised schoolgirl, I mumbled my apologies.

The frequent visitor to the Underhill Hotel was none other than the fist-shaking, hostile, bristling Billy Star of my surveillance photos. And get this — he always appeared in the company of a blond. A blond who crouched low in the seat while he signed in (W.P. Smith). Mrs. Presley even had the dates and room numbers — Room 10 (that was the mirror-ceilinged room) February 5, 12, and 19. Room 108 (vibrating bed) on March 12, April 2. Room 101 — that was April 9 — had a notation beside it: Fix light fixture, customer complained of shock. Briefly, I got sidetracked wondering what the hell they were doing in that room to get a jolt off a light fixture, but forced my focus back to the issue at hand.

There were other rooms and other dates. Usually twice a week, sometimes more. Until about a month ago, when the rendezvous ended suddenly. My mind roiled with questions. Who was the blond? Why the Underhill Motel? And why did it end so abruptly?

And most importantly, how was this connected to the murder of Jennifer Weatherby?

No, wait — the most important question was, how was this all going to save my ass?

Afterward, I'd driven back to the office with a death grip on the steering wheel and Mrs. Presley's spicy pepperoni churning on my insides. I think she'd spared her son the poison and fed it to me!

But no matter, I would surely live. I had to, if only to impart this juicy tidbit to Dylan. I couldn't wait to catch up with him, to find out what he'd found out, completely certain that my information could trump his information, in my best school-yard nyah-nyah, my-snitch-is-better-than-your-snitch-so-there mentality. Because, well, I was one to gloat too.

But Dylan had some pretty good information of his own.

The phone was just starting to ring as I took my coat off. My first thought was that it would be the police with more questions. Or worse, the press with some questions of their own.

"Not now, damn you." I decided to let it click to voice mail. But no sooner had it rung four times and flipped into voice mail, then it started ringing again. Then again.

Damn it. A glance at the display simply showed "Outside Call", which meant the caller was blocking caller ID. No messages either.

I'd been half surprised to see that Dylan wasn't back yet, but when I looked out the window I could see him pulling his bike into the parking lot. Damn, he looked good on that thing. My gaze took in long legs strad-dling the powerful bike. I also took in the fact that he didn't have his cell phone pressed to his ear. Whoever was calling, it wasn't Dylan Foreman.

"Oh, just give it up will you. Or leave a message already."

Who the hell calls ten times?

Truthfully, I didn't want to answer it. I just couldn't get my mind around the concept of new clients right now, not while the murder of Jennifer Weatherby still hung over my head. Worse, I thought it might be Detective Head asking me why the hell I'd not brought Jennifer Weatherby's receipt, deposit record and contract (yes, the non-existent paperwork) in to the station yet.

So I glared at the ringing phone and willed it to stop, scrunching my eyebrows in concentration. I wanted it to stop. Specifically, I wanted it to stop before Dylan walked in. The only thing worse than avoiding a call I really didn't want to take was having someone else know I was avoiding it. Having Dylan know it ...

The door to my office started to swing open. Shit. I dove across

Dylan's desk and lunged for the phone, making a very unflattering oomph/slide across the oak surface.

"Hello, Dix Dodd speaking."

Dylan arched a questioning eyebrow. I mouthed the words 'had to pee' and pressed the phone back to my ear in time to hear a female voice.

"Oh." A pause. "Oh, I was just about to hang up."

Well don't let me stop you.

"Just got in the door," I lied to the still unknown caller. "What can I do for you?"

"I'm calling for Dylan Foreman. Is he there?"

"Oh."

"Ma'am? Is he there?"

"Certainly. Just a moment, please."

I was just about to hand the phone over to Dylan when she said, "And er, sorry to rush your pee break."

Grrrr.

Oh, great, THIS I was able to mouth silently.

I handed the phone to Dylan.

"I'll be just a minute, Dix." Dylan hooked a leg casually over the edge of his desk. With the mouthpiece end of the receiver pressed against his shoulder, he waited. And waited until I got the message.

I turned and walked into my own office.

I closed the door between our offices. Well, almost closed it. I heard him laugh deeply, while my leather chair made a rude sound as I plunked my ass down on it. Nice, Dix. Chances were Dylan heard that, if not the caller on the other end of the line. Great, now they'll think I'm incontinent *and* a farter!

All I needed now was to … oh, crap!

Mrs. Presley's hospitality came back to haunt me. I belched spicy pepperoni.

Feeling about as attractive as Steve Buscemi, I sighed and turned my attention to my desk. Picking up the yellow legal pad I'd used when Jennifer Weatherby had been in the office, I examined my doodles. Stairs going nowhere; tight little circles. The crazy, meandering duck tracks. For some reason, I wanted to laugh. And not a good laugh.

"That's it! I'll just hand this over to Detective Head," I muttered to myself. "There you go, Detective! Proof positive Jennifer Weatherby was in my office. Case closed against Dix Dodd, your friendly neighborhood ball-buster!"

"Dix?" Dylan called from the outer office. "Did you say something?"

Damn. "I said I need another good ... wall duster." The smack of my hand to my forehead felt just about right.

He resumed his conversation, and I went back to glowering at my yellow pad.

About five minutes later, Dylan's voice went lower and I couldn't even make out bits and pieces of the conversation. Not that I'd been listening — like, a lot. I heard his deep chuckle — the one that just rolled itself up my spine. He hung up and before I could adjust my position from straining forward in my chair to casually leaning back with my feet up on the desk, the door opened.

"Sorry about that," he said, looking anything but sorry. "We're busy as hell, I know, but I really had to take that call."

"No problem," I said. "You know I don't mind personal calls at the office. Not at all."

Now was the time for Dylan to tell me it wasn't a personal call. I waited. I waited some more.

"Thanks." He smiled.

"Sure." I couldn't resist. But nor could I look at him as I asked. "How is your mother, anyway?"

"Great, Dix. Mother's great."

"So nice of her to call."

"She didn't."

Oh, wonderful, Dodd. Real mature!

It wasn't that I couldn't read his expression, it's that he didn't really have one. He was offering neither excuse nor explanation.

But I noticed he wasn't looking at me either as he'd answered — his eyes were staring into his own yellow legal pad full of notes.

I quickly (quickly before I said something even more stupid) told Dylan what I had learned from Mrs. Presley: that Billy Star had been a frequent visitor to the Underhill. With a blond. Dylan, of course, pointed out there were lots of blonds in the world.

"Maybe our boy Billy was with a hooker," Dylan offered. "A blond favorite, perhaps?"

I shook my head. "Hookers don't hide down in the seat and send the john in to register. It works the other way around. No, Mrs. Presley was positive she wasn't a prostitute, a regular or otherwise. And with her years at the desk of the Underhill, she would certainly know."

"Maybe Star had himself an under-aged girlfriend."

I considered that for a moment. But only a moment. I knew Mrs. Presley. If there were any underage hanky-panky going on, well, it wouldn't be for long.

But what was the connection between Billy Star, Ned Weatherby, the late Mrs. Jennifer Weatherby and the blond mistress we sought? I guess it could be coincidental, but it sure as hell didn't feel coincidental. It *felt* like there should be a connection there.

"Maybe we were right," I mused. "Maybe Billy and Ned were fighting over the same woman."

"Our mysterious mistress?"

"Yeah, Blondie gets around."

He sighed. "I don't know. I mean, that theory was just some wild speculation. And well, it kind of seems far-fetched."

"Far-fetched is all we've got to go on, Dylan."

I cleared my throat.

As if reading my mind, Dylan strode to the coffee pot in the corner. Ever ready, he flicked a switch and the hardest working thing in the office kicked into gear.

"What did you find out from talking to the neighbors?" I asked.

"It was interesting, to say the least."

"How so?"

He ran a hand over his chin, drawing it long. He often did this when carefully arranging his words. "According to everyone I talked to, they hardly knew Jennifer Weatherby."

"Hardly surprising. I mean in this day and age, it's not like people sit out on their front porch swings and chat over lemonade."

"Still, you'd think she'd have at least one friend in the neighborhood. But there was ... I don't know ... almost an animosity towards Jennifer."

I could feel my eyebrows arching. "Anything specific?"

The coffee gurgled and started sputtering into the pot and I silently blessed it.

"From what I understand, Mrs. Weatherby didn't much get along with the other rich ladies on Ashfield Drive. She wasn't one of them."

"Old money versus new money?"

He shook his head. "I don't think so. The homes are new out that way, so it's all new money. No, I think Jennifer was just one of those women that didn't fit in. You know, not the wine and cheese and charity ball kind of chick."

Dylan Foreman was one of those rare guys who could say 'chick' and not have it sound condescending. Actually, he made it sound downright sexy. Granted, he could probably make rice pudding sound sexy.

I shook my head to clear my thoughts. "Any specific incidents that would have made her enemies?"

"None that I could uncover. Just general stuff. You know, not attending neighborhood functions, not sending cards at Christmas, or pretending she didn't know the neighbors when they met at Ryder's."

"Ryder's on Main?" Ryder's was about as high end as it got, unless you wanted to jet off to New York or Paris.

He nodded. "Apparently, that's where all the ladies of Ashfield Drive shop. And apparently, whenever Jennifer bumped into one of them, she'd duck out of the store as quickly as possible. Wouldn't even say hi."

"Ryder's," I repeated.

On the one hand, it didn't really surprise me that Jennifer Weatherby shopped at Ryder's. She could certainly afford it. On the other hand, when she'd come to my office, she'd looked anything but stylishly dressed.

Stress? Maybe. It could do a helluva number on a person.

The coffee was ready, and I poured Dylan a mug as I got my own. "So Jennifer Weatherby wasn't popular with the ladies of Ashfield Drive. But did anyone hate her enough to kill her?"

"They're a cliquey bunch," he said. "But no. I don't think anyone wanted her dead."

I steered the conversation back to Billy Star, frequent flyer at the Underhill, and his skulking blond date. Again we tossed around the theory that the heated argument between Billy Star and Ned Weatherby had been over the same woman.

"Long shot," he said.

"It's a *shot* though." I held the cup in both hands, warming them even though they were far from cold.

Dylan nodded. "Okay, where do we go from here?"

The phone rang just exactly as I opened my mouth to speak.

Dylan rose to get it in the outer office. A bit too quickly.

"Here," I said. "I'll get it."

I thought it must be the same woman calling for Dylan again. This time, I was determined to show how mature I was. Coolest boss EVER. How what-a-great-boss-who-isn't-hot-for-her-much-younger-assistant I was. And this time, I wouldn't ask if it was his mother. I picked up the receiver before the second ring finished.

"Dix Dodd speaking."

"Well if it isn't the she-stalker herself."

Ah, fuck!

"Hello, Dickhead," I said. "How goes the quitting smoking? Bet you'd like one right now, huh?" Yes, it was dirty, but a girl had to score her points where she could. "Why don't I go pick you up a pack? I could have them delivered. Ahhh, can't you just feel that lovely tar filling your lungs right now?"

He laughed. Not his belly-shaking, everyone-run-here laugh, but a deep chuckle that unnerved me.

"Funny, Dixieland," he said. "Very funny. And here I was calling to give you some information. Just trying to be friendly."

Said the python to the rat.

"What's up?" I asked, cautiously curious.

"I just got off the phone with Ned Weatherby. He gave me his wife's itinerary for the last week." Detective Head paused, dramatically. My heart began to race.

"Well, good for you, Dick!" I said. "Itinerary's a pretty big word! Five syllables! Call back next week and we'll work on ..." — oh, shit, what was a good six-syllable word? — "... an even bigger word."

Okay, yes, the world's dumbest retort. But I was getting a little stressed here; he was so happy. *Just what did Dickhead know that I didn't?*

I forced up a chuckle.

"Laugh all you want now, Dix Dodd," Detective Head said. "You won't be laughing for long."

"You going to get to the point today, Detective?"

"The point is that Jennifer Weatherby wasn't anywhere near your office on Monday. The late Mrs. Weatherby was at the Bombay Spa for her weekly treatments. Left early in the morning, came home late at night. You lied, Dix. There is no way in hell that she was in your office."

I could feel my grip on calm slipping. Dylan moved closer, his gaze intent on my face, no doubt reading the growing panic there. "There has to be a mistake ..."

"The mistake is you messed with the wrong people, Dix. I'm going to haul you in."

"Give me forty-eight hours." The words were out before I'd clearly thought them over.

"Why should I?" Dickhead asked, clearly enjoying himself.

"Because I'll deliver the murderer to you by then."

Now I appreciated his pause. He was thinking it over. And then

I realized: there were no blaring sirens on the way to pick me up. No cops banging on the door. No police dogs sniffing my car. Detective Head, though he would dearly love to see me in jail, wouldn't let the real killer get away.

"Okay," he grumbled. "You got your forty-eight hours." Then he hung up the phone.

"Where do we go from here, Dylan?" God, was it just two minutes ago that he'd put that question to me? It felt like hours. I swallowed hard, but when I spoke, my voice was as strong as I could make it. "I'll tell you where we're going. To the Bombay Spa."

Dylan slowly nodded, erased the whiteboard and we began again.

And when the phone rang, we ignored the damn thing.

Chapter 7

FORTY-EIGHT HOURS.

Not too damn much time to save my butt. But it would be enough. It had to be.

As we sat down to brainstorm, it was clear that Dylan shared my anxiety.

Here's the thing about Dylan — he's not just good to look at; he's pretty damned good at this job. He is always intensely committed to solving the mystery at hand. I'll confess that over the period of our association, I've enjoyed watching him apply himself to a puzzle. There is something positively fascinating about watching an intelligent guy think. You can almost see the wheels churning, the adrenaline rushing. But this time, with this case ... well, I'd never seen him look so fiercely focused as we went over the details and attempted to chart the life of Mrs. Weatherby.

You'd think at first glance that Jennifer Weatherby had lived a fairy-tale existence. She'd grown up dirt poor, the stereotypical girl from the wrong side of the tracks. When she was barely twenty-one, she'd married the dashing young businessman, Ned Weatherby. Rumor had it that Ned's parents had never thought Jennifer was good enough for their Neddy, but he had fallen head over heels for the young and beautiful Jennifer. And some say it was Jennifer's fear of being poor again that lead Ned to work so hard, and be so ruthless in business over the years. To keep the dragons at bay.

After Ned had made the millions, Jennifer's life seemed to revolve around shopping at the most exclusive boutiques and spending her days at the Bombay Spa. Literally rags to riches. Safe and perfect.

But I never trusted fairytales. Too simplistic. Too black and white.

I'd been the one in grade school who'd scoffed all the way through the Sleeping Beauty play, finally yelling, "Wake the hell up!" After which, of course, I was escorted out of the tiny gymnasium. Little Red Riding Hood drove me nuts; she should have pulled a gun out of her handbag and just shot the damn wolf. Now *that* would have been happily ever after. Clint Eastwood-style happily ever after, but ... well, it would have put a smile on my face.

And I really, really didn't like Cinderella.

I never thought of it as a story of princess meets prince, falls in love. It just drove me crazy that Cinderella morphed into something to capture the heart of her true love, and that the fairy Godmother helped her do it! I mean, shouldn't she have shown up in her everyday clothes and seen what old Prince Charming thought of her then?

But yet, we all do that, don't we? We dress to impress. Play the part according to the audience. And yeah, okay, we judge on first impressions.

And whereas I was on my way to the Bombay Spa, I knew I'd have to play the part too. No way could I go in as Dix Dodd, Private Detective, with her assistant, Dylan Foreman. That would make me an outsider.

No, I would enter the spa as Dixie Davenport, rich bitch, needing a day of pampering. Rest and relaxation. Small talk and gossip. I had the wardrobe for it (okay, one outfit, an authentic Chanel charcoal blazer and pant suit that made me look like a million bucks rather than the hundred bucks I'd paid for it at a fire sale, and a decent pair of black pumps), and I could fake the attitude. Just throw those shoulders back, lift the chin and pretend you smell something vaguely unpleasant. And gossip? I could hold my own with the best of them. If there were any juicy details to be learned about the fairytale life of Jennifer Weatherby, I'd ferret them out.

When I called the spa and told them that I wanted to book for that very afternoon, I was told there was nothing available. The waiting list to get in was at least a month long. Remember those winged bills that had been flying overhead? My big payday? Well, they started flying toward the spa.

I told a few lies about being the wife of a movie producer from Hollywood, a producer who hoped to be shooting a Matt Damon thriller in the area. But, maybe I should tell hubby dearest to reconsider. No way could we make our temporary home in a podunk town where I couldn't get an appointment at the spa when I so desperately needed one.

The little squeally shriek that followed half convinced me the receptionist was having an orgasm. She put me on hold. Less than two minutes later, she came back on the line to inform me that they would certainly make an exception for any friend of Mr. Damon's.

That's how I got myself into the Bombay.

Dylan? Well, no way in hell would he sit around and be left behind.

"And just how," I'd asked, "do you propose to get in there? The clientele are all female."

"Way ahead of you, Dix." He had smiled. "I called the head of personnel. They're hiring."

"You got yourself an interview, just like that?"

"An interview?" He looked insulted. "Are you kidding? With my qualifications, I was hired on the spot, over the telephone."

I didn't even ask which qualification he was referring too.

I was appropriately gushed over as I entered the spa. One attendant took my coat, which I shoulder-shrugged out of perfectly. I caught the staffer sneaking a glance at the coat's tags, which made me glad I'd had the forethought to stitch a Hilary Radley label scavenged from a vintage coat I'd picked up at a yard sale over the real label. Another staffer offered me an herbal tea, which I declined with a wordless wave. I was then escorted to the office, where a nervous, bone-thin redhead in a thousand dollar pantsuit did her best to accommodate. Her name was Ms. Pipps, and she was as efficient as her name sounded. Crisply efficient. On such short notice, they'd put together a pretty comprehensive spa day. I'd start with a massage, move on to a mud wrap, followed by a manicure and pedicure, then a full facial. I ordered the lemon chicken for lunch, which I'd have out on the terrace.

But even as I made these elaborate arrangements, I had no intention of sticking out the day. I'd stick it out only as long as it took to get what I wanted. Then I'd pay up, drop the rich chick persona, grab a Big Mac and head back to the office.

"So a friend of mine comes here," I said, hoping to pique the interest of the redhead.

"Oh? Who would that be?"

"Jennifer Weatherby."

Ms. Pipps clapped her hands together forcefully, which scared the crap out of me, for I thought I heard something snap in her bony hands. "Yes, Jennifer Weatherby has graced the Bombay Spa with her presence on many occasions. She's taken advantage of not only our wonderful services and full line of beauty and relaxation products, but also the warm hospitality that is the Bombay's trademark."

I'd get nothing here. And it wasn't just the canned promo that the Redhead no doubt gave to everyone. It was the expression on her face — or rather lack of expression.

"I have another friend who's spoken of this place."

"Oh? Who would that be?"

"Justine Smithee. Married to Alan Smithee, the famous Hollywood director. Does that ring a bell?"

She clapped her hands again. "Oh, my goodness, yes. Justine has graced the Bombay Spa with her presence on many occasions …"

I tuned her out after that. I mean, I could have said Fanny Fartsalot or Ima Hoare and she'd have given me the same spiel.

Redhead insisted I must start with the top-to-toe relaxing massage. She assured me the Bombay was famous for their massages. Surely I'd heard that from Mrs. Smithee? I'd agreed, mainly because I wanted to play the part well. I mean, every day at the spa began with a relaxing massage, didn't it?

But here's my problem. Getting a full body massage means getting naked, and I don't like being naked around other people.

I'm not a prude by any means, and I'm certainly not ashamed of my figure. Sure, I could drop twenty pounds and it wouldn't kill me. And granted, things weren't as perky as they were when I was twenty, or even thirty, but I was happy enough with myself, a byproduct, I think, of turning forty and deciding *this is me, baby, and I like it*. But unless the circumstances are right — which reminded me they hadn't been for quite some time, dammit — I just have this … uncomfortableness about being naked around strangers. Bottom line, if the Jerry Springer Show had to depend on me, they'd be in bad shape.

So lying face down on the massage table in room 102 of the Bombay Spa with just a thin white sheet over my naked butt wasn't exactly the highlight of my week. Well, actually, maybe it was the highlight, considering how badly my week had sucked so far. Right after cleaning the bird crap off my car and that call from my mother *(shudder)* to tell me she'd nearly got caught skinny-dipping. Again. Now, that's a show for Jerry Springer. My seventy-year-old mother could do naked in a heartbeat.

Just then, the door opened. I reached back to make sure the sheet was covering my derriere, and in the process looking, I have no doubt, like an awkward flapping seal as I raised myself and slapped the sides of the sheet into place. With a sigh (oh God I hoped it didn't sound like a moan) I set my chin in my hands.

"Hi," said the petite young woman who now stood before me. I assumed she was the masseuse. "I'm Elizabeth Bee!"

"'B' as in ..."

"Just Bee, you know, like the bug. But don't say that, it drives me nuts."

She was in her bare feet.

"You're not going to walk on my back, are you, Elizabeth?" I glanced down at her feet and the toe ring that looked particularly menacing.

"No, Ms. Davenport." She smiled but gave the slightest suggestion of an eye roll at the same time — which didn't endear her to me. "I'm here to prepare the room."

"Prepare the room?"

"Oh, yes. You'll get the full pampering at the Bombay Spa. Scented candles, warm towels, music." She sent me a sidelong glance. "You'll be sure to pass all this along to your friends?"

She meant to my non-existent Hollywood friends.

I assured her I would.

"Actually," I said. "Another good friend of mine is a client here. Someone from Marport City."

"Oh, who's that?"

"Jennifer Weatherby."

There was no rocking back on the bare heels. There was no change in the expression, except for a shift of light in the eyes. A fast blink. And I knew, sure as anything, Elizabeth knew something about Jennifer Weatherby.

"Well," said Elizabeth, "Jennifer was certainly an ... interesting lady."

Yes, I caught it: *Was.*

"Wasn't it awful, what happened to her?" the young woman whispered in that hushed tone that habitual gossipers use, as if the walls might overhear and collapse with the news. As if the hushed tones made it less terrible. Or that much worse.

Okay, now she was endearing herself to me.

"It was terrible," I agreed. "And Jennifer was such a ... such a sweet lady."

Elizabeth's eyebrows crinkled skeptically, but she quickly recovered. "Why, yes. You're so right."

Mentally, I urged her to say more. With any luck, I could get the information I needed and get out of this popsicle stand before ten. But obviously my Jedi Mind Trick was not quite up to snuff this morning. She didn't say another word.

I knew the next step. I had to build up a friendly little atmosphere with Elizabeth.

"So tell me about yourself," I invited.

She blinked at me, clearly startled to be asked about herself by a client. "Oh, well, I'm twenty-three. I'm from Maine originally, but you know, just didn't seem to be anything left for me there anymore, once my mom died."

"Oh, I'm sorry to hear that." And I genuinely was.

"Oh," she said, "there were other things too."

That usually meant a man. And I knew at Elizabeth's age, that could sting.

"Have you been here at the spa long?" I wanted to change the conversation, from heavy to lighter.

"About two years now. I love it here. And, well, the pay's pretty good. With the tips I make, of course."

Yes, I caught the hint. And I'd tip her well.

"It must be an interesting job."

She smiled. "Oh, you've no idea! But I don't want to just assist forever, you know. I want to go back to school and take some courses in reflexology. I just ... you know ... need the cash first. I really don't have anyone to help me. My Dad is gone, too. And both sets of grandparents."

Why the lying little ... Then I smiled.

This was going to work out fine.

"Hand me my wallet, will you?" I'd left my purse behind, since it would never pass muster here, but I figured the Gucci-inspired wallet might be mistaken for the real thing.)

She did. I withdrew the fifty as though it meant nothing, folded it twice and handed it to her. "For your education fund."

"Oh, my gosh, Ms. Davenport I couldn't. I just —"

"Nonsense, Elizabeth. And at the end of the session, if I've enjoyed the services here, there'll be another of those."

"A glass of wine, Ms. Davenport?" Elizabeth asked me, smiling so wide I thought her face would crack. "Champagne? Fresh orange juice, perhaps? They'll have it down at the restaurant. Shall I go and get you some? It would be my pleasure."

"Actually, Elizabeth, what I wanted —"

My words were cut short by a knock on the door. Argh! Of all the crappy timing for the masseuse to arrive.

Then the door swung open and Dylan Foreman walked in with a mile-wide, unapologetic grin.

"Wine would be good, Elizabeth," I croaked.

Good? Wine would be *necessary* under the circumstances!

So this is the job he'd convinced the Bombay he was completely qualified for. It must have been a helluva sell-job he'd done for them to send him in to serve their newest VIP client. After all, I was Dixie Davenport, from Beverly Hills, wife of a Hollywood movie producer. Friend of Matt Damon's! And though he'd been hired over the phone, I had every confidence his good looks upon presentation had landed him with me. Movie star caliber eye candy for the woman who rubbed shoulders with movie stars.

Why couldn't I have thought of a more modest lie?

But even as I fumed about the situation (to wit, me lying naked on a table with my employee as my masseuse), I couldn't help but be a little proud. I'd trained Dylan well. If Harvard had a PhD in massage, he'd claim to have the same, and be able to identify all the professors. He'd have read up on everything he could.

"Oh, you're new," Elizabeth said.

Well, duh!

Dylan crossed the room to shake her hand. "I just started here this morning. I'm Dylan Pulse."

Pulse? That's the pseudonym he came up with?

"Wonderful!" Elizabeth gushed. "We've been short staffed for months now. I'm Elizabeth Bee. Like, you know, the bug."

Huh?

God, the girl was flustered.

I watched as she gave Dylan the once-over. Then the twice-over.

"Well," Dylan flirted. "You've got to be the cutest bug I've ever seen."

He was good; I'd give him that.

He looked good, too. The outfit for the male masseuses at the Bombay Spa was simple but classy — white t-shirts and crisp white twill pants. I'd known that from the brochures I'd looked through when I'd selected the day's services in Redhead's office. But apparently Dylan's six-foot-four frame wasn't what they were ready for. The t-shirt was about two sizes too small. The inch-high Bombay Spa logo (palm trees and happy coconuts) rode higher on his chest than I imagined it was supposed to, and the material hugged his abs like a second skin. And while I'm sure I'd noticed his biceps at one time or another, they'd never been displayed to quite such advantage before, the skin dark against the startling white of the t-shirt's snug sleeves. As for the trousers … well, his narrow waist let him get into them, but I suspected the inseam wasn't equal to his long legs. He'd obviously solved that problem by rolling them up almost to the knee, managing to look casually rugged while escaping the flood pants look.

If the Bombay Spa thought this was going to impress me …

Shit, how smart was that? They were going to be devastated when they discovered he wasn't going to stay.

"Elizabeth? My wine?"

"Oh, sorry." The girl dragged her attention away from Dylan, and in record time, she'd pulled a bottle of chilled Chardonnay from the mini-fridge, poured a glass and put it in my hands.

I tipped up my chin, completely conscious of my bare breasts against the table and lifted myself only enough to take a sip. An awkward sip. I had more of a slurp/drool thing happening.

"I think you're all set," Elizabeth said, "but I'll be back in about an hour to check on things."

"Wait!" Damnation! I couldn't let her get away. I'd buttered her up, but I had yet to get the dirt on Jennifer Weatherby. "Couldn't you hang around?"

She glanced at Dylan, then back to me, giving me a look that said, *'What, are you nuts, lady?'*

"I … I wanted to ask you some questions about the spa," I said. "And if … Mr. Pulse was it?"

"Yes," Dylan lied. "Dylan Pulse. As in heartbeat."

Oh good grief!

"If Mr. Pulse is a new hire here, I doubt he could help me as well as you would be able to."

Elizabeth brightened like I'd just slipped her another fifty. (And of course knowing I would). "I'd be pleased to. Just let me clear it with Ms. Pipps and I'll be right back."

Elizabeth made her exit, hips swiveling in the kind of model's runway gait I'd never get away with in a million years (or try in a million years).

With the world's coyest grin, Dylan turned to me. "Cool or what?"

"Or what!"

He put a finger to his lips, silently reminding me we were undercover.

Well, I was undercover. *Naked* under cover. Dylan was fully clothed.

"How the hell did you get in here?" I hissed.

He crossed his arms over his chest and leaned on the massage table. "Easy. I told them I was a graduate of the Cornick School of Massage in Chicago, class of 2003. Top of the class, mind you."

"And they took your word for it?"

"Once I showed them my credentials, resume and the glowing recommendations from two of my teachers." He shook his head. "Of course, I had to give a demonstration massage to the office administrator."

"Ms. Pipps?"

"The very one. Is that one uptight redhead or what? But she seemed impressed enough to hire me."

"What do you know about massage?" I demanded.

He feigned hurt. "Plenty."

"Let me guess, you really did attend the Cornick School."

"Nope." He linked his fingers, extended his arms, and cracked his knuckles. "Just the Dylan Foreman School. It's not that hard, really. I just kind of go on ... instinct. Slowly. Deeply. Instinctually."

I made a mental note to tell Elizabeth the first thing I needed upon her return was the heat turned down in here. "And that works?" I mocked. "Slowly. Deeply. Instinctually?"

"Well it certainly worked enough to fool Ms. Pipps."

Checkmate.

Elizabeth knocked and waited until Dylan called permission to enter. As if she didn't want to interrupt something. *Was that why this place was so popular with the ladies?*

"It's fine. Mrs. Pipps says I'm to accommodate your stay completely, Ms. Davenport."

"Thank you, Elizabeth."

Elizabeth went over to the prep area in the corner of the room and started shuffling through the bottles of lotions, towels and candles, trying to make herself look busy and efficient. To me, of course, but also to Dylan, I had no doubt.

"Well." Dylan cleared his throat. "I guess we'd better get started here."

Great. Just freaking great.

I closed my eyes and retreated into my brain. *"Hello, is this the Springer Show? I have an idea for you. Why don't you do a show where a forty-year old woman lies buck-naked on a table at the hands of a handsome, young, totally studly employee. Wouldn't that be a hoot!"*

Oh well, Mother would watch that episode.

And then I felt Dylan's hands on me. My eyes flew open as his hands glided up my back. Oh, yikes! I took a deep, steadying breath. This did not have to be awkward, I lectured myself. It didn't have to be sexual. I'd just close my eyes and pretend it was Elizabeth kneading my shoulders.

There. I let my breath out slowly. That was the trick.

Except Elizabeth's soft little hands could never feel like this. These hands were large and hard, the fingers strong. Despite my own lecture, I felt myself react to his touch. Then, because there didn't seem to be a damned thing I could do about it, I decided to just let myself feel. He started at my shoulders, finding and rubbing free the knots that I didn't even know were there. I could feel the strength of the man, but also the gentleness within the power. I felt the slickness of the oil, warm and penetrating, the lovely friction ...

"Anything I can get you two?"

I startled and tensed beneath Dylan's touch. How much time had passed? How many minutes had I allowed myself to fall under the spell of his hands. Oh my God! What was I thinking? This wasn't what I'd come here for!

Dylan's hands left me for a second, and when they returned to my back, his touch was much more clinical. More buddy-buddy than ... whatever that other thing was. I felt the heat rising in my cheeks. If I concentrated hard — *baseball, baseball* — surely it would abate in other places.

I cleared my throat. "Elizabeth, thank you for sticking around. You know, now that you mention it, my friend Jennifer told me about a particular incense that she always liked when she came here. I think it was ..."

"Jasmine! Mrs. Weatherby loved it. Whenever she was here, I made sure it was readied in the burner for her."

"Yes, Jennifer was a creature of habit." I forced a knowing chuckle.

Elizabeth smiled. "She liked room 102 always. She wanted the towels warmed, but not too warm. Sweet almond massage oil. She never wanted a glass of wine before or during the massage, but she always enjoyed a coffee afterward. She loved her Columbian dark roast. Then she'd have a seaweed body wrap just before lunch."

"Same routine every time?"

"Oh, yes. We had a standing appointment for her every Monday for the full day. She tipped well. Even the times she didn't make it, she made sure to send a cheque along."

Dylan's hands stilled. He'd caught the same thing I did. Not only the words, but the teasing little rise in Elizabeth's voice as she said the latter.

I tried to match it. "Yes," I said. "She was sometimes ... otherwise occupied."

"You know?"

I shrugged my shoulders, watching Elizabeth as she shot a look at Dylan. Whatever look he gave her back must have been encouraging, because she started talking.

"Oh, thank God! I thought I was the only one and that maybe I should go to the police with the information."

"Yes, well that was my instinct too."

"So you know about the affair."

Holy shit! "Oh, she told you, too?"

Elizabeth nodded vigorously. "She came in one day and I could tell she was very upset. And she ... she just broke down crying, you know? Said she just didn't fit in this society, and as much as Ned tried, she still felt so out of place. And she felt so horrible about the affair, but didn't know how to make it stop."

Apparently, someone did.

"It must have been so hard on her," I said, "to know that her husband was cheating on her."

Elizabeth shook her head. "Cheating on *her*? No, that's not right. *She* was cheating on *him*."

My eyes shot wide, and I forced myself to blink.

"With whom?"

"She never said his name. Only that she didn't know how to break it off. Actually, I think she was scared to break it off. But over the last month or so, she started keeping her spa appointments again, so I guess she finally dumped the asshole. She seemed kind of sad after that. Guilt, maybe. Worry. But she never said anything more about the guy."

I wet my lips. Things were falling into and out of place in my mind. "Elizabeth," I asked, nervously, "did Jennifer have an appointment here last Monday?"

"Yes, she did."

I prayed she'd say she hadn't kept it, but my prayer went unanswered. "She kept it."

I wrapped the sheet around myself and sat up, turned to Dylan. "We're out of here."

He grabbed a towel and started wiping the oil from his hands while

I headed for the change room.

"Oh!" Elizabeth looked startled. "Is ... is something wrong?"

"No, you did everything right. Perfect, in fact." I stopped long enough to tip her the fifty I'd promised. Dylan flashed her a smile. "Tell Ms. Pipps that Mr. Pulse and I hit it off extremely well," I called over my shoulder. "So well, in fact, I'm taking him with me." I shut the door behind me, but not before I turned and took a look at the dropped jaw, wide-eyed look from Elizabeth.

Chapter 8

So, I BLEW off the pedicure and manicure and everything else I'd booked. Unfortunately, it wasn't nearly so easy to brush off the memory of that massage. Dylan's hands on me, firm and soft at the same time. Commanding yet gentle. Powerful yet . . .

Shit.

It had been awhile since I'd been touched that personally. That deeply. And I just hoped that young Mr. Foreman couldn't see through me as easily as he seemed to see through most everyone else, considering how utterly aroused I'd been. Feelings had stirred that had not been stirred in a long, long time. And as every woman knows, there's danger in that. And now it was driving me crazy. But I knew I had to put such thoughts aside. I had more important things on my plate, like saving my backside before Dickhead's deadline expired.

I'd shot out of the Bombay spa, waving a goodbye to Ms. Pipps, calling out a wonderful recommendation of Elizabeth's services over my shoulder.

"Say hello to Mr. Damon!" Ms. Pipps called after me. "Please be sure to put in a good word for the Bombay Spa."

Right, good ol' Matt. "Absolutely!"

And if I ever had the good fortune to meet Matt Damon, I surely would.

So according to my well-tipped source, Ned Weatherby wasn't having an affair, but Jennifer Weatherby was. Or, maybe Elizabeth was lying to me in order to get the good tips? She could obviously tell I was a gossip hound. Maybe she lied to me. Or maybe Jennifer had lied to her?

Yet one thing seemed certain: Jennifer Weatherby had been at the Bombay Spa on Monday. Elizabeth backed up the information that Ned had given Dickhead, and which he'd been so delighted to give to me.

Double damn.

So who the hell had that been in my office that day? And why?

And that was just the beginning of the questions rolling through my mind.

Dylan and I agreed to meet at my apartment. Was I hiding out? Not yet. But I didn't want any interruptions. Dylan volunteered to go by the office before we met at the house. He'd pick up all the notes, all the pictures and recordings, and we'd start from scratch. While I changed from Rich Chick to Dix, he would check on the mail and the messages, and bring along only what needed my immediate attention.

You'd never guess what immediately needed my attention.

When my buzzer rang, I pushed the button to unlock the door without bothering to ask who it was. Yes, it could have been a mass murderer or burglar or someone selling salvation door-to-door, but the way I was feeling, any of the above would do. I'd tear a strip off them a foot wide.

Of course, it was Dylan.

I'd grabbed a change of clothes out of the small dryer — jeans and an oversized t-shirt. After having seen me in my birthday suit with only a sheet over my butt, I wanted to show him something as far away from that vision as possible. I was just coming out of the bedroom, baretting my hair high on my head, when he let himself in the unlocked door. I could tell instantly that something was wrong.

"What is it?"

Juggling the McFood he'd picked up for our lunch, he pulled a letter from his back pocket and handed it to me. An official looking letter, from the law offices of Constantine, Trodbridge and Poole.

"Shit." I tore it open and read it quickly. I could feel the tension in my jaw as I finished.

"What is it, Dix?"

"Apparently, Mr. Jeremy Poole has convinced the court that I'm a threat to his client."

"*What?*"

"It's a restraining order. I'm to stay at least a hundred yards away from Ned Weatherby, the Weatherby residence and Weatherby's office at all times."

I fell onto the sofa. I could feel the headache coming.

I looked at the damn document again. Dated today. Signed: *Judge*

Stella Q. Stephanapoulis. Ordering me to stay away from Ned Weatherby and his home and business.

I'm not one to feel sorry for myself. I have never labored under the illusion that life was fair. But holy shit, this was so wrong! How was I supposed to investigate, to clear my name, if I couldn't even access one of the main suspects?

"How about this, Dix?"

"How about what?"

Kicking off his boots, Dylan walked into the dining room with the fast food. *"Dix Dodd: call if your man is missing in action, or you're missing his action."*

"What?" I followed him to the dining room table.

"Yeah, that wasn't my favorite, either. Let me run this one by you, then." He cleared his throat. *"When the men are being pricks, it's time to call Dix."*

I groaned, rolled my eyes.

"Come on, Dix! I have to order the business cards next week."

"Why?"

"Because we'll need them."

I had to admire his faith in me. More and more I was concluding that there wouldn't be a business by next week.

"Let me think it over, Dylan," I said, to pacify him.

"Oh, you liked one of those? Nicccce."

"No," I said. "They both suckkkked."

"That's it!" Dylan shouted. *"Pay us the bucks if you think your guy sucks … and we'll find out if you're right!"* He said it in a singsong voice that sounded more like he was planning business cards for Dr. Seuss rather than a private detective currently specializing in busting cheating men.

"That sucks too."

He shrugged. "Yeah. But I'm not giving up on this, Dix."

Knowing his way around my apartment, Dylan deposited the burgers, fries and shakes (his strawberry, mine chocolate) on the dining room table. I pushed the pile of accumulated newspapers, magazines and un-ironed clothes (are there any other kind?) aside.

We sat to eat, but neither of us did so with much enthusiasm.

"I don't understand it." I chewed on a salty fry. "If Jennifer Weatherby kept her appointment, at the spa, then it can't have been her who hired me. And if that wasn't Jennifer who came to the office, then who was it?"

"There doesn't appear to be any *if* about it." Dylan reached inside his leather jacket and pulled out a rolled up copy of today's Marport City *Morning Edition.*

I took the paper from him, and there above the fold was a picture of Jennifer Weatherby.

Dammit. The fry I'd just swallowed turned leaden in my stomach. The women smiling back at me looked nothing like the woman who'd hired me. Now that I thought about it, even as her dead body had lain sprawled on that Persian rug, she hadn't looked anything like the woman who'd hired me.

"I'm a fucking idiot."

"I wouldn't say that, Dix."

"Oh, come on! That pantsuit, Dylan. The one she was wearing when she got plugged. It was definitely a quality garment, tasteful, understated, expensive. Jesus, why didn't I see it sooner?"

"You were upset," he said soothingly. "We all were. And you didn't see her face. I mean, you told the cops she was face down when you found her, right?"

Well, he was right about that. My first instinct had been to roll the victim over and do CPR, but one touch of that cold flesh and I'd known the woman was beyond help. And I'd had no desire for a closer look at death. Still, there were other things I should have noticed.

"No, I didn't see her face, but her clothing — I should have twigged to it then." My eyes widened as I remembered another detail. "And her shoe! For God's sake, it was right there in front of me! She'd lost one of her shoes, and it was normal-sized. Well, a little on the big side, maybe — a size 10, maybe — but nothing like the purple canoes that imposter bitch wore."

"Don't beat yourself up," Dylan advised. "Besides, maybe it's a good thing you didn't know. Maybe if you'd told the cops that, it might have gone even worse for you. I doubt if your favorite detective would have believed you, for starters."

Dylan was right. I really wasn't any worse off than I'd been before. And at least now we had another piece of the puzzle. "You're right." I tossed the newspaper and picked up my fries again. "So, Jennifer kept her spa appointment last Monday, but what about all the other Mondays she cancelled? What's with that? She paid in advance to keep the appointments. Heck, she *tipped* in advance. But then she cancelled without seeking refunds. I know money is no object to the Weatherbys, but shit, that's not a cheap place."

"Covering her ass?"

"That'd make sense if she *was* having an affair. Pretty smart, actually. All she'd have to do is show the receipts and debits on the accounts to prove to Ned she was at the Bombay."

"If they had a joint banking account or credit card account, Ned would see the transaction going through every week and have nothing to suspect."

"And…" I raised a salty french fry as I concluded the point. "Whoever was in our office posing as Jennifer Weatherby … maybe they knew this too. That Jennifer was at the Bombay on Mondays. So …"

Dylan's eyes widened. "So — holy shit! — they set us up."

Us. Yes, I caught that. Amazing how comforting "us" sounds when your ass is in a sling.

And dammit, Dylan was bang on. I'd been set up, all right. That, of course, put a whole new spoon into the pot. And the pot was getting so freakin' full already! "Shit, shit, shit!"

"Hold on, Dix. Let's not get too carried away."

Technically, he was right, but I didn't want to waste a good pissed off. "What the hell is it with people?" I ranted. "Okay, fine, I know I've made my fair share of enemies since I've been in business, but I only ever caught red-handed those with red hands."

"Huh?"

"Oh, you know what I mean."

"Dix, we don't know that this is about us. We still have to assume it's about Weatherby."

Okay, he had a point. Nobody would kill someone solely for the purpose of framing me, no matter how much they disliked me. Or if they did, they'd pick a victim I actually *knew*, someone I cared about one way or another, to make the frame job more plausible.

"Let's take the facts one at a time," he said. "What we *do* know is that the Flashing Fashion Queen who came to you posing as Jennifer Weatherby was not Jennifer Weatherby."

Dylan stood and took his milkshake with him over to the whiteboard I'd propped up on a dining room chair. He drew one of his famous stick figures on the board, and we started filling in the details. About five-ten in low heels, dressed horribly, a purse full of feminine hygiene products and five thousand dollars in cash. Dylan drew some dollar signs floating above the stick figure's head.

I sipped my shake. "How old do you think she was?"

He scratched his chin. "Hard to say with the big glasses on. Mid-forties, maybe."

Geez, he made mid-forty sound Jurassic. "That old?"

"Oh yeah, definitely."

Bummer.

"And here's a thought," I said. "We don't even know for certain our imposter was a female. If I can pass for a man, whose to say a man couldn't pass for a woman?"

Dylan lifted an eyebrow. "You might be onto something there. I mean, remember what she looked like?"

"I know, I know. A purple Amazon with the feet to match." My stomach sank. I'd only thrown the idea at Dylan because I was always trying to impress on him the need to keep an open mind on an investigation, but dammit, I think I was right. "Christ, Dylan, it could *easily* have been a man. Probably *was* a man." I reached for my yellow pad, looking at the tight pairs of circles I'd drawn, again and again. "Oh, for —" I ground back a curse. "*Gonads.* That's what I was doodling while she … oh, hell — *he* — was talking."

"Stones?" Dylan leaned close to look at the pad. "Ya think?"

"I think." I tossed the pad back on the desk in disgust. "How could I have missed something like that?"

"Hey, I missed it, too."

It was the money, of course. I'd been blinded by all that cash. How many times had I said it? People see what they want to see, and I'd wanted to see an easy payday.

"Or maybe not."

I glanced up at Dylan. "Huh?"

He shrugged. "Maybe she was just a masculine looking chick. My uncle married a woman who could pass for RuPaul, if you squint your eyes. And if RuPaul were a foot and a half shorter. And white. And quite a bit pudgier."

I rolled my eyes. "The spitting image, I'm sure."

"It's true. I swear. And you know how it can be with some women as they get older."

I resisted the urge to touch my upper lip. I'd had the latest go-round with the electrolysis needle less than a month ago. I did *not* have a moustache. Well, not much of one.

"Okay, I get the message. It might have been a woman. It equally well might have been a man. Which means we've effectively doubled our suspect pool."

He grimaced. "Looks like it. But it doesn't really change what we need to do, does it?"

"Not really."

We had to find out who Jennifer Weatherby had been seeing. Yes, this assumed that Elizabeth had been telling the truth, but I had little else to go on at this time.

"Shall we talk to the neighbors again?" Dylan asked.

"No. If they haven't told you anything before, chances are they won't now. So let's forget the new neighborhood and check out the old neighborhood."

"What are you thinking?"

"Maybe Jennifer kept in contact with someone from her old days before she married Ned. If she felt out of place in Ned's world, maybe she kept her place in the world she knew before him."

"The other side of the tracks."

I shrugged. "Worth a shot. We could talk to some of her old neighbors. See what the gossip was on that side of town."

Dylan looked at me, his blue eyes boring into me with concern and energy. He was chomping at the bit to get going on this. "So you want me on this one, Dix?"

"Yeah. This one's for you, Dylan."

I did want him on this. But not for the reasons he probably thought. Sure, he might find out something of use to us. But I also wanted something else. I wanted him safe. Because I had the niggling feeling again, that gut instinct that told me things were about to get a little dangerous.

"I'm all over it."

The minute I heard his motorcycle fire up and leave the lot, I grabbed my jacket.

Yes, I knew my next move. Knew who I had to talk to. And I was pretty sure it wasn't going to be a pretty conversation. I located my smallest, most efficient tape recorder, slid it into my pocket, and grabbed my purse. I tucked my cell phone inside.

And lastly, I grabbed my gun.

Chapter 9

SOMETHING SEEMED ODD about the restraining order. I'd seen a few of them over the years, both at Jones and Associates and since I'd been out on my own. Admittedly, I'd only glanced at the other orders, usually waved under my nose by agitated clients trying to underscore the danger they were in. But this order I had the joy (ha!) of examining more carefully.

I knew whose signature was at the bottom — Judge Stella Stephanopoulos. She was actually one of the smartest judges in Criminal Court; I'd known her by professional reputation for a long time. But more importantly, I knew her secretary Rochelle. I'd known her for years, actually, and had even arranged some *pro bono* work (a rarity for Jones and the boys, I assure you) for her little sister years ago. Her sister's husband was one-hundred-percent asshole with a pregnant girlfriend on the side, and exposing his assholic nature had been my pleasure. Rochelle's sister had been heartbroken, of course. But like all women, she eventually did what she had to do. Cried herself out, dusted herself off, and made a better life without the jerk.

Rochelle and I had been friends ever since. She trusted me; I trusted her. At the very least, I thought she'd have given me a heads up to let me know the order was coming. Not so I could dodge it, necessarily; just so I wouldn't be caught flat-footed. She'd been Johnny-on-the-spot (Jilly-on-the-spot?) on a number of things over the years, and, I was a little miffed that she hadn't called me on this.

The feeling that my friends were abandoning ship niggled at me, and it took all the will I had to push it aside.

The order had been obtained by that scrawny little poop of a lawyer, Jeremy Poole. You'd think Ned Weatherby was his only client, the way he was hanging off of him. Well, okay, they were obviously friends as well as business associates, judging by the photos I'd taken during that week I'd bird-dogged Ned.

Then again, Ned had so much money, maybe he truly was Jeremy Poole's only client.

Regardless, it was clearly the young lawyer's doing to get Judge Stephanopoulos to sign the order. One hundred yards away from Weatherby, the home, the business.

Yeah, right!

All of this to say that as I sat in my car immediately outside the Weatherby offices waiting for my mark to come back from lunch, I was in full disguise. The last thing I needed was to find myself in jail for breaching the restraining order. I had enough of a jail threat hanging over my head as it was.

So my disguise had to be a doozie. Ah, but all my disguises are doozies!

During my surveillance of the Weatherby Industries when I was supposedly in the employ of Ned's loving wife, I'd seen all kinds of workers entering and leaving. It was a twenty-story building, and it was fully occupied by Weatherby Industries. I'd memorized the faces of all the security guards first. That sorta came with the territory, noticing the 'heat' more than the others. But I'd managed to memorize a good chunk of the rest of the staff, too.

One thing I did notice was that the maintenance staff, a contracted service, wasn't consistent. I was familiar with the traditional (and butt-ugly) uniform for Watership Building Cleaning & Maintenance. It was solid navy except for the big yellow Watership logo (which looks like a pirate ship loaded with mops for sails and brooms for oars) and the Watership name emblazoned on the back. There were pockets and loops on the pants for carrying a variety of tools and products. And I just so happened to have one of these outfits. It was bulky enough to conceal my figure as well as hide any small recording devices or other equipment I might need. Like a gun.

I tucked my hair up under the equally ugly Watership cap and pressed on a blond mustache to my make-up free face. I snorted and spit (albeit into a tissue) to work myself up into man-mode. And I checked myself out in the mirror.

Not bad.

One would have to look long and hard to tell that I wasn't of the weaker (male) sex. But I didn't really worry about it. Like I said, people see what they expect to see. Even me, it seemed. A glimpse of mustache, and they think *guy*. A dress equals *female*. (Damn, but it burned that I hadn't looked harder at 'Jennifer'.) What I'm saying is, as long as I didn't stick around long enough for close investigation, I was safe. Sorta.

Shit, who was I kidding? Safe was the furthest thing from what I felt.

I crumpled the restraining order and stuck it in the glove compartment, and was just slamming it shut when I saw the reason for my trip to Weatherby Industries walking into the building. His head was bent and his strides scissored determinedly as he entered the front door. Two women stopped to talk to him, one going so far as to put a hand on his shoulder, but he just brushed past them and hurried away as if the devil himself were on his tail.

Nope, not the devil. Just me.

I got out of the car, and walked toward the building, determined to have a conversation with Mr. Billy Star.

And yes, as I walked toward the building, I checked for my gun, reassured by its cold weight. Even as I did it, I wondered if I was being overly paranoid.

On the other hand, someone had killed Jennifer Weatherby. The same someone had possibly set me up to take the fall. And I had no doubt that same someone wouldn't think twice about seeing me dead, too, should I get in the way. And I was always getting in the way; it was my job.

Overly paranoid, my ass.

I entered the Weatherby building directly after Mr. Billy Star — quickly enough so that I could see him getting on the elevator, lean to push a button, and turn with red-rimmed eyes to stare up at the top of the doors and watch the numbers. I had called his office right after Dylan left my apartment, and was only half surprised to find him working. Ned Weatherby would understandably be absent; Billy had to keep the business running smoothly. But there was more to his appearance at the office.

Red rimmed eyes didn't surprise me. If anything, they confirmed my suspicions.

I watched the elevator lights, rising steadily and stopping on the top floor.

I took the next elevator up, waiting impatiently then standing as inconspicuously as possible beside the two suited men. It worked. They didn't seem to notice my presence, or my listening in to their conversation.

"I heard Mrs. Weatherby had been shot three times."

"Maybe it was a suicide?"

"Three shots?"

"I heard old Ned had a lover. Bet it was that new girl in accounting."

"I heard Mrs. Weatherby was fooling around on Ned."

"Holy crap! I can believe it."

It didn't surprise me rumors were flying already. Stuff like that was always flying at times like these. But how much was rumor and how much was truth? Damn elevator. It moved too quickly and dropped my loose-lipped fellow travelers off on the 18th floor.

I quickly found the maintenance closet and jimmied the lock. I grabbed some Windex and hooked it onto my uniform. I loaded a maintenance trolley with what surely looked official and started heading down the hallway. Star's office, as I'd ascertained on my way down the hall, was the third to the right off the elevator. Right next to the corner office of Ned Weatherby. I cringed. That had to bite, considering that Star was the major partner just before the stock in the company went skyrocketing. Ned had made millions. And no doubt an enemy in the now under-his-employ Billy Star.

I passed a couple of other male janitors in the hallway, just as I was about to enter Star's office — their navy and yellow WATERSHIP uniforms visible from a mile away. They looked at me strangely, trying to place me.

"'lo," I said with a manly nod of acknowledgment. I adjusted the rolls of TP on the cart (like what the hell else was I supposed to do?).

They nodded back. These guys could have been a father and son team, they looked that similar.

"You new here?" the older one asked.

"New? Yeah, very new. First day." I deepened my voice and slowed my speech.

"Well, doesn't that fuckin' beat all." His coworker cast me a disgusted look. "Takes us five years to get this floor, and this dude comes in and day one, comes up here."

"Don't seem right."

I snorted a laugh and scratched my crotch. "Yeah, well, my uncle owns the company."

"Is that right?" the young one said, grinning a smartass grin. "Your uncle is Sophia Maria Watership?"

I rolled my eyes. "Don't be stupid. My uncle is her husband," I gambled. Poorly.

"You mean her *late* husband?"

"Yeah." I squared my shoulders (thanking myself for remembering to add the shoulders pads to the uniform for the decidedly male appearance). "You got a problem with that?" I said it with so much attitude, Steve McQueen would have been proud.

"I do," Shorty answered.

"Let's call head office, son." The old fellow shook his head. "Something isn't quite right here." They started walking away.

Aw shit!

"You do that," I called. "And when you talk to Aunt Sophia, you tell her I'll be over for supper at six tonight."

They halted and looked back at me.

"It's canasta night," I said, "and Aunt Sophia don't like me late on canasta night. Tell her I want her to make that seafood lasagna, but don't use those cheapie small shrimp like last time. And tell her I'll pick up some of the good rolls at the market on my way in. Oh, and tell her that if I catch my cousin Charlie cheating again, there'll be hell to pay. Oh, and be sure to tell her —"

"I look like your message boy?" Shorty called. "Tell her yourself!"

"Yeah," the other chimed in. "Tell her yourself! We've got work to do."

It worked. For now. But I wasn't foolish enough to think what I'd pulled on them would work for long.

They both gave me one last spiteful look before proceeding down the hall. And I had the sneaking feeling that though I wasn't yet busted, it wouldn't take Tweedledee and Tweedledumb long to check out my story.

I'd have to move fast.

Every indication I had of Billy Star from my week of running surveillance on his boss was that he was a hot head. And well, maybe there was a legitimate chip on his shoulder — I'd be pissed too if someone bought me out just before business skyrocketed. But really, what was Billy to do? He was well over fifty, had built the business alongside Ned from the ground up; it was all he knew. With a mortgage and an aging father to look after, not to mention two kids in college from his former marriage, he had to keep working for Ned.

That's why I packed the heat. Just in case I needed some motivation for him to calm down should he be inclined to go ballistic on me. He was a big man. Rugged. Obviously able to take care of himself, and though I wasn't intimidated by his size, I wasn't stupid either.

This was a murder investigation, after all.

And there had been tension, anger and hatred in the eyes of both Billy and Ned as they'd fought. It didn't take a trained private eye to come to that conclusion. But why would Ned keep Billy around if they got along so poorly? And oh, wait a minute, didn't I recall at the house when Jennifer's body was found, Ned and Jeremy Poole discussing calling Billy? Yes, they had.

Oh, man, I was missing something here.

Plus there was the information Mrs. Presley had provided about Billy's frequent trips to the Underhill Motel. Granted, that could be unrelated, but I was betting it wasn't.

Actually, I was betting my ass it wasn't.

Literally.

Suite 2002, Mr. William T. Star, Vice President.

His door was closed, but I doubted it was locked.

Slowly, quietly, I turned the doorknob right as far as it would go before I pushed the door open just enough to peek inside. I was hoping to catch a quick look at Billy Star before he noticed me, before his guard went up. I wanted an honest look at his emotions. An honest reaction.

I lucked out.

Now the scary thing about catching peeks at people is that you never know what you're going to catch peeks of. I've seen more guys surfing the net for porn that one could shake a ... okay, a stick at (no pun intended). I've caught more than a few people picking their noses and digging out their ears with their pens (these top my list of things I'd just as soon forget). I've overheard telephone conversations that would make a sailor blush. And certainly, I've caught people in all sorts of compromising positions. Hell, I've caught them in positions I didn't even know were physically possible. But the sight of Billy Star sitting at his desk without the knowledge that I was watching him is one sight that I will never forget.

He sat hunched over his desk with his head in his hands, crying softly. He made very little noise, and his shoulders shook with the effort of containing it. For such a big, powerful man, he looked very vulnerable to me then. As if a feather falling onto his shoulder would just break him.

"Billy Star?" I dropped the fake voice. "We need to talk."

Billy's head shot up as I walked into the office, and closed the door behind me. "I don't know who you think you are. But get the hell out of here right now."

"That's not possible, Billy," I said. I ripped off my fake mustache, slowly. Not for sake of drama, but because I'd used too much damn glue and it hurt like hell.

He looked at me incredulously. "What the — who are you?"

"Dix Dodd."

"And what the hell are you doing here, Dix Dodd?" He stood, all hulking muscle.

I braced myself as he started toward me, possibly to throttle me.

"I'm investigating the murder of Jennifer Weatherby," I said in a rush. "And I'm damn determined to find out who's responsible."

He stopped in his tracks. "Who hired you?"

I fought the urge to preface my comments with *Okay, here's where it gets tricky*. "Jennifer."

He blinked. "Jennifer hired you to find out who killed her before she was killed? Are you nuts? Are you … you …" He looked me up and down. "What the hell are you, anyway?"

"In answer to your last question, I told you, I'm a PI. In answer to your other query, yes, I probably am nuts."

"I'm calling security." Billy picked up his phone and stabbed the first button.

I had to talk quickly. "Jennifer hired me to find out who was having an affair with her husband. She was sure Ned was cheating on her, and I think her curiosity got her killed. And the only way I'm going to catch who killed her, is if you help me figure things out." I drew a shaky breath. "And dammit, I'm the only one who can figure this mess out. But not unless you help me, Billy."

Billy sat down heavily into his chair. "Jesus Christ." He put the phone back in the cradle, and shook his head. "Poor Jennifer. Poor, sweet Jennifer."

He cried. Big Billy Star was a broken man.

Okay, I've never been good with the right words, unless of course the right words were 'Aha, caught you!' But somehow I doubted those would fit this particular situation. It was clear that Billy was heartbroken over Jennifer. Clear that he'd loved her, which didn't come as a surprise to me. Because I was pretty damn sure which blond he had been hanging out with at the Underhill Motel and pretty sure why Jennifer had missed so many appointments at the Bombay Spa.

I didn't sit; that didn't feel right. But I did walk closer to Billy, deeper into the office. It was large, as offices go. Billy sat behind a beautiful mahogany desk. Above him hung a huge picture of Billy and Ned Weatherby shaking hands. Happier days, when each of them was twenty pounds lighter and a few gray hairs shorter. Days before the buyout, no doubt.

"I ... I can't believe Jennifer hired you," Billy said. He sat up straight and wiped a hand long over his face. "She had her suspicions of Ned, of course. Lots of suspicions over the years. And some of them, I know for a fact, were well founded. But ..." He shook his head again. "I can't believe it would matter to her anymore."

"Why's that?"

Billy hesitated. "Why should I tell you anything?"

"Because I think that you and I have the same interest here, Billy. We both want to find out who killed Jennifer."

He sighed long and shakily. "I saw you at the Weatherby house the night ... the night Jennifer was killed. Jesus Christ, I couldn't believe it when Ned's lawyer called me. What's his name ...?"

"Jeremy Poole," I supplied.

"Jeremy *Fool* if you ask me. That guy hangs off Ned like white on rice, or ..."

"Flies on crap?" I offered. Yes, I was truly starting to have a most negative opinion of the young lawyer, but my eloquent metaphor was an attempt to bring Billy more over to my side. Hopefully, it let Billy feel that I was a kindred spirit in his time of need. Hopefully, we'd semi-bond in our trashing of the lawyer.

He snorted a halfhearted laugh.

I drew a breath, and took the lead. "How long have you been sleeping with Jennifer Weatherby?" I asked with an authority I hoped to soon have.

He didn't hesitate a heartbeat. "A year, six months, twelve days."

"Continuously?"

His eyebrows knit. "I appreciate the vote of confidence, Ms. Dodd, but not even I can keep it up that long."

"I mean, were you having an affair the whole year, six months and twelve days, or did you have a hiatus in there?"

The look he gave me affirmed my suspicions that there had been a break, or at least an attempted break, by one of them. And if it was Jennifer, I could very well be sitting with her killer.

"Why do you ask?"

"Confirmation," I lied. "Just confirmation of what I already know."

"We ... cooled things down for a while. It was all part of the plan."

"What plan?"

His eyes misted over, and though I'm sure he realized he was still talking to me, it was as if he thought Jennifer could hear him herself. "I really loved that woman. With all my heart. And we were planning on making it happen. Planning on making a life together. Jennifer was the best thing that ever happened to me."

"And she loved you?"

He stirred in his seat. And paused for just one telltale heartbeat. "She did."

"Then why do you think she hired me, Billy?"

"You see," he said, clearly rattled, "that's what I don't understand. Why Jennifer would give a rat's ass about whether or not Ned was fooling around when we were planning on running away together."

"There's a possibility, Mr. Star, that whoever came into my office last week was merely posing as Jennifer. And it's possible that that imposter is responsible for her death."

"Then you'd better find her before I do, Dodd." I could see the clenching of his fists, a graphic reminder of his temper. "Because if I get my hands on whoever killed Jenny, I'll kill them."

I nodded, fully believing him.

"How did it start between Jennifer and you?"

Billy tensed visibly. "It was payback at first. Ned took from me, I wanted to take from him. For years, I wanted that bastard to hurt like he hurt me and so many others. So, I thought what better means of payback than to take his wife. Not that I had any initial interest in Jennifer." He paused for my reaction.

Which would have been *fuckin' pig* in other circumstances. "Go on," I said evenly.

"I'd known Jennifer for years, but always as Ned's wife. Nothing more. But I did know that she was lonely. And yes, I knew I could take full advantage of that. So I started to flirt with her whenever I saw her. I'd call her to say 'hello'. And it led to more. But then ... when I started to get to know her, how could I not fall in love with her? She was so smart, so witty and so very alone in the world."

"Alone?"

"Jennifer never fit into Ned's world. Not with his parents, not with the snooty neighbors. They all wanted her to be the same — quiet and polite and fucking plastic. She couldn't be. She wasn't a high-society snob. She wasn't the shopaholic doting daughter-in-law. So she kind of retreated from everything and everyone in her world. Know what I mean? She retreated into herself. But once I got to know her …"

"Did Ned know about the affair?"

"He thought it was over," Billy said. "We convinced him it was over. That was part of the plan, too. We didn't want him suspecting anything while we got our ducks in a row to get the hell out of here. We were going to leave before the renewal of the vows this weekend."

"I take it the vow renewing thing was Ned's idea?"

"Worse." Billy snorted with disgust. "It was the minister's. Can you believe it? But Ned got caught up in this new preacher's bullshit that that would make everything better. Renew the romance and all that. It's bad enough Ned got in with that new church — all the money he's donated to it would make your head spin — but now the minister is trying to re-cement the marriage? Just makes me sick!"

"So he knew about the infidelity?"

"Yeah."

"Was Jennifer scared of her husband?"

Billy hesitated a moment too long. I could tell he was picking and choosing his words carefully. That always made me suspicious.

"Not really. She just didn't want the public hassle. The pictures on page four, the in-laws growling her out …"

"Did Jennifer have a pre-nup?"

"No. When she and Ned were married, Weatherby Industries was in its infancy, hardly worth a thing. Actually," Billy's jaw tightened with anger, "it was Weatherby and Star Industries back then."

"So once the divorce was through," I offered carefully, "half the assets — including half the business would be Jennifer's, and then yours and Jennifer's if she married you. Financially, you'd be on top again. Right, Billy?"

He stared at me unblinking, and I stared back.

"I think you'd better get your ass out of here, Dodd. I don't like what you're implying."

He stood, towering a good eight inches taller than me, his clenched fists shaking.

"I just have one more question?"

"We're done," he said coming around the desk and advancing

toward me.

My mind shrieked *skedaddle!* but my gut told me to stay.

"Why didn't Ned fire you?" I asked.

He stopped in his tracks and looked at me, startled. "Christ! You're not too damn good at this job, are you, Dodd?"

Ouch. "What do you mean?"

"He can't. If that son of a bitch ever tried to —"

He shut up. Too quickly; too thoroughly.

And at the sound of the cigarette-scratchy voice from behind me, I realized why.

"What's going on here, Billy?" Luanne marched into Billy's office, followed by two burley security guards that looked absolutely clueless as to what to do. And bringing up the rear, of course, were Tweedledumb and Tweedledee.

Busted!

"Nothing, Luanne. Nothing at all. This lady was just leaving."

She hissed at him. "I hope you weren't telling any of your lies against Mr. Weatherby." The woman stood close to him. He dwarfed her in height, but it was easy to see she was scaring the crap out of Billy.

"I ... I didn't say a thing, Luanne."

"Gentlemen, you know what to do." Luanne nodded to the security guards.

"Yes, Miss Laney."

Left-side guy grabbed a little too roughly. The maintenance staff were dismissed with a wave. I expected to be steered toward the elevator, but was turned right and directed down the staircase, away from prying eyes. Unceremoniously, I was escorted/tossed/shoved out the back door.

"If you ever come back here, Dix Dodd," Luanne said, "I'll have a restraining order filed against you so fast your ugly little head will snap!"

I was about to tag her with my best "Ha! There's already one against me," but I thought better of it.

And I couldn't help but wonder as I got to my feet and dusted off my butt, how the hell did she know who I was?

Chapter 10

I WAS SITTING at my desk, reading and re-reading the notes I'd taken that day the mysterious blond had come into my office when I heard the police sirens in the distance.

Uh-oh.

Tensing, I sat there and listened for the sirens to draw closer and closer until they converged in my parking lot. Just how many cruisers would Detective Head send my way when he heard I'd violated the restraining order? Two? Six? Would he call in the military from the nearby base? A helicopter and a half-dozen tanks, maybe? But as I sat there, the sirens peaked then faded until I could no longer hear them.

Huh.

I'd thought that Luanne Laney, a.k.a. Weatherby's psycho secretary from hell, would have had the police on my doorstep in no time. Damn, she was like a crazed German shepherd on Red Bull. True, she didn't seem to know about the restraining order being in place when she threatened to slap me with another one. But I figured when she raised the matter of my incognito visit with Ned, or worse, lawyer dude, my ass would be grass. I pictured Ned and his lawyer racing each other to the phone to call the cops to report my transgression.

I glanced down at the yellow legal pad I'd been studying. Too damn sunny of a yellow, if you asked me. It lay there on my desk, mocking me with its happy yellowness. I picked it up and looked over my notes and doodles again. Was I missing something? Maybe the answer was there, if I could just see it.

I stared into the pad, like when you're looking at one of those 3D thingies and the hidden picture suddenly leaps out at you from behind all those dots and squiggles if you can let your eyes drift out of focus.

Nope. Nothing leapt out at me.

I looked at the pad again. The tight little circles I'd already decoded.

That was my subconscious saying, Dix, honey, your client could be a dude. Although looking at them now, they could also be my nerves. Lord knows they were wound tight enough.

But the other stuff ... stairs going to nowhere. Was that significant? Did it relate to the many floors of the Weatherby building?

I'd learned a long time ago that women were better off when they trusted their instincts. What had my intuition been telling me that day when I'd made those scribbles?

Damned if I knew.

With a sigh, I tossed the pad down and picked up the phone. I punched in my password and checked the voice mail. No messages, but there were 33 hang-ups since Dylan and I had last been at the office, all from an unknown number.

Dylan's female friend? Something fluttered in my stomach.

Okay, Dix, what'd you think? That the guy was celibate? Ha! Not in a hundred years. But he'd never talked about anyone seriously, never invited a guest up to the office. Not that I'd be jealous if he did. Not that we had the kind of relationship where I had the right to be jealous. No, it was strictly professional between Dylan and me.

My mind flashed to the memories of the massage room and his strong hands ...

The phone rang, scaring the shit out of me. I glanced at the call display. Unknown number. This should be fun. I picked up the receiver.

"Dix Dodd," I said in my sweetest, I-am-so-*not*-jealous voice.

Click.

Grrrrr. All that feigned sweetness for nothing.

I thumped my boots onto the desk, and turned my mind to the more pressing matter at hand.

Apparently my hunch had been right. Billy Star's frequent guest at the Underhill Motel was none other than his boss's wife, Jennifer Weatherby. (I made a mental note to send Mrs. Presley a basket of goodies for her help.) I must admit, my stomach turned at the thought of Billy seducing Jennifer to revenge himself on Ned. What a selfish asshole. Yes, Billy Star was definitely a rat. But I really doubted that he was a killer rat. He'd said everything changed when he fell in love with Jennifer, and I believed him. He'd been torn apart when I'd come across him at the office. I doubted that he was that good of an actor, especially since he had no idea he'd had an audience.

Still, Billy Star knew something. Something that I'm sure he would have told me had Luanne not walked into the office just then. And the way his face dropped when she did told me something else. I'd never seen a man pale so quickly. Clearly Billy was scared of her.

She kind of scared me, too, in a knuckle-rapping Nazi-bitch teacher kind of a way. She was ferociously protective of her boss.

"Okay, Dix," I muttered. "Just the facts. What do you know so far?" I was swimming in information; I had to compartmentalize.

The fact was, Ned was looking more and more suspicious to me. Maybe he wasn't so in-the-dark on the affair continuing as Billy seemed to think he was? And even if he were, even if he truly believed it was over, there was bound to be residual jealousy. People didn't just forgive and forget overnight, especially when it came to something as volatile as infidelity and sexual jealousy. Could Ned have orchestrated all the events that were now in motion? Could he have had Jennifer killed, and set me up accordingly?

If he did kill his wife and set me up, one thing was for certain. He'd hired an actress (actor?) to play Jennifer. Neddybear was at least 6' 2" without heels. If he'd presented himself in drag, I'd have drawn a frank to go with those beans. And if he were responsible for Jennifer's death, he would have hired out the hit, too. Made sense, really. Hire a PI to watch him all week so when the hit went down, he'd have a rock solid alibi.

And Billy had told me that he knew Ned had had mistresses in the past. Maybe he did again. Maybe someone he wanted to replace as the current Mrs. Weatherby? Was the planned renewal of vows all a hoax? Or was the mistress usurped when Ned 'found' the new religion and the pastor he seemed so very fond of?

Except Ned as the killer felt too neat. Plus he'd looked so horrified when he'd found Jennifer.

As I wrestled with all this, another fact dawned on me — I was hellishly tired. Sometimes the rush of adrenaline can backfire. It suits you fine when you need it, but the coming down from it usually means a crash.

I slouched down in my seat, my butt hanging precariously close to the edge of the chair. Before my bleary eyes closed, I looked at the coffee pot in the corner that seemed to be calling me. Ah, sweet, sweet caffeine. Dylan should be here any minute. I could start the coffee for us. Or I could grab a few minutes sleep, something I hadn't had in almost 24 hours. It was a short contest. Within minutes I'd drifted into dreamland.

And of course, The Flashing Fashion Queen, was waiting for me there.

She was as blond as ever, this dream lady of mine. But she no longer was the mysterious lady in my mind; now she was the Flashing Fashion Queen. Purple clad, hat wearing, Flashing Fashion Queen. And she was pissing me off.

It was not uncommon for me to dream of the cases I was currently working. It was not uncommon for 'aha' moments to come within the dreams. And even as I slept, I knew better than to dismiss the dream lady before me. I knew she wasn't Jennifer, but she had something to tell me.

Again she flounced into my dream, swirling her purple skirt around. It flew up over her knees to about thigh-high on her smooth legs. The scene was hazy around her, and this time again, she twirled away and eluded my reaching grasp. Coyly, she turned from me, and I still couldn't see her face.

"So what shall I call you?" I asked.

"Why, Jennifer, of course."

"But that's not your name."

She giggled. "Jennifer's a lovely name. I think I'll keep it."

"But you're not her."

"Oh, poop!" She stopped dead in her tracks. Her back was to me but I could see the stiffening of her shoulders. "Given the chance, I'd make a wonderful Jennifer." Her voice turned pouty. "How did you know I wasn't her?"

"I'm smarter than you think," I said. "I figured it out."

She laughed out loud. "Oh, you're not half as smart as you think, Dix Dodd."

I ran a hand through my hair. God, I knew I was dreaming . . . why was I so very tired? "What am I missing, Blondie?"

She began to walk away. "You're not missing anything, Dix. Everything's right before your eyes. Always has been."

"But who are you?" I screamed at her. "Just tell me who the hell you are!"

It was then that she stopped and turned back to me. Her face was now obscured by the haze of the dream and by the same glasses, hat and ton of makeup she'd worn into my office the day we'd met, the day I'd dubbed her the Flashing Fashion Queen. She snarled at me. "I'm you're worst nightmare, Dix Dodd! Because you're just too damn stupid to figure it out!" She ran then and I could barely hear her trailing-off voice.

I awoke with a teeth-rattling jolt as I slid from my chair and my butt hit the floor.

Damn! Even in my dreams I was thought of as incompetent.

I ran a hand over my sore rear as I stood and climbed back into the chair. My legal pad stared up at me. I grabbed it quickly and started to write under the doodles I'd drawn. I wanted to get all the elements of the dream before they drifted away.

She's a bitch ... and not in the good way.

Okay, now that that was out of my system:

She'd swirled and swirled and swirled.

She wore the same clothing: bright purple dress with the mile-wide shoulder pads (or mile-wide shoulders?), floppy hat and dark sunglasses.

"I would make a lovely Jennifer."

Jealousy.

No, not me. My dream mind was telling me that jealousy was the motive for this whole mess. Responsible for Jennifer's dying.

I pressed the pencil to breaking as I wrote down the last glimpse of dream I retained.

"You're just too damn stupid to figure it out."

The phone rang again.

I snatched up the receiver without looking at the call display.

"Dix Dodd," I answered. And yes, to hell with the sweet voice. My tailbone hurt, dammit!

Silence.

Well, almost silence. I could hear someone breathing very heavily on the other end of the line. Okay, kind of breathing, kind of panting. I glanced at the call display, and *surprise, surprise*, it displayed unknown. Either Dylan's girlfriend had worked herself into an, um ... frenzy and had breathlessly been expecting him to answer, or the caller of the day had just finished running a marathon.

Or maybe he was some pervert looking for a little phone fun?

And if this latter reason was the plan, boy, did he have the wrong number.

The heavy breathing continued.

"Listen, pal, I don't know what kind of kinky stuff you think you're going to pull here. Maybe you get your kicks by shocking women, but I've heard it all. Hell, I've *seen* it all, and it ain't as pretty as they make it sound. And let me tell you, you depraved little shit, if you think for one fuckin' minute —"

"Dix Dodd, don't you remember me?"

Oh shit. It was *her.* For a moment I wondered if I was still asleep. Because the voice on the phone belonged to the one and only Flashing Fashion Queen. The selfsame lady who'd been in my office just a few short days ago, and in my dreams a few minutes ago.

"Ah, Jennifer Weatherby," I said. "I thought you were dead."

"Maybe ... maybe I am. Maybe I'm calling from beyond the grave?"

"Beyond the grave? Wouldn't that be one hell of a long-distance charge?"

"You don't believe me?" She was mocking me in her slow, throaty voice. "Oh boo."

"Boo?" I scoffed. "I don't believe in ghosts, Blondie! Who the hell are you?"

She ignored my question. Not that I expected a direct answer, but a clue would have been nice.

"You might not believe in ghosts. But you do believe in money, Dix Dodd."

Okay, she had me on that one. "What the —"

"I left the rest of the payment in your car. The other five thousand dollars for your week of service. You certainly earned it."

"Why would you do that?"

"Because you did what I asked you to do. And I always keep my promises."

"I repeat, why would you do that?"

She laughed, one of those forced, out loud laughs that always bugged the shit out of me. "You're not all that smart, are you Dodd?"

I had to retort with something professional. "Bite me."

"No, thank you," she replied, "you're not my type."

Okay, now I was ticked. "Listen, Blondie, I've had just about enough of this —"

"Just check the car, Dix. You left it open, again. And I left the envelope on the front seat. Your payment's in there. The other five thousand dollars for a job well done."

"You're lying."

She snorted a most unladylike laugh. "Go see."

Click.

Ah ... ffffff-hell!

I had every confidence that this mysterious caller was playing games with me. Every confidence this woman was having the time of her life, yanking my chain. And every freakin' confidence that I'd find no envelope of money awaiting me in the car.

Yes, my car probably *was* unlocked, because nine times out of ten, I left it that way. Bad habit, I know, but how did the caller know this?

I had to go see, of course. Stopping just long enough to start a pot of coffee, I headed out the door. As I strode across the parking lot, it occurred to me the Flashing Fashion Queen was probably watching me. I paused, scanning every window, every doorway. Nothing. I could feel myself getting angrier by the minute. I almost turned in my tracks and headed back to the office, because, of course, there would be nothing there!

I glanced in the car window.

There was something there.

"Holy shit."

On the seat, rested a plain brown envelope. *Dix Dodd* was printed on the package in wide black marker. It was thick — just thick enough to be a wad of bills equaling five thousand dollars.

Or possibly a bomb.

The thought froze my hand on the door handle. Softly, slowly, I started to back away. That's when I heard the squeal of tires as a car came speeding around the corner. The engine revved as it changed gears and shot forward. It took me all of a heartbeat to realize it was coming straight for me. It took another heartbeat to realize it was *her* behind the wheel. She wore the same floppy hat, same blond wig and wide sunglasses. And a mile-wide evil grin as she sped toward me. The damned envelope, the call, it was all a set up to draw me out here!

I dove across the hood of my car, half on my elbows and half on my side, landing hard on the asphalt on the other side. I sat up, and watched as the car sped off. It had barely missed me.

YPC 389, YPC 389, YPC 389. I repeated it another half dozen times until it was burned in my memory.

"Shitttttttttt!" I climbed to my feet, swearing as I looked at my bleeding elbow. "Okay, bitch," I muttered. "I'll bite."

I opened the passenger door and retrieved the envelope, which was surprisingly heavy. I was so shaky I wanted to slip into the passenger seat, but I didn't think that was prudent in case YPC 389 came roaring back to take another swipe at me. Instead, I closed the door and leaned on the car's fender, letting it take some of the weight off my trembling legs.

Ears tuned for a racing motor, I ripped the envelope open.

Of course, I was no longer expecting a bomb. Because — duh — had the Flashing Fashion Queen wanted me dead by means of a car bomb, she'd have slid it under the seat and used her phone call to prod me into hopping into the car to race off somewhere, triggering the big *ka-boom* when I keyed the ignition.

Nor did I expect the other five thousand dollars. And I sure didn't expect a plate of warm cookies. But what I *really* didn't expect was what slid out onto my hand as I opened the envelope.

A gun. A gun that I had no doubt had been recently fired.

I heard the sirens again, but this time, I had no illusion that the sound of them would drift off into the distance. And as I held the gun, the very gun that I knew had to have killed Jennifer, I could see the flashing red and blue bar lights of a squad car turning into my parking lot. It came to a stop squarely in front of my car. At the squeal of tires from another direction, I turned to see an unmarked Taurus barreling towards me. Instinctively, I raised my hands in the age-old gesture as the unmarked car swung in behind my vehicle, effectively blocking escape. And then — oh, God, my day just kept getting better and better — a snarling, toothpick chewing Detective Richard Head emerged from the second car.

She'd set me up. The Flashing Fashion Queen had planted the evidence, lured me to my car, and called the police to tip them off. And she had left me with the literal smoking gun.

And I couldn't help but hear her words flipping me off in my brain: *"You're not all that smart, are you, Dodd?"*

Okay, even I was beginning to wonder.

Chapter 11

YOU KNOW, MY high school guidance counselor, Mr. LeCarrier, had suggested I be a funeral home director. Or maybe a chiropractor. "How about orthodontics?" he'd said. Of course, he suggested the latter to everyone who managed to scrape by in science. The standing joke was that he was hoping at least one of us would become an orthodontist and remember him fondly by the time his six kids needed braces. As for the other suggestions for me, Mother and I had both laughed. And I'd rejected them all. Too boring, I'd told him.

A nice quiet life, Mr. LeCarrier suggested, would be perfect for a girl like me.

That's what he told all the female students.

Well, this girl had gone into a different line of work. Dangerous, exciting, and anything but quiet.

But right now, I was beginning to think Mr. LeCarrier might have known his ass from his elbow after all. Right now, boring and quiet sounded pretty damned appealing.

Yes, she was one up on me. No, she was two ... wait, make that ... oh, fuck it. Let's just say she was a *few* up on me. The Flashing Fashion Queen — a.k.a. impersonator of the late Mrs. Jennifer Weatherby, a.k.a. My Nemesis from Hell — had me by the short and curlies.

She was framing me big time. Hell, she was trying to kill me big time.

Okay, she hadn't done so great with the killing me part, but the frame job ... man, it was brilliant. Calling the office to get me out to the car (I now had a pretty good idea what the thirty three hang ups were about), putting the murder weapon into my hands, and tipping off the police. It was a masterpiece of timing.

Yeah, she was damned clever.

And I was getting damned worried.

The police cars screeched to a stop, arrayed strategically around me, their blue and red bar lights flashing. Not having a death wish, I didn't wait for an order to be barked over a bullhorn. I immediately raised my hands high, stepped away from my car, then slowly bent to deposit the gun on the asphalt. Still moving slowly, I stood and kicked the Glock toward the closest car.

The doors on the two cruisers popped open and the officers slid into position behind the safety of their doors, weapons drawn and trained on me. A curse dragged my attention to Detective Richard Head, who had just heaved himself from his unmarked Taurus. Unlike the patrol cops, he didn't unholster his weapon. Nor did he hide behind the door of his car. Rather, he strode right up to me.

"What the fuck are you doing, Dix?"

"I'm counting my limbs, dammit, because someone just tried to deprive me of a few of them." In a rush, I told him about the attempt on my life. Told him about the crazed imposter who just tried to run me down. And told him if he'd get his ugly ass in gear, he might catch her!

To his credit, Detective Head instructed the officers to stand down. He also sent a patrol car in the direction I indicated, and radioed in the vehicle description and plates I'd supplied. Of course, I would have felt better about these developments if I thought he believed me. Or if he hadn't put me in bracelets.

"Standard operating procedure, until we sort this out," he said. "Now, would you like to explain why you were waving a handgun around the parking lot?"

"Sure. Right after you explain why half the police force is here staring at me when some maniac woman just tried to run me down."

"We got a 9-1-1 call about a maniac woman waving a gun around in a parking lot. Now, spill. What's going on here?"

Which is when Dylan Foreman showed up. He pulled up on his motorcycle right in the middle of Detective Richard Head's grilling of/ yelling at me, as I tried to explain what had happened. And as I tried to explain why he'd come upon me in the possession of the gun that had most likely — *shit, shit, shit* — killed Jennifer Weatherby.

I suppose I could have tried to pass the gun off as my own, claiming I'd whipped it out in self-defense after that maniac tried to mow me down with her car, but under the circumstances, it didn't seem advisable to play fast and loose with the facts. Especially since an officer had already collected the gun and stuck it in an evidence bag. Especially since they would very shortly know it was not registered to me.

No question about it. Things looked bleak. Even Dylan, always my cheerleader, couldn't quite hide the depth of his concern. Despite all that was going on around us, I felt the tightening lump in my throat.

"Just a setback, Dix," Dylan whispered to me. "Nothing we can't handle."

Come on, Dix, suck it up. I nodded an affirmative *you bet*. It was the best I could manage.

With a nod/grunt from Dickhead, soon there were two police officers from Ident doing a cursory search of my car. I could probably have stopped them; they had no warrant. On the other hand, they *did* have me brandishing a gun in a public parking lot, which no doubt gave them fairly broad scope. On yet another hand (clearly, we are dealing with a six-armed Mahakala here), if my nemesis had been in my car, she might have left trace evidence behind. If so, I wanted the cops to find it with their high-tech searching gear. So I let them have a look.

Moments later, my faced flamed. And no, I'm not talking about the humiliation of standing there in handcuffs while cops searched my car. They may have been officers of the law, but they were still men. Thus, when they drew out the fake boobs I kept stuffed under the seat, the whole place went up in snickers. Eyebrows soared over the fake mustache I'd left in the glove compartment from my stint as Maintenance Man. All they needed now was to find my blow-up doll (a.k.a. Betty, the decoy), and I'm sure they would have pissed themselves laughing. Thankfully, Betty was standing in the closet of my office, behind my truck-driver flannel shirts and nun's outfit.

The first officer was pulling little plastic evidence bags out of his pocket, while the second officer was tweezering things into them. I rolled my eyes as they placed a month-old wrapper from a DQ burger into a bag. Right. Like that was going to have a mountain of clues on it.

"Got a hair here, Detective," one of the cops called to Dickhead. He held the tweezers up like a prize ribbon, as if we could actually see from that distance. "It's blond."

"Well, duh. I'm blond!" I called over.

"Shut up, Dix." Detective Head returned his attention to the men in my car. "Bag it, Edson," he said. "Bag every damn shred of evidence you get. No, wait, even better. Call dispatch and have them send a hook. We'll haul that piece of crap in and have forensics give it a thorough going over."

Dylan shifted beside me. "You can't just —"

"It's okay, Dylan," I said. "Let them."

The way I figured it, the Flashing Fashion Queen had already planted the biggie, the literal smoking gun, and nothing else they found could trump that. I hoped. But I had to risk it, in the hope the CSIs would find some evidence against her. The cops already had my DNA from the night Jennifer was killed when Detective Head had scraped it from my cheek. So hopefully, something else would turn up pointing a finger toward the real killer.

"Do a good job, boys," I called over to the officers in the car. "That car hasn't had a good cleaning in a dog's age. Be sure to get the vacuum deep down in the seats. And under the floor mats. And it's kind of grungy there in the cup holder — too many spilled lattes. I'd wear gloves if I were you."

Detective Head dug in his pocket and pulled out one of the mint toothpicks. I held off on any remarks about comparative phallic symbolism here.

"You just don't realize what shit you're really in, do you, Dodd?" he said.

I snorted. But actually I did fully understand the severity of the situation.

I was being framed for murder.

And well, even on the best of days, that sucked.

"You all right, Dix?" Dylan asked.

"Fine."

Detective Head did a dramatic double take. "All right? You want to know if she's *all right*? Let's see what we got here. Obsessed, love-sick stalker who not only followed the husband of the murder victim around for a week taking pictures, taping conversations, crying herself to sleep, wringing her hands and moaning 'why me' —"

I growled. I mean, I *growled*. This guy was pulling my chain and it was working. I would have liked nothing better than to rip a strip off him. And unfortunately that just would not do. Not now, at least. Beside me, Dylan tensed. I could tell he wanted to rip something off Detective Head himself. I shot him a look that said 'wait', and thankfully, he picked it up.

Detective Head continued, "And now what do we find in the

possession of this lonely spinster? The very same gun that killed Jennifer Weatherby."

"We don't know that it's the gun that killed Jennifer, Detective. That's merely what I've speculated. And as I told you, that gun was left in my car by the woman who came into the office posing as Jennifer Weatherby. That's the woman you should be harassing, not me."

"Right," he said sarcastically. "And you just happen to be the only one to have seen her."

"I saw her," Dylan answered.

"Today?" Detective Head asked, but he knew the answer. "You saw this blond today as she put the gun in the car? As she tried to run down your boss?"

Dylan shook his head. "No. Not today. I saw her the day she came into the office. But, holy hell, just look at —"

Dickhead's lip curled. "Let's move this party along, shall we? We'll get to the bottom of this downtown. I got a nice cozy interview room I can house you in until we get around to asking you a few questions."

Downtown? This I couldn't allow.

If Detective Head got me locked up, I could be there for days. As long as he could possibly keep me. And I had no doubt that during my detention the Flashing Fashion Queen would keep her blond self busy planting more evidence against me. If this woman was to be caught, it was going to have to be by me.

Thus there was no way in hell I could go downtown. I sent a sideways look at Dylan, who, with an almost non-existent flash of eye contact and a barely perceptible nod, signaled his understanding.

"Okay, fine," I said. "I'll be thrilled to ride downtown with you and answer your questions. But first, I have some business to take care of in the office, some stuff I need to hand off to my associate before I go. It'll only take a few minutes. So if you'd take the bracelets off ..." I angled myself to present my cuffed hands to Detective Head.

He raised an eyebrow. "Why would I want to do that?"

"Because no one's arrested me yet?"

The toothpick bobbed. "I could rectify that. Hell, I probably will."

"Come on, Detective," Dylan interjected. "I appreciate you guys felt you were coming into a potentially hairy situation, so I understand cuffing her until you secured the scene. But everything's under control now. No firearms, no resistance. Dix consented to the search of her car, and has said she will answer questions. You don't need to arrest her and you sure as hell don't need handcuffs."

"Whether to cuff or not is my call, and mine only."

"Precisely," Dylan agreed. "But you're supposed to use the minimum force necessary to accomplish the mission. Do you really think you need handcuffs to get Dix downtown?"

"Huh!" I put in. "He probably figures he has to cuff a woman to get her in the car with him."

"Dix," Dylan warned, putting me behind him.

Detective Head's eyes bulged, and his jaw clamped so tight, I'm sure I heard his molars cracking. But after a few seconds, he produced his keys and removed the bracelets. "Ten minutes, Dix. If you're not back down here by then, I'll drag you out."

"Okay, ten minutes." I grabbed Dylan's arm and we headed for the office. "See you then."

"Hold your horses there, Dixiepicker."

I stopped in my tracks. "Oh, what now!" With a huff of exaggeration, I turned toward him again.

Detective Head took the toothpick out of his mouth long enough to bark an order at one of his junior boys in blue. "Go with them. Make sure she comes back out."

"Come on, Detective," I said. "You can trust me."

He couldn't of course, but that wasn't the point.

"Not as far as I could throw you, Dodd."

I chose to make that statement a reflection on his manly strength rather than my size. "Fine!" I shouted at the young officer. "Just hurry up, Junior, I have work to do."

I felt half bad when the young guy paled.

"On second thought," Dickhead said. "Why don't I escort you myself? Yeah, that would work much better."

Damn.

I'd left the office door open, but pretended to fumble with keys in the lock so I could cast another look at Dylan. This is where a smart employee would start rethinking his commitment to his employer and start thinking about covering his own ass. But what I saw in his eyes was a clear, steady message. *I'm with you, Dix.* And oh, Jesus God, my throat got all tight and painful again.

While Detective Head waited behind us, I winked at Dylan in what I hoped he would interpret as an I-have-a-plan message.

The moment we walked into my outer office, I turned to Dylan.

"Get my lawyer on the phone."

"Now wait, Dodd —"

"I know my rights, Detective. And yeah, I know yours too. You can take me downtown and I'll go. I'll answer any and all of your questions, but be damned if I will be downtown without my lawyer waiting there. I have the right to call her, and I'm calling her now. Dylan'll get her on the phone."

I didn't have a lawyer. And of course Dylan knew this too.

"Sure thing, Dix."

Dylan sat down at his desk, picked up the phone, and starting pushing buttons — to nowhere.

I walked from the outer office into my own.

Dickhead had never been into my office. I didn't care about the dust in the corners, or the clutter on my desk. I didn't give a rat's ass what he thought about the one aloe vera plant dead in front of the window. But I knew that his presence, rather than one of the junior officer's, would make my disappearing act harder.

"Geez, Dixie," he said, "what stinks in here?"

"Funny," I answered, crinkling my nose. "Didn't smell a thing till you walked through the door yourself."

He chuckled. Which meant he felt he could afford to chuckle. "You got ten minutes, Dodd," he said. "Then it's downtown with me."

He studied my desk. As I've said, I didn't give a rat's ass about the mess left there, but I didn't want him to see my notes. As if reading my mind, Dickhead picked up the yellow legal pad off the desk. He snarled/laughed/made some guy guttural sound. "What do you do here all day, Dix," he asked eyeing the pad, "draw dirty pictures?"

He truly was an asshole. I ripped the pad from his hand. "These notes are none of your business."

"If it concerns this case, it is."

"What? You think Jennifer Weatherby's case is the only one I have?" Well, it was but he didn't have to know that. "Why, at any given time, I probably have a dozen cases on the go." I waved an arm to the door, indicating he was to leave. "Now if you'll excuse me, I have to get a couple things done before we take our lovely little trip to the precinct."

"I need to keep an eye on you."

Damn.

"You're kidding," I said.

"Not a chance."

"Look, I have some personal things to take care of. The glass is beveled. You might not be able to make googly eyes at me, but you'll be able to see that I'm sitting right at my desk."

"No way in hell, Dixieshit. Whatever you have to do you can do in front of me."

"Fine, at least let me go to the bathroom."

"You can go when we get downtown."

"I can't wait."

"You can!"

I nodded. "Okay, then, you got it." I walked over to my desk, sat, and opened the bottom drawer. And I pulled out a handy-dandy king-sized value pack of my favorite tampons. Yep, a pack of sixty Playtex Supers. (Is there anything higher for a woman in brand loyalty than feminine hygiene products?) I dug around a bit more, and pulled out the box of maxi pads and smacked them down in the middle of the desk beside the tampons. If this didn't get Detective Head out of the office nothing would. I turned to look at a wide-eyed Detective.

"What the hell are you doing?"

I rolled my eyes. "Well, you see, Detective, boys and girls are built differently. While boys have a penis, or rather some of you do, we girls have —"

"Smartass," he growled.

"And since you won't give me a few minutes alone in the bathroom, well, you're about to get a very detailed lesson of those things." I nodded to my closet as I unzipped my jeans and started to shimmy out of them (all the while thankful for the granny panties I wore underneath). "Hand me my the feminine spray from the top shelf will you, the scented one. And while you're at it, there's a spare portable douche Bidet on the top shelf. It takes a minute longer, but *so* very worth it."

"You don't need all that! I was married you know!"

I stopped mid shimmy. "Well I got this itch you see. And my gynecologist prescribed the douche Bidet to relieve the swelling. Just wait, I'll show you."

"Christ! Dodd," he yelled. But he yelled while he headed for the door. I knew it would work. Detailed descriptions of feminine hygiene products scare the shit out of most any man. "You've got ten minutes — no, *eight* minutes — to do whatever the hell you have to do."

At that precise moment — damn the lad could read my mind — the phone on my desk rang. Dylan answered from the outer office, then yelled to me. "Dix, I've got Ms. Bee on the phone."

"Good," I said. "Give me a minute, Dylan, then send the call in."

With a grumble, Dickhead closed the door behind him. I had to work fast.

The cabinet I had directed him to for the douche Bidet (to my knowledge there was no such thing, but I guessed Dickhead wasn't up on these things) — was a cabinet I knew he'd never open in a million years if I asked him to. And of course it was the one that contained good old Blow-Up Betty. I kicked a box on the floor to make it sound like I was rummaging around. And while I did so, I pulled her out, whispered hello, and removed the jacket I'd been wearing. I stuck her plastic arms into it.

She looked better behind my desk than I did. Quietly, I pushed my chair out and sat on the floor. "Okay, Dylan," I yelled. "Give me Ms. Bee."

I picked up on the first ring, glancing only a minute at the call display before I erased it — Dylan's cell phone of course. With my number on speed dial, it had been easy for him to call the office, pretend it was the non-existent lawyer, and buy me some time.

With duct tape I kept in the drawer for such emergencies (and there were a surprisingly number of them), I taped the phone to the blow-up doll's hand, then taped that up to her head as if she were listening. If, and when, Detective Head looked through the beveled glass, he would see the outline of the doll and the black phone positioned against the blond head. And, where he thought I was talking to my lawyer, he maybe would give me a few extra minutes. Maybe.

God, I hoped this worked.

I turned to head toward the window leading to the fire exit. Not a venture I would enjoy. The rusty contraption hadn't been used in years, and it emptied into a narrow alley between my building and the next one. I knew for a fact the alley was full of broken bottles and smelled of urine, but it was a way out.

I had one leg out the window when a thought occurred to me. I went back, grabbed the duct tape and positioned Betty's free hand palm up on the desk in the classic middle finger salute, ready to properly greet Dickhead when he stormed in. Hell, maybe he'd think it *was* me for a moment, after all.

Task completed, I made my way down the fire escape and tiptoed through the broken bottles and other things I didn't want to examine too closely. And just like that, I was officially on the lam.

Chapter 12

I N MY WILDEST dreams, I couldn't have foreseen what would happen to me that day.

Possibly because my wildest dreams do not involve my life going into the dumpster. And there could be no question that's where I was headed. Literally.

The alley, if you could call it an alley when it was bisected by a freaking nine-foot fence, proved a tricky escape route. The fence, a solid wood proposition, was too tall and too foothold-free for me to scale. Fortunately, a dumpster squatted right up against the fence. A dumpster that was no longer covered, its lid having been wrenched off by vandals not long after I'd moved into the building. I'd given up harping to the landlord about it months ago. So, there I am with an open dumpster and a nine-foot fence between me and freedom. No problem, I think. I'd just climb up on the dumpster, edge my way around to the fence and boost myself over.

Great plan, until I lost my footing and fell into the damned thing. And oh, Jesus, what a smell! Cursing, I pushed myself up out of the pizza boxes, rotting vegetables and rolled up disposable diapers. Ugh.

Goddamned leather soled flats. Next time I went on the lam, I wanted better footwear.

And then — oh, shit! — something small and fast moved under my foot. I came up out of that dumpster like a rocket and over the fence, slippery footwear notwithstanding.

As I pulled the cold, green pasta from my hair brushing the ... whatever-the-hell-that-was from my jeans, I realized how very much this whole situation ... well, stank.

But I'd seen a lot over the years as a PI, and if there's one thing I know, it's that women are resilient. When we have to face our dark hours, we do. And we usually find a silver lining there.

Don't we?

My silver lining, as I loped off down the street, was picturing Dickhead, patience exhausted, finally barging through my office door and finding me gone. Finding Blow-Up Betty holding the phone in one hand and flipping him off with the other. He'd be frothing at the mouth!

I felt a tinge of guilt for leaving Dylan behind to handle the wrath of Detective Dickhead. He might not be spitting bullets, but certainly he'd be spitting toothpicks around the office as he raged and made ever more colorful expletives from my name. I knew he'd take it out on Dylan, blame him for my escape. Of course, there was nothing to link my escape to Dylan. Nothing anyone could prove, anyway. But Dickhead was the kind of man who needed to blame others for his fuck-ups — you know, the kind of guy to shoot the messenger (thus back again to his blaming me when his wife found out he was cheating and left him). But Dylan could handle Dickhead. That law degree did come in handy sometimes. Hell, if I knew Dylan, he'd be hard pressed trying to hold back the laughs when he saw Blow-Up Betty so artfully posed. In any case, I'd know soon enough what had gone down between Dylan and the detective.

Because Dylan would know where to find me.

You see, we had it all worked out. Granted, we'd worked it out not so much in anticipation of my escaping lawful custody, but rather as a hedge against the possibility of my having to go into deep cover some time.

If I'd moved the dead aloe vera plant from the window and tipped it over on the floor to the left of said window, he'd have met me at the airport with some cash. If I'd left the plant upside down directly in front of the window, we would meet at the university library (third floor, stack twelve in the BFs). But I'd set it to the right of the window, and he'd know what that meant.

Of course, he also had to know that the cops would be tailing him to see if he would lead him to me. But I had faith in Dylan Foreman. He'd be patient. He'd be smart.

And he'd be there tonight.

I'd slowed to a brisk walk now, partly because I'd developed a stitch in my side (despite my gymnastics in clearing that fence back there, I am no athlete), and partly because I knew I'd attract less attention. But even with an ache in my side, even with the black cloud of a waiting jail cell hanging over me, I couldn't suppress a small smile. The Flashing Fashion Queen thought she was pretty smart. But I was willing to bet she wasn't counting on me running. She'd wanted my ass sitting helplessly in lockup while she dug a deeper hole for me by the minute. Well, bite me, baby! I wasn't going to be her victim. I wasn't going to be anyone's victim. And as far as the Flashing Fashion Queen was concerned, I was about to become her worst fucking nightmare.

Did I finally have one up on her? I couldn't help but grin as I wondered how that would make her feel when she realized I was still at liberty. The control was slipping out of her hands. She'd fucked up this once, and I had to believe that would rattle her.

"Geez, Dix, what's wrong? You look all shook up." Mrs. Presley winked and elbowed me hard. "Get it ...'all shook up'?"

"Yeah, I get it Mrs. P."

For a woman who day in and day out worked below a sign that emphatically told the world she was not related to Elvis, Mrs. Presley had no qualms about stealing a line to get a good laugh. Even if it was her own good laugh.

God, I liked this woman.

We were sitting side by side on the lone bed in Room 111 of the Underhill Motel. This was her 'special' room, reserved for 'special guests'. For the drop of a few quarters, the bed would start vibrating. The lampshades were red and when the lights were on, cast a red haze around the room. There were mirrors on every wall and built into the headboard of the bed. And I'd bet anything that the light fixture hanging from the ceiling would support the swinging weight of at least one nimble person. Hell, the toilet seats were even padded! (God, I hated the deflating sounds those things made when you sat on them, but far be it from me to complain.)

But that's not what made Room 111 special. What made it special was its location, far away from the street at the other end of the motel, with a view that was unobstructed by trees or other structures. A person could keep a pretty good watch on traffic in and out of the motel — be that traffic irate husbands/boyfriends, johns, or in my case, the cops.

But even better, Room 111 had a secret back door. Not one with a doorknob, but a hidden one in the back of the never-used closet. A solid hip to the left of it, and it would open, but only when unlocked from the other side. That back door just happened to lead to a narrow, unlit hallway, low-ceilinged but straight. Those in the know (and few of us were) knew that there was a small penlight stashed up over the doorway. And that passageway led right into Mrs. Presley's kitchen, and thence to the outside via a private exit.

Room 111 was always the last to be rented out. And the door was locked to most clientele, who were unwitting of its existence. But I knew for a fact that at least two women had escaped from abusive ex-husbands that way. And here was the best part — if anyone unwanted were foolish enough to find and burst through that hidden door, they'd receive a lovely how-do-you-do from one of Mrs. Presley's hulking sons at the other end of it, neither of whom would have qualms about beating the crap out of an intruder. Those boys were just that protective of their mom.

"I don't want to get you into trouble, Mrs. Presley," I'd said, when I'd landed on her doorstep. "But holy shit, I'm in trouble!"

She'd raised an eyebrow. "Cops after you?"

"Yeah," I admitted. "I can understand if you don't want to —"

"Trouble? Ah hell, we all have troubles. Quit complaining! You need a room? I got a room. That's it; case closed."

No need to sign the register. She just slipped me the key.

I slipped her a couple hundred from the Jennifer Weatherby advance, which Mrs. Presley promptly pocketed behind her pencil-pen-pencil combination. She was a businesswoman, after all. But I know Mrs. Presley, if I'd come there flat broke and on my ass, there'd be the same room and the same hospitality for me.

And yes, the same old Elvis jokes.

With a gentle suggestion that I might want a shower (okay, more like a 'phew, you really stink'), Mrs. Presley left me. She took the back door, the one that led directly through her apartment and out. She was short enough so that she didn't have to stoop to pass through, and knew the route well enough she didn't bother with a light.

"Usually, I lock this door, but sometimes I forget," she said with an obvious wink. "I'll send that handsome young assistant of yours through when he gets here."

If anyone happened to see Dylan enter the Underhill Motel, they'd only know he entered the main lobby and he'd exit from the same. They'd not see him entering Room 111.

As if in afterthought Mrs. Presley added, "Oh, and when you get in that shower — and I hope that's soon — stick those old clothes in the passage, I'll send Cal or Craig down to get them and throw them in the wash for you. I'll have 'em back in an hour."

"Thanks, Mrs. Presley."

She headed for the closet/back door and gave it a hip check that would have taken out Tai Domi. "Take care, Dix. I mean that. And you get your ass down that hallway double time if you need help. Me and my boys'll be home all night."

The door snapped back into place as she left — back into near invisibility. And I let out a shaky breath I hadn't even known I was holding. And when I took a breath back in — holy shit — even I had to grimace.

Mrs. Presley was right. I *did* need that shower.

I stripped from my standard uniform — jeans, t-shirt, granny panties and sports bra. I hip checked the door open and quickly (as in I'm naked here, quickly) shoved the soiled clothes into the hallway to await retrieval by one of the Presley boys. Then I ran into the bathroom, closed the door and ran the water as hot as I could.

The warmth of the water felt amazing. I shampooed my hair twice, emptying the little hotel bottle of shampoo, and scrubbed every inch of me for a good ten minutes. With the side of my hand, I wiped clear the bathroom mirror, and I combed out my long blond hair. Despite having opened the lone, small window, the bathroom was steamy when I'd finished. Hot. And when I let myself out, despite the terrycloth bathrobe Mrs. Presley had provided, the cool air hit me.

I grabbed the remote and clicked on the room's small TV, not at all surprised to find it tuned to a program that gave new meaning to the phrase 'love triangle'. Hell, I was never that flexible. Quickly … well within an hour … I clicked to another channel, one that displayed the time. It was just after two o'clock. Dylan wouldn't be along for hours, possibly not until after dark. And I knew better than to be out and about in Marport City. Every cop in town would be seeking my hide. I'd leave the TV on, volume muted. When I awoke, it would be easier to open one bleary eye to check the time than to move an actual major muscle to reach for my watch on the nightstand.

With the shower, the heat, and the coziness of the bathrobe, that bed looked damn inviting, despite its garish red bedcover. Of course, a reasonably clean floor would look inviting, considering I'd been sleeping in spurts of about 40 minutes since I embarked on the surveillance of Ned Weatherby just one week ago. I removed the bedcover, revealing red sheets beneath. Figured. I folded the bedspread and dropped it on the lone chair in the room. I tossed the heavy, warm quilt Mrs. Presley had provided over me.

"I'll just snooze for a little while," I mumbled, crawling into the sea of red.

Of course this was the logical choice, I assured myself, closing my eyes. Just until Dylan came.

Dylan. The thought of him was comforting to me. I wanted to see him. Okay, I'll admit it, I really wanted to see him. I couldn't wait to see him.

Strictly professional, I assured myself. *You're just tired and anxious to get working on the case and find out what he knows and needing a coffee and horny as a sailor on shore leave* ...

My eyes opened wide.

It's been a long, lonnng time since I'd been with a man. Okay, if I was honest with myself, it had been a long time since I'd *wanted* to be with a man. Not that I didn't have the physical desires — hell, I wasn't dead. But it had been a long time since I'd thought of one specific man in that way. A long time since I had allowed myself, if only for the briefest moment, to think that way ...

Geez, snap out of it, Dix.

But whatever I was feeling — however I got there and however I justified it, professionally or completely unprofessionally — I couldn't deny the end result. I wished Dylan were here. He would be soon. As I drifted off to sleep, I allowed myself the self-indulgence of thinking of him.

But only for a moment, because wrapped in the snuggliness of the soft housecoat, I wasn't long drifting off.

I dreamed of being back in high school, wandering the hallways in my PJs while the cool kids looked on. Then I was riding an escalator wearing just a pair of old blue fuzzy slippers. That morphed into the one where I was riding an elevator that just wouldn't stop on the damn floor I needed. Okay, normal dreams. But then the dream elevator finally stopped on the floor I wanted. The door opened. And it didn't surprise me that she was there again. There to taunt and torment me. The Flashing Fashion Queen.

I stared at her. She stood on one side of the elevator threshold, and I stood within it. Her back was to me. Why could I never see her face clearly?

"Hiya Dixie," she said, her voice gritty.

"Still got that throaty thing going on, I see. Maybe you should see a doctor." *But for what? A polyp on the larynx or a sex change?*

"You're concerned about me! How sweeeet."

Even as I slept, I could feel my blood beginning to boil. "Concerned? Not a chance. The only thing I'm concerned about is that your stint in jail is nice and long."

"But you'll have to catch me first, Dix Dodd. And I bet you can't." She waved a backward hand at me.

"I'd be careful on what bets I placed," I goaded. "After all, I'm not in jail, and I know you wagered that I would be."

She huffed. "That's just a technicality. You'll be there soon enough."

"Still think you're too smart for me, Blondie?"

She laughed. "Oh, I know it, honey. If I didn't, then why would I —"

Quick as lighting, I reached and grabbed her. I jumped that quickly and that forcefully and grabbed this dream apparition. In my dream, I tossed her down onto the elevator floor beside me. No way in hell was she getting away this time. Not until I had some answers. Not until I saw her face. Not until —

"Dix! Wake up."

And in that instant, murky turned to clear-as-glass as I awoke and discovered that I'd not pulled my nemesis down beside me after all.

It was Dylan who lay there in the red-sheeted bed beside me, eyes wide, his t-shirt pulled taut in my white-knuckled grip.

"You must have been dreaming, Dix," he said.

"Yeah. I . . . I was."

"Her again?"

I nodded, and released my grip on his shirt. I braced myself for the whiplash effect that would ensue as he jumped off the bed like it was on fire.

But he didn't jump up off the bed in a hurry. He didn't jump off the bed at all. He didn't run away screaming. Dylan didn't do any of those things. He hadn't when I'd grabbed his shirt and hauled him down beside me. And damn — *oh freakin' freakin' damnity damn damn damn!* — not even when I leaned over and kissed him.

So much for wildest dreams.

Chapter 13

OKAY, HERE'S THE scoop (excuse/justification/explanation) on how Dylan Foreman ended up in my bed at the Underhill Motel.

For my fortieth birthday, my mother sent me glow-in-the-dark thong panties and matching push-up bra (did I mention Jerry Springer would love her?). My sister Peaches Marie (it's okay, she likes her name), bless her, sent me tickets to the Stones. I'd taken Rochelle, and Judge Stephanopoulos had been jealous as hell. Jokingly, she'd threatened to throw me in jail and confiscate the tickets. (At least I'd hoped she was joking.) Even Dylan had gotten me a present for the big 4-o — a bottle of wine and a set of two wine glasses. He'd given them to me at the office, just as we were preparing to leave for the night. The wine, he explained, was a 1989 Australian Shiraz. Full-flavored, a little peppery, but luscious. It had gotten better over the years, he'd said, just as I had. (I'd have felt better about that if I hadn't seen the Museum Wine sticker on the bottle.)

God, I remember that night so clearly. A weeknight, Dylan had hung around late. No plans, he'd told me. Just kicking around the office. I guess he felt like chatting. Mainly about the wine. Of course, I'm more of a rum cooler gal myself, and all I knew about wine was that I preferred red to white. After listening to him sing the praises of this particular vintage yet again, I'd thanked him effusively, set the bottle and glasses in my bottom desk drawer, and yawned widely. I was anxious to get out of there; there was a new CSI on. But man, I didn't think Dylan was ever going to leave. So I stretched and yawned a little wider, then stretched and yawned again.

Finally, with a long sigh, he'd left, and finally I was able to go home to a frozen dinner and murder on the tube. Geez, hard to figure men sometimes. They just do not pick up hints.

But what did I give myself on my fortieth?

I gave myself one hell of a sleep disorder. And that's why Dylan

Foreman had landed so unceremoniously in my bed.

It had been at a particularly stressful time in my life with the new business. Of course, in retrospect, comparing the stress I was under back then with what was going on in my life right now was like comparing pilling a house cat to declawing a Bengal tiger.

Still, it's little wonder I started 'acting out' in my sleep. Smacking lampshades across the room, ruining mini blinds with karate kicks. I had woken up on more than one occasion with the sheets completely off the bed and my ass on the floor rolled up in them. The wilder my dreams got, the bigger the mess I'd make of my bedroom at nights.

After weeks of thinking I was going crazy, I finally saw my family doc, who sent me to a sleep specialist who promptly diagnosed me as having REM-Sleep Behavior Disorder, or RBD. He said it was more common in men than women, as if I should be either amazed or proud that I'd managed to develop it. "Yeah well, so are hemorrhoids," I'd groused. He'd replied that I might prefer hemorrhoids, and went on to explain RBD.

See, normally when you're in REM sleep — the period when you dream — you lose muscle tone, resulting in a kind of a paralysis. This is a good thing; it stops you from acting out your dreams and hurting yourself or anyone in your proximity. But with RBD, that's exactly what you do — act out your dreams. Obviously, that can get pretty intense. (Nightmares, anyone?) I'm told that they see RBD sometimes in people suffering from booze or sedative withdrawal, but it can crop up in anyone, particularly after they've reached — you guessed it — middle age. In my particular case, as the stress goes up, my dream mind tries to sort out the details of whatever case I'm working on. I dream more; I act out more.

It's usually not a problem. I mean, I've knocked over a lamp or two. I've woken up on the floor a few times. I buy the cheapest of alarm clocks because I've found the expensive ones break just as easily when they hit the far wall of my bedroom. It's frustrating, of course. And weird, I know. But though I have to replace the odd appliance and apologize to the odd motel desk clerk for the trouble, I can certainly live with it. Nothing too out of the ordinary has ever happened. Nothing too embarrassing.

That is, until my dream mind caused me to reach out for my blond nemesis and capture Dylan Foreman instead. Until I'd found myself lying in bed beside him. Lying on red silk sheets, wearing only a housecoat pulled not so tightly around me. Yep, my eyes had been shut tight during all of this. Fast asleep in dreamland.

But when I kissed Dylan, my eyes had been wide open.

But you know what else? So were Dylan's eyes when he kissed me back.

It was an impulse, really. A simple curiosity to know how his lips would feel under mine, how he would taste. Innocent, almost. But the moment I leaned into the solid heat of his chest, the moment his mouth opened under mine, it was no longer simple, and it sure as hell wasn't innocent.

He tasted like sin. And, oh Christmas, he kissed just exactly the way I liked. His mouth was mobile, now hard, now soft, as he nipped and licked and swept his way into my mouth and invited me to return the favor. I did, enthusiastically, bearing him down further into the mattress. And once my hands touched his chest, I couldn't seem to stop touching him. As my hands skimmed under his shirt, I felt his hands fist in my hair. Ahhhhh! If I hadn't already gone from zero to sixty, that would have done it for me — gentle yet firm, curious and claiming. There's just something about a man with his hands in my hair like that when we're making out —

"Holy hell, Dix." His hands gripped my arms, putting me away slightly. Not a great deal of distance, but enough so that I knew this wouldn't be going any further. Enough so I knew he'd come to his senses. Enough to start the wave of embarrassment washing over me.

"I can't do this." He shook his head. "Sorry, Dix, I can't. Not like this."

I moved away and he rolled off the bed. With a quick hand to the nether regions and a bow-legged dip to his walk as he took his first steps, he adjusted himself in his jeans and walked into the bathroom. I closed my eyes. *Stupid. Stupid. Stupid!* What had I been thinking?

I jumped up, pulling the housecoat around me so tightly it could have acted as a tourniquet. I checked the door leading to the Presley apartment. Unlocked, of course. That's how Dylan had gotten in. But a quick glance revealed my clothes hadn't yet been returned as Mrs. Presley promised they would be. I checked the clock. A peek out the window confirmed it was just about dusk. Holy crap! I'd slept more than three hours. And it had been nearly four hours since Mrs. Presley had taken my clothes. More than enough time to wash and dry them, yet Dylan had arrived and my clothes hadn't.

Coincidence? *Not!*

Thank you, Mrs. Presley. *Not.*

I could just picture her now sipping her tea, looking at my clean clothes in her laundry basket and chuckling over it all. But I wasn't chuckling as I closed the door and pulled the housecoat even tighter. *Stupid, stupid, stupid.*

"Er, Dix?"

I looked up to see Dylan standing in the bathroom doorway.

"Sorry," I said, rubbing my forehead.

Dylan shoved his hands in his pockets, then pulled them out again. "Dix, don't … don't read anything into this." With a quick wave of the hand he gestured to the bed. "I mean, don't think I got up —"

I lifted an eyebrow. I could have sworn that he was 'up'.

He ran a hand through his hair. "What I mean is, I stopped because —"

"Don't worry about it, Dylan."

"But you don't understand. And I want to make sure you do."

"Remember that sleep disorder I told you about? Well, you just witnessed it firsthand. I was dreaming of that goddamn Flashing Fashion Queen. When I reached for you, I was sound asleep. I thought I was grabbing her. Nothing more."

"And is that why you kissed me? Because you were thinking about her?"

Damn.

"Damn."

He did a poor job of trying to hide a smile.

"Of course not." I let out an exasperated breath. "Look, let's not ruin the good thing we have going here. I made a mistake. I was dreaming; I was caught up in the moment. You … you know the stress I've been under."

"Yeah, Dix," he answered, "I *do* know. And that's why I couldn't take —"

I raised a hand. "It's okay." I cut his words short again. I knew I did. Part of me knew I shouldn't, but a stronger part of me knew I damn well had to.

We stood there awkwardly staring at everything but each other for a few minutes. Then, my stare turned to the coffee he'd brought. Coffee, muffin box and a brown paper bag (which I assumed, correctly at it turned out) held a change of clothing he'd picked up for me. Dylan had a key to my condo of course, for emergencies such as this. He followed my gaze to the motel dresser where he'd set the things down.

"Got your toothbrush and stuff. Grabbed the first things I came to," he said. "Jeans, shirt and underwear from the bottom dresser drawer."

After what had just happened, I was surprised to see him blush on saying the word 'underwear'.

But if he'd gone to my apartment ... "Can you be sure you weren't followed?" I asked.

He grinned. "The cops they had tailing me are probably still parked in front of Camellia's."

"The peeler bar?"

His grin grew wider. "Yeah. I parked out front, then slipped out the back. Camellia said she'd send a couple of the girls out to flirt with the uniforms. Bought me all the time I needed to do some snooping around."

"You left your bike there?"

"Hell, no. I left your mother's car there." He tapped his pocket to jingle the keys. "Then Camellia gave me a drive in her Hummer back to the office to pick up my bike."

Brilliant of course. Mother had left her tiny Beemer at my place last time she was home — hanging the hot pink DO ME key tag on the cork board in my kitchen and telling me to use it any old time. Then she'd hopped on a plane and flown back to Florida with the new gentleman friend she'd hooked up with. She couldn't wait to show him (him being 'Frankie Dear') off to the girls at the Retirement Residence. Gentleman friend, my eye. More like a sleaze bucket in a bad toupee. But I hadn't been too worried about Mother; she could handle herself.

"Dickhead will kill them when he finds out you gave them the slip."

"He won't find out. When I leave here, I'll double back to the club and come out the front door again."

"With a grin on your face and a swagger in your walk, no doubt?"

"Is there any other way to exit Camillia's?"

This thought left both of us finally smiling easily as we sat and sipped our coffees. The tension had eased a bit. I could feel the release of it in my shoulders and reached up to rub my right one. The coffee was unjangling my nerves.

"Why do you think you keep having that dream, Dix?"

Nerves jangling! Nerves jangling!

"I thought we were going to forget about that. I don't dream of you that often."

Dylan's lips twitched in a grin. Lips I'd felt beneath mine, tasted ... Oh, damn. He meant the sleeping dream, not the waking one.

"I meant, why do you keep dreaming of the Flashing Fashion Queen?

With that intuition of yours, it always means something."

"Oh, that." My throat burned with the large gulp of coffee I tried to hide behind. "I'm dreaming because there's something I'm missing. There has to be. The damn woman just keeps teasing me, flouncing around in her puff of purple dress. And I can never, ever see her — or his — face clearly."

"That day she came into the office, she was hiding her face too. The big glasses, the make-up, the blond wig."

"Of course she was. She didn't want us to know she wasn't Jennifer Weatherby."

"Agreed. But that was the easy part, since Mrs. Weatherby stayed well out of the spotlight despite the attention her husband got from the media."

"True," I said.

"And it was a pretty safe bet that a PI with our address wouldn't move in Jennifer's circle, so there'd be very little chance you'd know her socially."

I lifted an eyebrow. "Did you just call our office a *dive*?"

He grinned. "Your word, not mine. But what I *am* saying is that our Flashing Fashion Queen was hiding her face because she didn't want you to know who she *was*, not so much because she didn't want you to see who she *wasn't*."

I frowned. "This dream woman ... she told me she wanted to *be* Jennifer. Told me she'd make a wonderful Jennifer."

"Rich bitch wannabe?" he offered.

"A rejected mistress of the former philandering Ned Weatherby?" I countered.

"Transvestite lover?"

We sat there a moment in silence. My mind whirled, rearranged things, then did it again. Nothing. Dammit. With a fisted hand I punched my pillow. "Argh! This is so goddamned frustrating!"

"It'll come to you. Just give it time."

"Unfortunately, time is something we seem to be running out of." I wasn't worried about Dickhead's 48-hour time limit. That kind of went out the window when he'd found me holding the murder weapon. Or rather what I suspected was the murder weapon. As if reading my mind, Dylan spoke.

"I did some calling around about the gun. Called in some favors."

"You called Rochelle?" As secretary to Judge Stephanopoulos,

Rochelle had her fingertips on the pulse of whatever was going on in the various law enforcement departments in Marport City.

"I tried, but she's away this week. Her sister got re-married and she flew down to Hawaii for the wedding."

"So who did you call?"

"My mother," he answered sheepishly.

Marjorie Foreman, Dylan's mother, was not only a well-loved politician in Marport City, she was also known for being tough on crime. Without a doubt, she'd have been kept abreast on what was happening on such a high profile case as the Jennifer Weatherby murder.

"You were right about the gun. Initial ballistics tests confirm that the 9mm you were holding was the same one that killed Jennifer."

"Unregistered?" I asked, suspecting it would be."

"Surprisingly, it *is* registered."

I sat up straight. Was a bubble of hope beginning to form? "To whom?"

"That's the problem. It's registered to Talbert K. Washington."

"*The* Talbert K. Washington?"

He nodded.

Pop goes the bubble.

The name Talbert K. Washington was a name everyone in Marport City remembered. And would remember for a long time to come. About five years ago, there had been a double homicide. The only double murder in Marport City's history. Washington's car had broken down on the highway just inside the town limits. An elderly couple had stopped, offered to help, and he'd murdered the two and stolen their brand new Lexus. He'd driven it clear to Toronto before the police had caught up with him. Caught him and the fifteen-year-old girl he'd picked up along the way. In other words, Washington was a real slime bag.

There was plenty of evidence against Talbert K. Washington — the stolen Lexus, traces of the victims' blood on his clothing and under his fingernails, the testimony from the girl whom Washington had amused himself with by relating again and again the details of the murder to the terrified kid. But most damning of all had been the 9mm handgun he'd used to kill the couple. It was registered to Washington and had his prints all over it when the cops found it in the glove compartment of the Lexus. You'd think the case would be a slam-dunk.

But nothing is ever that simple.

Talbert K. Washington's father was Harland Washington, a rich

lumberman from Maine. He hired a team of lawyers with specific instructions: *Clear my boy. Clear my son at all costs. And I'll make you all rich men.*

It became a legal and media circus. The Washington team of ten lawyers — five from New York and five from a local law firm — had marched
into court every day to face the frazzled team of two crown attorneys.
The local paper had carried pictures of Talbert K. Washington in his
younger days — doing everything from selling apples to raising money
for Boy Scouts to petting puppies at the local animal shelter. There
were glowing testimonials about his character from everyone from his
high school drama coach to his earliest Sunday school teacher — who
was photographed wiping a tear from her eyes as she held a picture of
Talbert K. close to her chest. Not to mention the smear campaign that
Harland Washington started against one of the crown lawyers, Carrie
Press. Marjorie Foreman had made it clear that in Marport City, Talbert
K. Washington would get a fair trial, but no one was going to be intimidated. Actually, I'd always suspected that's why Carrie had gotten the
case. Judge Stephanopoulos had heard the matter. Too bad for Talbert
K., Rochelle told me that the defense's posturing had backfired, especially
the trash that was dished out against Carrie Press. The young Crown
Prosecutor had been embarrassed, sure. But worse for the Washington
team, she'd been extremely pissed off.

But the media frenzy peaked when it became public that key
evidence had gone missing — the 9mm that had been used to kill the
old couple.

The lawyers for Talbert K. Washington had wanted the case thrown
out, but Judge Stephanopoulos held firm. And fortunately, there was
enough other evidence to convict. And the jury wasn't too impressed
with the defense argument that Talbert K. Washington had been too
rich to steal a Lexus; he could have just bought one himself. And that
the kidnapped girl was lying and perhaps the killer herself. And that
the blood all over Harland Washington's boy was just bad luck when
he tried to help out the poor little hitchhiking girl. It must have flown
from her and onto him.

Talbert K. Washington was now doing life with no chance of parole
for 25 years.

And that was a very good thing.

But the very bad thing... how the hell did the missing gun now turn
up in my possession? Was I cursed? Did I have a sign on my back that
read *kick me*? Or perhaps, *frame me*? So now I was wanted for murder,

escaping police custody and being in possession of stolen evidence from a murder/kidnapping trial.

I knew better than to think that it couldn't get any worse.

"Let me guess," I said. "The car that tried to run me down ... the news you have on that sucks, too."

He lifted his shoulders in an apologetic gesture. "Sorry Dix. The car belongs to Mrs. Levana Fyffe. Ninety years old. She tripped over her geriatric poodle and broke her ankle last month. Hasn't driven since. Her nephew has been doing errands for her while she's been housebound, and she swears the car hasn't left the yard. Detective Head checked it out. The car was parked in her yard when he got there. And Mrs. Fyffe has been home all day."

"Please tell me Dickhead hauled it downtown for forensic testing anyway."

"Unfortunately, Mrs. Fyffe wouldn't let him. Told him he'd have to apply for a warrant if he wanted to steal her fuckin' car. She knew the fuckin' law better than all 'you young bastards'. Those were her exact words. Then she kicked the lot of them off her property."

"Feisty old thing, eh?" I just was not catching a break on this. "Think Detective Head will get the warrant?"

He shrugged his shoulders. "I don't know."

Things were bleak. No, not just bleak. They were horribly bleak. Yeah, that just about described them. But at least I wasn't behind bars. And I knew what my next move was. What it had to be. I was going to the source of the matter.

"I'm going to the Weatherby house," I announced.

"Are you forgetting about the restraining order?" he asked. "To say nothing of the BOLO that will have gone out by now."

"Ah, but they'll *be on the lookout* for Dix Dodd. I don't plan on looking like Dix Dodd. Nor am I planning to announce my presence, if you know what I mean."

"I'm afraid I *do* know what you mean." He shook his head, a look of concern clouding his blue eyes.

"Don't worry. You know I never met a lock I couldn't finesse. I won't get caught."

"Do you really think you'll find evidence there?"

"Don't know, but it's where I have to start."

"What are the chances you'd let me do it for you?" he asked.

"Non-existent. You have no charges against you. Let's keep it that way."

"Yeah, but it would be safer for me to go than you. You get caught, you're toast."

"Yeah, and if *you* get caught, then who the hell proves my innocence when I'm behind bars? Who the hell else believes in me at this point?"

That sobered him. Hell, it sobered me.

He straightened one long leg as he reached into his pocket. "Here's Ned's schedule for tomorrow. Or the best I could figure it, anyway."

Why didn't Dylan's having this surprise me?

"He's picking his parents up at the airport at 6:30 in the morning," he said. "He'll have to leave home by six at the latest. By the time the plane lands, his folks go through customs and they drive back, you'll have at least a couple of hours there. The place should be empty. I'll stake it out early in the a.m. and call you."

"Is there a security system?" I asked. Usually, these high-dollar places were alarmed liked Fort Knox.

"There was," Dylan answered. "But no alarm went off the day Jennifer was murdered."

"Which goes to prove," I offered, "that the killer was someone she knew."

"You'd think," Dylan said. "But Ned cancelled his account with the security company. Right after Jennifer's murder. Said he had nothing left to protect."

I reached for my cell, and checked that it was on vibrate in preparation for the morning. Just in case, turning off the ringer while I was thinking of it. Nothing like having the phone ring when you're hiding in the bushes, in a closet or under a bed. "What'll you pursue?" I asked.

"Tonight I'm going to go back over the pictures, notes and tapes we got."

I blinked. "Wait a minute … I thought Detective Head would have confiscated those?"

Dylan smiled. "Yeah, there was some kind of a mix up. I accidentally gave the Detective the wrong stuff."

"What stuff did you give him?"

He cringed. "The stuff from your mother's seventieth birthday party. You know, the tapes of the party your sister sent you. The one with the dozen male strippers and the penis shaped piñatas."

Dickhead would have a toothpick snapping fit. I laughed out loud. And that felt pretty damn good.

Dylan laughed, too. "Wait'll he gets a load of the pictures where they're doing the limbo."

I moved to put the now-empty coffee cup on the nightstand, and sat back against the head of the bed, still chuckling.

"Er, Dix," Dylan said. "You're kind of . . . kind of coming undone there."

I sighed. "No, I'm fine Dylan. Just thinking."

"No, I mean, you're . . . falling apart."

He just was not listening!

"I'm fine, Dylan. Really."

He drew a breath. "I mean that your housecoat is coming undone and I can see your breasts."

Well, that sat me up straight. "I'd better get dressed."

With a pinching grip on the collar of my housecoat that would have made any Mother Superior proud, I grabbed the brown paper bag of clothing Dylan had brought, and raced to the bathroom.

I'd just exposed myself to my employee. No wait, that wasn't quite accurate — not quite the *whole* truth. I'd exposed myself to my employee after hauling him into bed and kissing him thoroughly and running my hands all over his chest. My life was on a roller coaster. One big freaking loop-de-loop. I opened the bag of clothing and pulled out the jeans and sweater Dylan had packed. But my hand stilled to the knock on the bathroom door.

"Dix?"

"Yeah?"

"I . . . I don't want you to think that what happened . . . or rather what didn't happen here between us, was because I didn't think it could. Okay, what I mean is, it *could*. Really could. I mean, hey, I certainly could . . . if you know what I mean. Shit, I didn't mean it like that. But I didn't think it should happen. Not that it shouldn't. But that if it should, it should be . . . you know, when it should."

Apparently, in all the excitement, I'd missed the alien invading the body of the usually eloquent Dylan Foreman. I'd never heard the man tongue-tied before. Yes, I know I should have let him off the hook. But it was kind of fun. Kind of cute. And damn it, kind of hitting home.

From the other side of the door, I heard his exasperated sigh. "Oh, to hell with it. I'll just say it straight out. Dix, you're vulnerable right now. Only a jerk would take advantage of that. And I'm trying really, really hard not to be a jerk."

I sat on the edge of the tub. Not that my knees had gone weak, but

… well, I just needed to sit.

Oh, Dix, don't do this. Don't feel this.

Okay, this was Dylan … but still, he was a man. I was too smart for that. Too tough. Too cynical. I wasn't going to fall for any man, especially one so young and handsome, while I …

While I what? What excuse should I make up this time?

I gave myself a mental kick in the ass. And I continued to listen. Apparently the door between us gave him as much freedom to speak as it did me to listen.

"Dix, I just don't want to make love to you when you've got so much trouble on your mind. I don't want to do anything that would fill you with regrets after. I don't want us to share mind-blowing orgasms and then have to race away into hiding again. I want it to be like it should be for us. I want it to —"

"Wait!" Oh, Jesus, he was scaring the shit out of me. Give me a mugger in a dark alley. Give me a cheating boyfriend who's just been busted charging my way. Hell, give me Dickhead on a wild-eyed rampage. All of those things at once couldn't scare me the way Dylan was scaring me right now. Dix Dodd didn't do close. Close hurt. I squeezed my hands into tight fists until my nails bit into my palms. "What happened shouldn't have happened, Dylan. Let's just leave it at that."

"But Dix …"

"We're both under pressure here. That's it. That explains everything. It was nothing."

Please, I prayed, as the minutes ticked by in silence, not even sure what I was praying for.

"All right, Dix. You got it. It was nothing."

I should have felt relief. Yep, sure should have.

"Good. Great. Glad we cleared that up."

His voice was flat in its return. "I've gotta get going. Need to sneak back into Camillia's, then out again. I'll keep working this, of course. And I'll call you in the morning like I said."

I sat there for a moment, my insides shredding in the silence. Then I leapt up.

"Dylan! Wait."

I dropped the jeans and shirt I'd been holding and held the housecoat around me as I raced from the room. But Dylan was gone. The backdoor was closed. I was alone with only the muted glow from the television flooding the room.

"Just like you wanted, Dix," I mumbled.
But no one answered back.

Chapter 14

EVENTUALLY, MRS. PRESLEY did return my clothing. Washed, ironed (people still did that?), folded perfectly and smelling of Tide. My underwear had never been so soft. Mrs. P brought them to me herself, just after Dylan left. Which was good, because as I'd discovered when I searched the bag Dylan brought me, he'd packed the be-tasseled glow-in-the-dark abomination my mother had given me for my birthday. Could I be any more humiliated?

I'm sure Dylan hadn't planned to grab this set, especially. Yes, it was the only matched set of underwear I owned, but I doubt if that factored into it. I couldn't see him rummaging around in my underwear drawer until he found a match. No, he probably just grabbed the first things he saw, which in the dimness of my unlit bedroom, would be the glow-in-the-dark green nestled there among ... oh, shit, among my granny panty collection!

To think I'd thought I'd bottomed out on the humiliation scale. Argh!

But Dylan Foreman had seen more than just my underwear as of late I reminded myself. And that thought was causing me a little more consternation than I wanted to acknowledge.

I barely slept that night. Tossed and turned, tangled the sheets up good all by myself. Thinking of ... thinking of everything. The Flashing Fashion Queen. Dylan's kiss that still lingered on my lips. No wonder the mattress was half off the bed when I awoke.

It was not yet dawn. The curtains were not tightly drawn and I watched the sky. I found myself staring into the stars as I waited for my bedside phone to ring with the 4:45 a.m. wake-up call I'd requested. I no longer needed the call to awaken me, but I did need it. I needed it to cue me into getting a move on ... getting ready for today's criminal offense.

But that wake-up call came in the form of a petite woman in blue suede shoes, knocking softly on the door, and tiptoeing her way into

Room 111 where she'd hidden me.

"You're not going out without breakfast, Dix Dodd," Mrs. Presley said. "Don't even try to argue."

I didn't.

She set the tray — complete with two fresh blueberry muffins, the butter already melting into them, orange juice and a steaming cup of my beloved nectar of the Gods (black coffee) — on the night table. The tray also contained a red rose in a tiny vase and morning paper, rolled up and held tight with a thin elastic band. The newspaper was spotted a darker gray in a place or two. It was raining. Good. Fewer early morning joggers to worry about when I broke into the Weatherby home. Just the fanatics, heads down and hunkered in on themselves against the rain.

"Thanks, Mrs. Presley. But you didn't have to do this. I could have grabbed something ... somewhere."

"Ha. Are you kidding me? You don't want to be coming eyeball to eyeball with the counter staff of any convenience stores or coffee joints today. You haven't seen today's paper yet!"

Oh no.

"I got Craig to pick it up when I sent him out for that other thing you wanted."

"He got it?"

"He did."

I reached for the paper, but Mrs. Presley snatched it away before I could grip it.

"First," she said, with a stabbing finger toward the muffins. "You eat."

"I really don't think —"

"Well, I really do." Her tone brooked no argument. "You're no good to yourself fainting from hunger."

Resigned, I choked down one of the muffins and washed it down with some orange juice before Mrs. Presley relinquished the paper.

Yes, there I was. Front page, of course.

"Shit."

Mrs. P handed me my coffee with one hand, and set the other gently on my back as I looked at the paper.

Murder Suspect Dix Dodd On the Loose. And in smaller letters below this lovely 80-point headline, *Murder appears to have been crime of passion.*

The picture they put below the caption, of all things, was my driver's license photo. I don't take a good picture on the best of days, but after an hour of standing in line at the DMV when their air conditioning was on the fritz while some guy who must have bathed in ripe cheese stood in front of me digging who knows what out of his ears, I had a bit of a snarl on my face when the bubble-gum snapping employee clicked my pic. And omigod, it looked exactly like a mug shot.

As picture ID, it worked fine. In fact, I kind of liked the kick-ass-and-take-names-later snarling edge to it. However, had I known it was going to wind up plastered larger than life on the front page of the Marport City's *Morning Edition*, I'd have fled the DMV office that day and not come back until I'd been to the esthetician.

"So much for my modeling career," I mumbled.

I rushed to read the story, and quickly decided that the mug shot that made me look like Quasimodo's ugly stepsister was the least of my troubles.

> *Marport City Police have asked residents to be on the look-out for local private detective Dix Dodd, who is wanted for escaping police custody and resisting arrest. Police sources confirm she is a person of interest in the investigation of the recent brutal murder of Jennifer Weatherby, wife of millionaire businessman Ned Weatherby. Dodd is considered dangerous, and citizens are advised not to approach, but to immediately call police at 555-8250 or 911 should they see her.*
>
> *Though police declined to give more details, Jeremy Poole, lawyer and friend of Ned Weatherby, elaborated on the situation. "From what we've been able to ascertain, Dix Dodd apparently had an obsession with Ned. She'd been stalking him for at least a week — recording his every movement, snapping pictures, even going so far as to sleep outside his house in her car at night. You have to feel sorry for a woman like that." But Poole quickly changed his tone when asked if perhaps Ned Weatherby had returned Dodd's romantic interest. "He'd never be interested in a floozy like that." (see 'Floozy' page A-4)*

I recognized the 555 number, of course. It was Dickhead's cell phone.

He must want me badly to give that number out to the paper.

I turned to page A-4 and quickly scanned the pictures. It would serve no purpose at this point to read further. What more could they add that I didn't already know? *Breaking news! Dix Dodd totally fucked!*

No, I reminded myself, not totally. I was still free, still able to investigate, and I intended to remain that way.

There were no other pictures of me. There was one of the parking area outside my office, with uniformed cops heading every which way (in the wake of my giving Dickhead the slip, no doubt). In one frame, Dickhead, in a moment of total frustration, was launching a small package across the yard. Toothpicks, I figured. There was a picture of Jennifer Weatherby — the real Jennifer Weatherby, not the phony who'd posed as her in my office — and my heart ached for her. There was a picture of Ned, leaving the church, I assumed after making funeral arrangements. Pastor Ravenspire had one arm around Ned's shoulders, providing whatever comfort he could. The other arm was raised in a failing effort to block the access by the flashing cameras. Luanne Laney stood looking severe and efficient behind them. There was a picture of Jeremy Poole, too, standing in front of the Court House, looking very lawyerly in his long black robe. Looking serious. And looking like he had a stick so far up his ass, he'd need three surgeons and a skilled dentist to extract it.

"Good call, Mrs. Presley," I said.

"Getting Craig to pick up the paper?"

"No, getting me to eat before I saw these pictures."

She laughed, and handed me the other muffin.

"I'm not hungry." I put the paper aside.

"Put the muffin in your pocket for later. When you've got your appetite back."

Pocket, right. That reminded me. "Were you able to put together an outfit for me?"

She smiled. "Of course."

One of the ... er ... benefits, of running an establishment such as Mrs. Presley's was that clients sometimes left things behind when they dashed away in a hurry. And when they did, they often didn't want to risk coming back for them. After thirty days, Mrs. Presley claimed the articles as her own. She got such a kick out of these little treasures. Money was her favorite (and least frequent) find, followed by jewelry, mostly of the costume variety. But Mrs. Presley also had a wide assortment of clothing and accessories that had been left behind. The undergarments (or what was left of the undergarments after some enthusiastic nights) she tossed out. But the other stuff, she kept. Feather boas, fur-lined handcuffs, tight-fitting skirts, dark glasses, assorted scarves. Oh, and lots of trench coats with high collars.

"Oh, yes, I got you an outfit, Dix. You're gonna love it!"

She went to the closet, hip checked the door open and popped herself out for just a moment. And when she returned with the outfit on a hanger, she held it out to me like the girl at the car show, showing off the latest model.

"Oh, my."

One look at the skirt, told me it would be a tight squeeze. A very tight squeeze. And my knees would be pressed together so tightly, I'd be doing that penguin walk. It was black and straight and leather. Mrs. Presley had also provided me with a blouse. Sparkling white, of all things. But judging by the dated style, I knew it would have been a dingy white had it not been for Mrs. Presley's meticulous domestic skills. The topper of the outfit, the most important ingredient, was a bright red blazer. The latter was classy-looking, and I knew without a doubt that it was new. And not cheap by any means. Two hundred bucks, easy. Two hundred of *Mrs. Presley's bucks*. It would take a dose of sodium pentothal to make her admit it, but I knew she'd gone out and bought it for me.

"This ... this is wonderful, Mrs. Presley."

"Ah hell," she said, "I'm glad to get rid of the old stuff. Been gathering dust in my closet for too long."

Now I *knew* she was lying. Dust wouldn't dare settle in her closet.

"Oh, I almost forgot this." She reached into the deep pocket of her flowered skirt, and pulled out two things: a bottle of black hair dye and a bright pink disposable razor.

Okay, the hair dye I could understand, along with the finger-wagging warning not to get any on the bedding. Black hair would be great for my disguise/transformation.

But just how did she know I needed to shave my legs?

I looked at her quizzically. "The razor, Mrs. Presley?"

She waved a dismissive hand. "Oh, Dylan told me I'd better send that along. He said you should probably give your legs the once-over before you headed out."

My jaw dropped. "He *didn't*."

"No, he didn't." She smiled like the cat that swallowed the canary. "But now that I know how close you two got, I'll be on my way." With a nudge and a wink and a laugh at my expense, she leapt up and left through the regular door.

I groaned and covered my face.

Great morning so far.

Chapter 15

IT WAS BARELY dawn when I prepared to leave the Underhill Motel.
The hair dye Mrs. Presley had gotten me was a temporary one,
thank God, but somehow I couldn't see getting my natural blond hair
back in one shampoo as promised on the label. Maybe a week of shampoos, if I was lucky. It was so ... well, *black*.

I'd piled my hair up high on my head, and set it in place with bobby
pins. And before you groan, it looked great. Really. Just because my
underwear isn't that fashionable and I seldom bother plugging in an
iron doesn't mean I'm not damned good with my hair. Hell, I can fix it
a dozen ways, and I can do it faster than a runway model can change
outfits. All part of the job. The quick change, the ability to convert my
looks on a dame.

Get it ... on a 'dame'?

But I digress.

By the time I perfected my makeup and put on the Roberto Cavalli
shades Mrs. Presley had provided (at least one guest must have left the
Underhill in a hell of a hurry to forget those puppies), I hardly recognized
myself. Now as long as no one else did. Maybe the horrible picture of
me in the Marport City *Morning Edition* had been a blessing after all.

As I stood looking at my reflection and admiring my handiwork, I let
myself think the thought I'd been trying to suppress: You could run, Dix.

I closed my eyes and pressed a thumb and forefinger against my lids
as though I could push the thought back. But there was no budging it.

Because, dammit, I knew I could do it. I could disappear. With my
skills and resiliency, not to mention the five large in cash that the Flashing
Fashion Queen had given me, most of which I still had, I could get away.
With my connections, I could easily score fake ID, after which I could
just evaporate. Poof into thin air. Granted, five grand wouldn't carry me
far, but it wouldn't have to. I could certainly get far enough away from

Marport City to start a new, anonymous, keep-to-myself life, with a nice, boring job. Hell, I could fly under the radar forever.

But that would mean the Flashing Fashion Queen would have won. And oh, God, it would mean Dickhead had won. And dammit, when I really thought about it, it would mean all those chauvinistic bastards at the Jones Agency had won. I could still hear their snickers when I told them I was going into business on my own. Still see the condescending eye-rolls.

I shook my head. No way in hell was I going to rabbit. No Plan B for me. It was Plan A all the way. The only plan I needed. The only plan that cleared me of the murder of Jennifer Weatherby, and put the guilty party, whoever she was, behind bars.

I put on the red blazer, which clashed slightly with my shades but matched perfectly the tint of my lipstick, and presto change-o, there I stood, the quintessential real estate agent.

The item I'd asked Mrs. P to get for me was a Marport First Realty Ltd. sign. I had no doubt she'd asked Craig to borrow one, and even less doubt he'd have to sneak back with it this evening. Craig had set the sign in the back seat of Mrs. P's red Hyundai. Mrs. Presley was taking a chance lending me her car, but when I mentioned this to her, she waved me off with a flick of the hand.

"Someday, Dix Dodd, it might be me needing the favor."

My throat tight, I just nodded. I'd do my damnedest to make sure that car wasn't noticed. Starting with smearing dirt on the immaculate license place, which I did as soon as Mrs. P went back inside (she'd have had a bird to see me sully her baby). I stood back and examined my work. Upon close inspection, it wouldn't hold up, but on not-so-close inspection, it would do just fine. And fortunately, there was enough of a lip over the license plate that the rain wouldn't directly hit it. Not unless a wind came up, which was entirely possible. No, it wasn't a perfect plan, but it had to do.

I wiped my hands best I could on rain-damped tissues and climbed into the car — no small feat considering how tightly my lower half was packed into that pencil skirt Mrs. Presley had provided. Automatically, I checked my cell to make sure it was set on vibrate, then dumped it in the inside pocket of my red blazer. All set for Dylan's call.

Dylan's call …

It struck me then that I was more nervous about that than I was about the pending break-and-enter. Schoolgirl nervous instead of jail-time nervous? Ack! The hair dye must be affecting my brain.

I stuck the key in the ignition, then checked my watch. It was time.

I parked a few streets away from the Weatherby mansion, near a walking trail, to await Dylan's call. I checked my watch again. I wanted the chatter of morning radio to keep me company, but I wasn't quite up to hearing about myself on the news. It was just quarter to six. Figuring it would be a news-free zone until the top of the hour, I flicked the radio on and quickly tuned it to the local station, the one with the ultra-cheery early-morning DJ banter.

"So it looks like another rainy day in Marport City, Kevin."

"Great weather for ducks, Caroline. Ha ha ha."

Someone pushed a sound effects button and a canned rim shot sounded.

Lame.

Well, no one said they were *original* ultra-cheery early-morning DJs. I turned the radio off again.

A couple walked by. They wore matched walking suits — his navy blue and hers pink — that must have cost what I spend on clothing in a year. And which perfectly matched the navy blue and pink jackets on their two pugs. Double Income, No Kids, I decided. They held close under Mr. DINK's umbrella, while Mrs. DINK held the leashes of the two straining pugs. As I watched, I noticed them give more than just a sideways glance my way. I lowered my head and busied myself going through a stack of papers (which turned out to be takeout menus upon this close examination) I'd picked up from the seat beside me. Then I faked a sneeze, grabbing a tissue from the box squeezed between the seats to cover my face in an over-zealous nose-blowing effort. Eventually, the DINKS moved on, but not before the pink-clad one (the human, not the pug) gave a good hard look back at me.

"Okay," I counseled myself, "don't overreact. It's raining. Any glimpse through the windshield would be blurred. I'm in disguise — a damn good disguise. Nobody is out this morning looking for a dark-haired real estate agent. They're looking for a blond Dix Dodd, not …"

Which reminded me I needed a name. Not just to put me in character (though that was important), but in case I was asked and had to think of something quick. I glanced back again at the real estate sign in the back seat. There would be a name on the sign, of course. I turned and leaned back to read it. "Okay, they're looking for Dix. Not ... Bert Cartsell."

Damn.

I glanced in the rearview mirror, staring into my well made-up eyes. "Hello there, Bert. How's it hanging? Oh, it's not hanging? Well, that's probably a good thing."

Had Mrs. DINK seen the sign? Would she necessarily put two and two together if she did? Maybe she knew Bert Cartsell? Who the hell sells carts anyway in this day and age? Apparently Bert.

"Argh!" Sometimes, I swear, I was my own worst enemy. Yeah, me and the Flashing Fashion Queen.

I felt the vibration in my pocket and glanced at my watch. Almost six. It had to be Dylan; I knew this before I even flipped the cell open and glanced at the number. "Bert here."

"What's that, Dix?"

"Never mind."

"Coast is clear. Ned Weatherby just left."

"House is empty?" He'd pretty much told me that, but I wanted to keep him on the line. We'd left things tense last night, and I wanted to make sure that was going to blow over.

"Empty," he repeated.

"Well," I said stupidly. "Empty is good."

"Yep."

"Yep."

I waited for him to say something. Desperately hoped that he would. The tension was too heavy. And I didn't want to lose my best friend. My best employee. Hell, I didn't want to lose Dylan in any respect. "Well, I'll head over, then."

"Dix?"

"Yeah?"

"Want to know if this love is true? Call me and I'll make sure you do."

Jesus! I nearly dropped the phone. "Dylan, I —"

"For the business cards, Dix," he said, and damned if I couldn't hear the grin in his voice. "I know it's not as catchy as my other suggestions, but I kind of like it. Cute, you know?"

I kind of liked it too. And I found myself smiling for the first time since last night.

"Not too bad," I agreed. "If I ever get out of this mess ..."

"When," he corrected. "*When* we get out of this mess."

I swallowed. "Thank you, Dylan."

"You're welcome, Dix." His voice turned serious. "I've got an excellent view of the Weatherby house. I'm parked across the street, in the driveway two houses down."

"Where are the owners?"

"Japan for four months while renovations are being done. Which I discovered the other day when I was talking to the neighbors, asking about Jennifer."

"Are you in the same car?"

"Give me a break. I'm in a white van marked CHESTNUT CARPET SERVICE," he huffed. "I'm not a rookie at this. I'm a big boy, you know."

Totally inappropriate 'big boy' visions filled my mind, and I answered with a too-husky, "I know."

Then I heard Dylan's soft, amused laughter coming through the cell.

Way to go, Dix. I cleared my throat. "I'm going to head over to the Weatherby House now."

Dylan sobered. "I'll keep watch. Keep your cell on, all right?"

"I will."

A pause. I could hear him drawing a breath. "Call me as soon as you can."

The line went dead, and I looked at the cell a moment before I plunked it into my pocket. I started the Hyundai, and drove the short distance to the Weatherby house.

I parked alongside the road. Not quite in front of the Weatherby house as to say I was at the Weatherby house, but close enough that I looked like I *might* be at the Weatherby house. I glanced at the white van and the form of Dylan sitting in it.

Ducking under the black umbrella that Mrs. Presley had provided, I tugged the real estate sign from the back seat of the car and headed toward the house.

Awkward. The sign was heavier than it looked. I tucked it under my arm but was careful not to hold it against the expensive blazer Mrs. P had gotten for me. I imagined Bert Cartsell for a moment slinging the sucker around — sign in one hand, hefty sledgehammer in the other to pound the post into the ground.

But I wasn't going to pound it into the ground.

I stepped carefully over the flowerbed, and leaned the sign up against the house. That would hopefully ward off any nosy neighbors who spied me this early morning. And I had every intention of being gone by the time Ned Weatherby returned, sign safely stashed in Mrs. P's car as I sped back to the Underhill. Hopefully, with the information I sought.

Whatever the hell that turned out to be.

Okay, sign placed. Now I had to go into full real-estate-lady mode.

I stood back and took a businesslike look at the windows, and then further back to examine the roof (it had windows; it had a roof ... good, good). Very quickly, I poked at the flowers. I rapped my knuckles on the siding in a few places — this seemed efficient. In fact, I rapped my knuckles along the entire length of the house. In fact I rapped my knuckles right around the corner of that house. Then I made a mad dash to the back of it.

Yes, I was good with locks, but not so good that I would chance spending a few awkward minutes trying to pick the front door lock in broad daylight. A back door would do just fine.

I was in luck. Which, I realized as I mentally high-fived myself, was a change for me these days.

Not only was there a back door, but there was a sliding glass patio door, and I bit down on the 'bingo' I wanted to shout. As long as the security bar wasn't down ...

The security bar wasn't down.

Things were starting to go my way — the rainy day, Ned leaving on time, the easy access to the house. I quickly jimmied the lock. Easily. No alarm, just as Dylan had told me. No barking dogs. No surprises waiting on the other side.

Just smooth sailing from here on out.

I might have known better.

Chapter 16

YOU KNOW, I would have made a lousy real estate agent. As you will have figured out by now, I'm not exactly a people person. But I must have looked passably convincing as a realtor. I stepped inside the Weatherby mansion (thank you, easy-to-open sliding door) and no alarms and whistles blared. No sirens came roaring down Ashfield Drive, summoned by suspicious neighbors. Mentally, I gave myself a pat on the back at my transformation skills.

Okay, yeah, I wouldn't pass for Bert Cartsell, but hopefully no one would read the pilfered sign that closely. Or if they did, they'd probably assume I was an office underling sent to do the boss's bidding.

Now, as long as old Bert himself didn't drive by …

I glanced around the study. It was an eerie feeling being in the room — the very room — where Jennifer Weatherby had been murdered. It's not that I felt the presence of her ghost, or a tingling up my spine or a rise in the hairs on the back of my neck. It was just that not so long ago, this room had been full of life, until, in one violent instant, it had been turned into a scene of death. Not that there was any lingering physical evidence of the crime. The bio-cleanup crew had been in and erased all trace. But it still felt like a murder scene. Especially in the quiet of the closed-off room.

And even though it had been an imposter who'd been in my office that day, I still felt I owed the real Jennifer something. Still felt for the victim in this crime. And if I didn't catch her murderer, no one would.

Now, that was a scary thought.

Of course, the police tape had long since come down. The forensics team had done their work. Every fabric and fiber would have been examined; every surface would have been dusted for prints and — if I knew Dickhead — dusted again. And when the police finished processing the room, the cleaners had moved in and restored everything to its former state. Still, the place felt just as totally off limits as though yellow barrier tape still screamed CRIME SCENE — DO NOT ENTER. The double doors on the opposite side of the room from which I entered were closed firmly and the drapes were drawn. Dust didn't lay heavy on the furniture yet, but a few motes swirled in a thin steam of sunlight that came through a slight parting of the drapes. Other indicators around the room attested to the loss of life. Memories of Jennifer were everywhere — a scarf carefully folded on a chair in the corner, a pair of sunglasses on top of the well-stacked bookcase. No wonder Ned had chosen to keep this room closed off.

Of course, I had every confidence Detective Head would have already searched this room thoroughly. But I also had every confidence that we were looking for different things.

In fact, I was growing more confident of this by the minute.

Of course my heart was racing. Not in a holy-shit-I'd-better-get-outta-here racing, nor a kid-at-Christmas racing. But more of an I'm-getting-warmer racing. I knew it; I just freakin' *knew* there was something here. Kind of reminded me of that game we played when we were kids, where one person would hide an object and the other would direct her to it by leading with degrees of *you're getting hotter-warmer-colder-freezing*. This room definitely gave me hot vibes. So hot in fact, I doffed my red blazer and set it (neatly, with visions of a finger-wagging Mrs. Presley) on the first chair by the door from which I just entered.

This had been Jennifer's room. Her sanctuary. The walls were femininely decorated. The carpeting was a rosy pink. It was cozy and comfortable feeling. Gracious.

My eyes swept past the beautiful Tiffany lamps in each corner. And then over the rows of bookshelves that spanned an entire wall of the room, stacked tightly and neatly with hardcover books. Fiction titles mostly, with a few nonfiction thrown in. I looked past the black leather club chair that sat in front of the giant office-style mahogany desk, past the coordinating leather office chair on the business side of the desk. And directly behind that chair, larger than life, hung the wedding picture of Ned and Jennifer Weatherby. He had been a dashing young man in a tailored tuxedo, while she looked almost consumed by the white gown she wore. The veil, the gloves, and oh, Lord, the pearls that seemed to snug just a bit too tightly around her neck. My heart dipped. Even on her wedding day, Jennifer had looked so out of place.

Turning from the depressing portrait, I tugged off the dress gloves I'd used to jimmy the door, stashed them in my purse and pulled on the latex gloves I'd dug from the same bag. Dexterity, baby. That's what I needed now. Well, that and to keep my fingerprints — which Dickhead had from the other night when he'd found me at the murder scene — from getting all over Jennifer's study again. Contrary to what PI novels might lead you to believe, private detectives do not make a habit of breaking and entering. No way in hell would they risk their license by engaging in clear-cut criminal conduct. But under the circumstances, losing my license was a little further down on my list of worries these days. And hell, what was a little B&E when I was already unlawfully at large? Not to mention that little ol' murder charge hanging over my head.

My first thought, of course, was to search the desk, but I quickly scooted it away.

Reason one: Dickhead would have certainly gone through that desk and every scrap of paper in it. If there'd been anything of significance in that mahogany monstrosity, he'd have confiscated it. (And yes, it did just about kill me to give him this credit, if only in my thoughts.)

Reason two: If Jennifer had been hiding something, the last place she would try to conceal it would be in her desk. See, I've had lots of practice studying cheating spouses. And if the jealous husband or jealous wife is going to be snooping, someone's private desk would be the first place to look for evidence of an affair. No, Jennifer would be more cautious than that.

And the third reason I didn't start with the desk, it just didn't *feel* right. My intuition was tingling, but not in the direction of the desk.

I looked around the room again, letting my mind lead me to where I should begin.

The books. Definitely, the books.

There was something about them that was calling me over. The shelves seemed neatly arranged. No books upside down, pulled out a little too far or pushed in a little much. But still ... I walked closer and scanned the titles. They were arranged alphabetically, by author. No surprise there. Alcott's *Little Women* came before Austen's *Pride and Prejudice. Even the Stars Look Lonesome*, by Maya Angelou was neatly shelved before Margaret Atwood's *The Blind Assassin* and *The Handmaid's Tale. Life of the Bombay Dung Beetle* by Elizabeth Bee came before

Brontë's *Wuthering Heights.*

Whoa, wait a minute — Elizabeth Bee? *Life of the Bombay Dung Beetle?*

With shaking hands, I pulled the book down and began flipping through the pages. Eureka! Jennifer's journal, wrapped in a very professional looking dust jacket — complete with graphics and a back-cover write up — which she'd no doubt printed from her computer. I took a moment to marvel at her ingenuity. Hidden virtually in plain sight, it had escaped a forensic search. Obviously, Jennifer had put a lot of work into hiding her journal. Obviously she felt that she had to. So much for sanctuary.

I again glanced at the wedding picture of Jennifer and Ned hanging over the desk.

I didn't dare turn on a light to get a closer look at Jennifer's journal entries. I'd pressed my luck about as far as I wanted to with the neighbors. Fortunately, there was sufficient sunlight coming through the slight part in the drapes, spilling across an edge Jennifer's desk. I crossed to the desk and settled my ass in what proved to be the most comfortable chair I'd ever sat in, ignoring the rude sounds of leather skirt on leather chair that would have sent any twelve-year-old boy into a fit of laughter. I felt now the kid-at-Christmas kind of heart racing as I held Jennifer's journal in my hands. Her *hidden* journal. Surely it would hold the key to fingering her killer and to proving my innocence.

I moved the journal into the strip of sunlight on the desk. I was just beginning to relax, to feel the situation was coming under my control, when the desk phone rang, scaring the bejeezus out of me.

"Shut up," I hissed. Which was more of a frustrated venting rather than a plea that I thought would work. (I'd long ago finished with talking to appliances, but that's another story.)

Closing my eyes, I gathered my severely fraycd cool, reminding myself I was alone in the house. Dylan had made sure of that. No one was going to hustle in here to answer the phone and find me sitting in Jennifer's chair. But there's just something about a phone ringing into an empty house when you're doing something you'd rather not be caught doing. Looking through what you're not supposed to have. Sitting where you're not supposed to be sitting. You immediately want to put your hands up in an I-didn't-do-it gesture.

After three rings, the answering machine clicked on.

It was a female voice, and I knew it had to be Jennifer's. "Thank you for calling the Weatherby residence. We cannot take your call right now, please leave a message." I wondered how long Ned would leave that message on the machine. It struck me as strange. Usually a grieving spouse would change a message like that as soon as possible to avoid the repeated heartache of hearing the voice of the deceased loved one over and over again. Or to avoid creeping out callers.

"Er, yeah, is this Pepper's Pizza? Huh? Is it? 'Cuz I really need to get me a pizza with some spicy pepperoni. *Hot* pepperoni. *Very hot* pepperoni! Right this minute!"

Click.

Dylan? Pizza? What the hell? It had sounded like him. But he would have called me on my cell. Right? Right. He was probably just horsing around. Flirting maybe? I had to grin at that. "I got it, Dylan. Hot and spicy. Cute."

Okay, in retrospect, I probably should have given that call more thought. But as it was, I was little distracted by my find. I have to admit, I felt a little smug as I held the journal in my hand. The journal that Detective Dickhead had missed when he'd searched the room.

Okay, I felt a *lot* smug. He wasn't as smart as me ... er, I mean as smart as I. Right ... I. (Yes, mentally, I corrected my grammar to prove the point.) And he wasn't as motivated by any means. And mostly, he wasn't a woman. He wouldn't know what to look for. I most definitely would.

I glanced at my watch before I opened the journal. It was about a quarter to seven, I had some time yet. Still, I knew better than to dally.

As I flipped through the pages, a few things spilled out into my lap. There was a birthday card for Jennifer from an aunt in Toledo. Jennifer's aunt had tucked a cheque for five dollars in it, which struck me as both a little sweet and a little sad. There was a receipt for two very expensive men's watches from Hardy Jewelers on Main Street. For Billy Star? For her husband Ned? Next was a flyer from Pastor Ravenspire's church, clearly promoting the pastor himself more than anything else. Someone — presumably Jennifer — had drawn a circle around the pastor's head, and drew a small line and a large question mark out from this.

But what caught my attention under these odds and ends and bits of life was what Jennifer Weatherby had written in the pages of her journal. And how she'd written it.

Every entry was written in peacock blue in flowing, feminine script. Jennifer had her codes — her shorthand — but after glancing at a few pages, I could easily figure these out. She put J when she was writing a note to herself. (*J* — *return dress to Ryder's. J* — *watch should be ready at Jewelers*) Anything pertaining to Ned was prefaced with an N. *N* — *evening meeting with Pastor Ravenspire. Again.* The 'again' was underlined twice. Underlined so hard the pen had torn the page. Clearly, Jennifer wasn't very happy with Ned's newfound faith. I pondered over other shorthand notations.

BS? I thought on that one for a moment. Billy Star? Bull shit? But I realized it was referring to the Bombay Spa when I read the next line. A note to Jennifer herself.

J: be sure to tip EB well at the BS. Mother in Ohio still sick.

Wait a minute? Ohio? Elizabeth had told me she was from Maine. And that her mother had passed on when she was just a girl. Obviously this one was working for tips. Stretching the truth somewhat. Padding the story. I had to smile. Good little liar, that one.

Remembering the dates Mrs. Presley had given me that Billy Star had rented out a room at the Underhill, I scanned those dates in Jennifer's journal. They matched, of course, without exception. The dates Billy had booked a room at the Underhill were days that Jennifer had written in her journal *BS: call, confirm EVERYTHING.* Emphasis on "Everything". Which told me two things. One, that Jennifer'd called the spa to cover her ass. Annnnnnd, because she wrote it in such a manner, she was concerned that Dear Old Ned would be peeking at her journal should he ever find it.

I turned to the last few pages before the day Jennifer was killed. No, I didn't expect to see my name there. No appointment with *DD* was entered on her to-do list. Nothing close to *Frame private detective for murder.* But something else leapt out at me, something that sent a chill along my spine. *J* — *called Kenny Kent to cancel caterer for weekend.* That was the last entry — the last in Jennifer's writing, that is.

But there was more. One final note beneath Jennifer's dainty peacock blue notation about canceling the caterer. A bold, slashing, all-caps message in dark black that clearly wasn't Jennifer's doing: *NO WAY IN HELL.*

I could feel the cold along my spine.

While all of Jennifer's entries had consistently been written in a dainty peacock blue, this one was written in dark black. Bold. Commanding. Right under the 'called to cancel caterer' ... *NO WAY IN HELL.*

Someone had found Jennifer's journal before I had. My eyes moved slowly up to the date on the page. It was May 30. Exactly six days before Jennifer had been murdered. And exactly one day before the Flashing

Fashion Queen had made her way into my office.

The phone rang, but it didn't startle me so much this time. I didn't snap at it to 'shut up'. Which was a good thing, because just then from the hallway beyond the office, beyond the locked doors that were just now being rattled by the sound of a key in the lock, someone else *did* hiss, "Shut up!"

Oh, shit.

Third ring, answering machine, Jennifer's ghostly voice, then Dylan's panicked one.

"Okay, I NEED a freakin' pizza. Yes, pepperoni. Yes, smokin' freakin' hot pepperoni. I need it with the works. But I need it now. Do you understand? NOW!"

Click.

I clutched the journal to my chest. Why the hell hadn't Dylan called me on my cell? Why hadn't he ... Oh shit! Just as I dove under the desk, I realized my cell was in my red 'realtor' jacket. The very same red jacket that I had draped over the chair on the other side of the room when I had entered. Shit. There'd be at least a dozen calls on that cell from a freaking-out Dylan warning me I was no longer alone in the house.

I slid myself under the desk — thank God for the desk's modesty panel that went practically to the floor — and pushed myself up against it, both surprised and grateful that leather slides well on carpet. My heart beat so loudly I was sure whoever was on the other side of that door could hear it. Certainly would hear it as they approached. I thought again of my red jacket. No way in hell did I dare crawl back out to make a mad dash to retrieve it. *Geez, Dix, why didn't you just leave a damned banner? Maybe hire a marching band to announce your presence. Hire a sky writer. Hire a bus with a bullhorn.* I pulled my knees up close to my chin, scrunching myself up tightly as the rattling of key in lock stopped, and someone entered the room.

Silence. But not the comforting silence of being alone. This was the silence of someone crossing the room on very expensive, cushy carpet. I watched the chair glide out from the desk on noiseless casters, and the intruder — no, wait I was the intruder ... make that Intruder Number Two — sat down. Sneakered feet inched toward me, coming within a gnat's hair of brushing against me. I tried to shrink smaller, feeling the bite of the journal's edges clutched so tight to my chest as I did. Were they looking for this? What would happen when they didn't find it? Crap! Worse, what would happen if they found it attached to me?

I waited (okay, there wasn't much else I could do, was there?) as this second intruder rattled keys, opened drawers, and rummaged through the desk. I heard the distinctive thump of papers being plopped on top of the desk. *Were they cleaning Jennifer's desk out? Oh my word, I'd be here all day!*

Or maybe I wouldn't. Because I realized whoever it was above me, was moving things around at one hell of a fast pace. Not a tidy/organized pack-things-up pace. But a my-life-depends-upon-it pace.

Drawers began opening with a sharp yank and closing with a loud bang. Papers were shuffled through frantically. A few fell on the floor and were left there at the intruder's feet/my knees. I heard an audible gasp above me and a few panicked words. "Where the hell is it! Jesus Christ, I've got to find that damn journal."

A chill needled along my back, down my arms that cradled the journal. Holy shit! My grip on the book tightened, and I crunched back a little further. How the hell would I get out of here? How the hell would I —

The doorbell rang.

Thank you, Dylan!

At least, I hoped it was Dylan. That would be all I needed to be caught in the middle of a meeting here or some damned thing. What if it was Bert Cartsell, real estate agent in the flesh who'd driven by and happened to notice he was selling a house he wasn't selling? Maybe old Ned would have Jennifer's wake here and the caterers were coming in? Caterers and mourners. In this very room. Hell, I could be stuck under this desk for days!

The doorbell rang a second time. Then a third and fourth time, frantically. The chair pushed back so hard it tipped over. Quickly the second intruder gathered the papers that had fallen onto the floor (and I pushed a few into the grasping fingers rather than have them venture further under the desk toward me), before running the hell out of there. Not via the front doors, but by the way I entered, through the sliding glass doors, and past the red jacket without so much as a glance.

I let out a breath and knew I had to get the hell out of the Weatherby home myself. Fast. But I was good with that as I clutched the journal tighter.

I slid out from under the desk and raced — or as close to racing as one can manage in a too-small leather skirt — for the door, grabbing my jacket on the way out. I could feel the vibration of the cell phone in the jacket pocket like a recrimination as I did.

Yes, it had been a close shave, thanks to my brain cramp in separating myself from my phone, but I'd escaped detection. I had Jennifer's journal clutched tightly in my arms. And bonus upon bonus: I knew the identity of the second intruder, one who apparently had a heck of a lot to lose.

Chapter 17

DIX IS MY nickname, of course. Short for ... well, short because my mother is weird. When she named me, she did so ... um, originally. I swear my late father must have been having a Frank Zappa flashback when he went along with her on that one. She actually told me once that she'd scoured every baby name book, every telephone book, every birth announcement in every newspaper she could get her hands on — all to make sure that my name was 'one of a kind'. And it is.

Thanks, Mom.

At the age of five, I'd sworn her to secrecy on that name. I wanted to pinkie swear (it seemed appropriate), but she said a pinkie swear wasn't real unless we did it over chocolate-frosted cupcakes and Mountain Dew. Then we had a burping contest. She won.

Yes, my mother is weird.

But to get to the point of this preamble, I've been called a lot of things besides Dix over the years. Dickhead had his favorites, Dixieshit of course being a most recent addition to the ever-growing list. My first boyfriend used to call me DixieDoo. I know — gag. But I was thirteen and in love. In my defense, I called him Pookieboo, which made the love poems easier to write. But even back then when I dubbed him Pookieboo, it was largely in case I needed to blackmail him at some future point to keep him quiet about DixieDoo. (Hey, I might have been young and in love, but I was always a realist.) And then there was "the girl". That's what the guys at the old detective agency used to call me. And let's not forget the men I've busted the last six months of business. Oh, you'd better believe they all had colorful names for me.

Yet, what Ned Weatherby called me when he came home to find me scooting around from the back of his house, hell-bent on grabbing the real estate sign and getting my butt out of there, I'd never heard before. And sincerely hoped to never hear again.

"Oh, go ahead, Dylan. Just do what you've got to do. Just get it over with."

"No, I'm fine. Really." He nodded firmly, resolutely, but I could see the strain on his face.

"Dylan, you're about to explode. So just go ahead and —"

He didn't need any more coaxing.

He exploded, all right — with laughter.

And not with a manly *ha ha* chuckle or even a curled-lip snort. He collapsed on the motel room bed with peels of helpless mirth. Tears streamed from the corners of his eyes. He held onto his sides.

Did I mention he was rolling on the bed?

He'd seen the whole lovely scene unfold outside the Weatherby house as I'd made my hasty and not so graceful exit.

"Oh, you *vulture!*"

That was the name that greeted me when I came barreling around to the front of the house. I stopped — or rather, skidded to a stop — in my high-heeled tracks.

Shit, shit, shit!

Ned was back. Back with grieving parents in tow. Right freaking in front of me! With mouth gaping open, he kept looking, first to me, then to the real estate agency sign I'd propped against the house. His parents had to have grabbed an earlier flight, one that hadn't been available when Dylan had checked for me. Or maybe Ned had chartered a private plane.

His shocked parents gave me — that is to say, the dark haired, pink-sunglasses-wearing, tight-skirted real estate agent me — a look of utter disdain. Cockroach-on-the-dinner-plate revulsion.

"Who are you?" Ned demanded.

Wordlessly, I held the real estate sign up in front of me. Partly as a shield, and partly to hide Jennifer's journal, which I'd tucked into the (ever more tight now — circulation slowly becoming non-existent) waistband of my skirt.

"Oh, you work for that Cartsell fellow, do you?"

"Yes." After my initial squeak of an answer, I lowered my voice to what I liked to think of as my slow, breathy, lets-have-phone-sex voice. Not because I was feeling particularly sexy. But because, apparently, Ned hadn't yet made me. True, the night we'd met, the night he'd found Jennifer dead, he'd been somewhat distracted. But even so very cleverly disguised as I was (God, I *hoped* I was cleverly disguised!), I wasn't taking any chances. "Yes, that's right, Mr. Weatherby." I could literally feel the words purring in the back of my throat as I spoke. "I work for Mr. Bert Cartsell. And he —"

"Well, doesn't that beat all? That son of a bitch just doesn't give up, does he?" Ned's face turned so red, it looked as if his head might explode. "That no-good, rotten, money-grubbing bastard!"

'Breathe, breathe' I silently coached. To both of us.

"Mr. Weatherby." I took my phone-sex voice a notch lower, added a deep-south accent. "I assure you that Mr. Cartsell —"

"I told him to stay the hell away!"

Oh shit! Of all the real estate agents in Marport City, *this* was the one from whom Craig had to steal the sign!

Ned continued to rant, "I've no intention of selling this house. Not now, not ever, and not for any amount of money. The first day Jennifer's obituary was in the paper, you goddamned people start nosing around, trying to make a buck off my wife's murder. Well let me tell you, missy, I've had enough." Ned opened his jacket. For the briefest of moments, I thought he was going to haul out a gun. Worse luck. He hauled out his cell phone. "I'm calling that Cartsell son of a bitch! No, wait, I'll call Luanne! She'll get his boss on the phone. She won't let him get away with this. She'll —"

"M-Mr. Weatherby," I stammered. "I really don't think —"

I could tell by the flick of his thumb, he'd pushed number one on the speed dial. And as he waited, and waited, he pointed a demanding finger at me. "And you stand right here."

Not in this lifetime.

There was no way in hell I was going to maneuver down the walkway, past Ned and his parents (his mother's walker looked dangerous, like a weapon now, in her grip), so I veered off across the rain-soaked lawn, making a mad dash for the street.

Bad idea.

My spiked heels sank to the hilt in the soggy lawn, causing my hips to move in ways hips weren't meant to. After a few more heel-sinking, Frankenstein lurches, I stepped right out of them (my shoes not my hips). Barefoot now, I pulled Jennifer's journal from the waistband of the skirt, clutched it to me with one hand, hiked the skirt up to my ass with the other hand, and with the red blazer fanning out behind me, I ran like hell to Mrs. Presley's Hyundai. I peeled out of there so quickly you'd think I was trying to qualify for the Indy 500.

Well, at least Dylan was getting a good laugh out of it now.

"Asshat," I mumbled, loud enough for him to hear me. I faked annoy-ance even as I bit down on my own grin.

"Sorry," he said, wiping at his eyes. "But all I can see is you trying to run across that lawn in that skin-tight skirt and those high heels. The look on your face when the shoes stuck in the lawn! Omigod, it was priceless. And when you hiked up your skirt and really ran …" He started laughing again, so hard the bed shook.

"Look who's talking." I sat on the red sheets beside him, giving him a poke (okay, a damn good knuckle jab) in the ribs. "You were a sight yourself, Boy Wonder. Creeping along on your hands and knees, peeking through the neighbors' bushes."

The laughter subsided, but the smile remained. "Oh, you caught that, did you?"

"Ha!" My turn to tease. "How could I not catch that? All six-foot-four of you, crawling along the length of the hedge like some kind of long-legged, studly bug or something."

As soon as the words passed my lips — the very freakin' *millisec-ond* — I realized what I'd said. *Studly*. Should I try a quick recover and say 'ugly bug'? Like, five times really fast. That would sound intelligent!

Dylan said nothing. Didn't so much as falter in his grin, or blink. But I could tell by the glint in his eyes that he'd caught my slip of the tongue.

And I wanted to slip my tongue …

Whoa, Dix.

I busied myself re-belting the old brown housecoat Mrs. Presley had provided, cinching it even tighter, telling myself I needed the extra bit of warmth after the long, increasingly cool shower. It had taken so many shampoos to get the temporary dye out of my hair that I'd used up all Mrs. P's hot water. But at last, I was blond again. And though I was fully clad in underwear (no, not the be-tasseled stuff that Dylan had brought over), jeans and t-shirt, the housecoat felt good around my shoulders. Protective. Defensive.

Butt-ugly.

"Had to make sure you got safely out of there, Dix." His voice dropped a notch. Though his eyes still showed a bit of teasing, he'd stopped laughing altogether. "I'd crawl through worse than a few bushes to do that."

"Well, thanks. If you hadn't been watching my ass —" *Oh, just shut up, Dix!* "— I'd still be stuck under that desk."

"Yeah, well." He cleared his throat, then said, "If you need a hand checking up on the man, I'm the one to call."

"Let me guess — another business card?"

He pulled himself up on the bed so both of us were leaning against the headboard. "It's a good one, don't you think? Straight-shooting from the hip. Gets right to the point. Clever and witty."

"Ummm, that would be a no."

"Geez, you're hard to please, woman. We gotta come up with something."

"I know, I know. But it has to be the *right* thing. The exact thing."

And it felt kind of good just then, when I realized what I'd said. Dylan felt it too, I could tell by the impish grin on his face. We were talking positively about the business cards again. Talking about the future. Hope.

Things were beginning to look up. Jennifer's journal had been an amazing find. And though I was far from out of the fire, I had maybe moved a little to the periphery of it. Maybe.

I heard a siren in the distance growing closer. Dylan's eyes widened along with mine. Only when the siren sound began to fade again did I realize I'd been holding my breath. I let it out again. Just a little reminder that I was far from burn-free yet. This was no time to get lazy. No time to let my guard down.

It was time to get to work.

I told Dylan about the second intruder to the Weatherby home — Luanne Laney. Turns out it wasn't news, of course. He'd seen Ned's psycho-secretary walk up to the front door and let herself into the Weatherby house with a key.

That was why he'd called frantically on Ned and Jennifer's home phone line after I failed to answer my cell. He'd ID'd her from all the surveillance pictures I'd taken over the course of the week I'd trailed Ned, even though she'd drawn her hat down over her eyes and pulled her coat collar up around her ears.

"I'm telling you, she might have had a key, but she wasn't supposed to be there," Dylan said. "Even without the turned-up-collar routine, her posture would have said it all. Self-conscious and guilty."

"Odd for a woman known to scare the bejeezus out of just about everyone who knew her."

Luanne's presence there put a new spin on things. Why had she been sneaking around? Why had she wanted Jennifer's journal? And, perhaps most importantly, how the hell had she even known about it?

"Do you think it was Luanne who came to the office dressed as Jennifer that day?"

"No," I answered, without having to put too much effort into the thought. "For one thing, even in heels Luanne isn't tall enough. And yes, I realize the impostor was putting on a fake voice, but I think it was too throaty for Luanne Laney under the best of circumstances."

"Luanne could have hired someone. There's a very good chance that whoever killed Jennifer and set us up did just that — hired an actress for that stint. And I'm betting that if that's the case, that's one scared actress right about now."

I nodded in agreement. "Scared and close-mouthed, no doubt."

Dylan scratched a hand along his unshaven jaw as he thought. "You said Jennifer hid the journal somewhere other than in the desk?"

"Right, the bookshelf."

"So who was she hiding it from? Ned or Luanne?"

"And what the hell is so very important in this journal that Luanne Laney would risk breaking in to retrieve it?"

Dylan and I barely breathed into the silence now, as I opened Jennifer's journal. The bed dipped between us as we leaned in closer together to look through the pages. Dylan was seeing this for the first time, of course, and studying it with all the intensity that I'd come to admire about him. I was giving the journal a second but substantially more thorough look — a more purposeful one now that I had the time to do so, and now that I'd had the chance to think things over.

I looked at the time correlation of the journal entries again:

J - return six dresses to Ryder's.
N - meeting with PR.
J - buy three watches, choose one (return others within the week)
N - church meeting after supper
J - cancel first-class tickets to New York.

"She didn't go to New York?" Dylan asked.

"She did." I flipped forward a few pages, and pointed to an entry.

J - see Mrs. E at Tiffany's on Fifth re: refund policy

"That's Tiffany's in New York," I pointed out helpfully. "She went. She just didn't go first class."

Dylan huffed a laugh. "So she downgraded her ticket, and flew *economy* to New York? Why?"

I smiled. "Think about it. What's the only logical reason someone would chose economy."

Dylan was still for a moment, then nodded slowly. "Money. Jennifer downgraded the ticket and pocketed the difference."

"That's my guess." I leaned closer to Dylan and started flipping through the pages — back and forth as I compared. "And look at the way purchases and refunds are aligned here. Every time Jennifer contemplates she should 'return' something, it corresponds with the times her husband is in church, *at first*."

"Feeling guilty for excesses?"

"Orrrrrr," I said. "Every time he goes to church, she got concerned. So she'd write a note to return a costly item. That's the way Jennifer kept her entries — always what she 'planned to do'. This wasn't so much of a diary as an events calendar. And the more her husband went to church, the more Jennifer bought and returned."

"I don't know ..."

"Think about it, Dylan. She puts items on her virtually limitless credit card. Returns them for cash. Husband, pays the credit card bills every month and is none the wiser as Jennifer tucks the money away. What would an outfit from Ryder's run? At least fifteen hundred or two thousand, I'm thinking. That would certainly add up after a while — build a little nest egg. Little backup cash just in case."

Just in case of what? That was the question pounding through my mind.

"Nice theory," Dylan offered. "Except stores would simply credit the amount of the refund back to the credit card, wouldn't they? I've never known a retailer to do otherwise. I don't think they *can* do anything else."

"Sure, to you and me and the rest of us plebs. But this is Jennifer Weatherby we're talking about here. You gotta figure the proprietors of those shops would bend over backwards to keep her business, especially in this fairly small backwater. Hell, they'd probably turn a blind eye while she *stole* the stuff, then send the bill to Ned."

Dylan grunted agreement.

"I've got it!" I said, my eyes widening. "I betcha my best RF tracker that Ned Weatherby's arrangement with Ryder's doesn't involve credit cards at all. I'm betting he has a free standing line of credit. You know, rack up the purchases, settle up once a month."

"Oh, hell, yeah. That's gotta be it. They could give her a cash refund, no problem, because they'd still get paid by Ned."

"Oh, and hey, maybe they even levied a little surcharge," I suggested. "Say five or ten percent, to make it worth their while. Then everybody's happy."

"Okay, that works for the local dress shops," Dylan said, "but what about the airlines?"

I shrugged. "Maybe not the airlines, but certainly any travel agent that was interested in keeping the substantial Weatherby account could figure out a way to accommodate."

He looked further through the journal. "But the consistent correlation of notes to self and Ned's church times *ends*. And in the last few weeks, Jennifer was buying and returning up a storm whether she writes of Ned going to church or not. In fact …" He jumped up and rummaged through the pics on the bed. "In fact, the last time he went to church, when you snuck into choir practice, Jennifer didn't even make an entry that day."

And we both knew why.

"Church attendance was no longer noteworthy," he said. "It was expected. Part of Ned's everyday life now. She might as well have written in he brushed his teeth and wore a tie. Going to church was that common."

"Right," I said. "But Jennifer wasn't a big Ravenspire fan." I flipped around the pages. "Other than the first two Sundays Ned attended, Jennifer never returned to Ravenspire's church."

"We need to look into this guy some more," he said.

"Oh yeah. Do we ever."

Proud as oh-so-smart peacocks, we sat grinning at each other. This felt good. This felt like good old-fashioned private detective work. This felt like a bit of control here.

As we'd poured over the journal, we'd drawn closer together on the bed. Getting more casual, getting more at ease as we sat there. Together. Almost touching. Dylan looked at me closely, his eyes soft but unreadable.

"We … we still don't know who killed Jennifer Weatherby," I said.

"But, we're getting warmer, aren't we, Dix?" His voice was slow and deep.

I nodded. "Damn right we're getting warmer."

I tossed the journal on the bed beside us, and it fell open. A chill raced up my spine as I glanced over and saw where the book had opened, as if willed to this page by some other force. Some other spirit.

J cancelled caterer, in Jennifer's handwriting.

And beneath it, contrasting sharply and angrily, the bold, black-inked *NO WAY IN HELL*.

Dylan and I both stared at it. And we both knew. The answer was here. Had to be here.

"Jennifer didn't write that last part," he said. "That's not her blue; that's not her hand writing. Someone else could just as easily have found out what she was up to."

"Someone else did."

"But who?"

"We'll figure it out."

Dylan nodded. He reached out and touched my hand. And I didn't pull away.

Yep. Damn right we were getting warmer.

Chapter 18

L UANNE WAS NOTHING if not ultra-efficient.

But was she an ultra-efficient murderer?

Dylan and I were motel-bound for the rest of that rainy afternoon. When Mrs. Presley saw us coming in, she said she'd fix up some sandwiches for our supper.

"Or should I fix up some oysters on the half shell?" she asked. "Strawberries dipped in chocolate? Want me to send down a bottle of wine for you two? Candles? I got some old 45s out back. What if I hook up a record player so you two can have some music to dine by. *Love me Tender* kind of stuff. You like love songs, Dix?"

Subtle, Mrs. Presley. Real subtle.

I told her — emphatically — that sandwiches would be fine, and that I'd be back in a little while to pick it up. But truly, food was the farthest thing from my mind right then, as Dylan and I headed down the hidden hallway to Room 111. We had work to do.

We got down to business immediately, poring again and again over Jennifer's journal. That was strange in itself, looking so intimately at the life of this poor dead woman. She'd clearly been taken by the attention of Billy Star. And again, that made me cringe as I reflected on Billy's initial motivation for wooing Jennifer, i.e., to revenge himself on Ned. And, oh, how she'd soaked up that attention! At least at first. But, if I was reading the cues correctly — and I'm a woman so, hell, of course I was — love was waning as of late.

May 12
J - return (mail) necklace to BS
LL - needs to confirm things for reception — call the bitch
and make sure she does.
May 16

J - call EB at spa, re-confirm all my Monday's
May 20
J - must find that lost BS letter!
May 22
J - tell BS to go FCK himself once and for all!

Now, that last one was a shorthand code you didn't have to be a detective to decipher. And I doubted very much if the BS here was the Bombay Spa. No, Jennifer was done with Billy Star. There were a couple more references to Luanne (LL), snarkily written. Complete with little frowning faces all over the page — and a fair number of devil's pitchforks. The (PR) Pastor Ravenspire mentions were equally negative, but the accompanying graphics were a little more intense. And there were many N (for Ned) entries, of course. EB — Elizabeth Bee popped up every so often, always with a note to be sure to tip her for one thing or another. For one who apparently had been saving her money, Jennifer had no qualms about tipping Elizabeth very well. Genuine generosity? Buying her silence? There were a few references to neighbors, appointments to be kept, but nothing out of the ordinary.

And it wasn't just the re-reading of the journal that kept us occupied that rainy day and evening. Dylan and I also listened to every taped conversation, again and again. We looked over every photo. We went over every note, the crumpled restraining order, every receipt. I swear, Dylan and I could have recited verbatim the contents of any of those documents or recordings.

It was about 6 p.m. when, with a mutual huff, we set the pages down. The whiteboard Dylan had brought along had been written upon and erased time and time again until it was more gray than white.

"I'm missing something, Dylan. Any one of these folks," I waved a hand over the pictures and pages before us on the bed, "could have killed Jennifer. Could have hired someone to come into the offices to pose as her and set me up. Could have written that NO WAY IN HELL in her journal."

I groaned in frustration, then yawned on the next indrawn breath. I glanced at my watch. Holy crap, I was tired. And getting a little hungry.

I'd long abandoned the comfy brown housecoat. In fact, the room was warm enough that I'd shucked my socks hours ago. Now, weary and tired, I linked my fingers together and curled my back as I stretched out my arms. My neck was sore from the strain of hunching so long over papers. I rolled my head gingerly, then put a hand to the tight muscles on right side of my neck. Ouch.

"Let me, Dix."

And before I could utter a word in protest (funny, I'm not usually such a slow talker), Dylan had his hands on my neck. "Whoa!" he said. "You're tense."

Well, duh. "Just ... long, hard day, Dylan."

He grinned. "Lucky for you, a master masseuse from the Bombay Spa is here."

I arched an eyebrow. The mental picture of me beneath the white sheet, naked on the massage table flashed through my mind. I felt the heat rising in my cheeks, and lowering in other places. "And here I thought that diploma from the Cordick School was a fake."

"It's Cor*nick* School. Not *dick*."

"Of course."

"And yeah, it's a fake, but I'm damn good with my hands anyway. So let me get that tension out."

"Oh well, no need. I'm just —"

He cocked his head. "Do I make you nervous, Dix?"

I snorted. "Of course not."

Technically it wasn't a lie. He didn't make me axe-murderer nervous.

"Then just let me help you here."

Why not? Dylan had made it clear the other night when he'd jumped out of my bed that he wasn't interested in me that way, hadn't he? And surely, I didn't have feelings here myself that I couldn't handle. No way. Not hard-assed Dix Dodd.

I lay down on the bed, fully clothed. He turned down the light. And I felt the anticipation rise unchecked within me as the mattress depressed, then I felt his hands on my back once again. But this time, it was even more intimate. This time there was no pretense, no Elizabeth Bee in the corner. This time there was nothing to stop us. Except ourselves.

Careful, Dix. Remember the trouble last time you let yourself feel.

But even as I reproached myself, I knew ... I could *be* here. I could drift into this feeling. Give into this feeling. If only —

Though his voice was low, I startled when Dylan spoke into the quiet, darkened room. "You know Dix, sometimes when you're so busy looking for the bad guys all the time, you miss the good guys. You don't always have to be on the defensive. You might be missing something pretty good here."

Maybe it was his voice. Maybe it was his hands. But, holy hell, whatever it was it was working. I was melting under the touch of this man. And that did make me nervous, paling in comparison to any axe-murderer at the door.

"Dylan, I—"

"Just hear me out, Dix. The other night when I held you was … I felt something and you felt it too. I know you did."

He waited, and though I was sorely tempted to, I didn't jump into that pause. I could feel his warmth—all of his warmth as he touched me gently. I could hear his breathing. Goddamn it, I wanted to be this close to this man. We were alone in the world just then—in the quiet of our room.

"Dix," he continued, his voice deep and soft as it curled along my spine. He was leaning down toward me. Leaning in to kiss me, I knew. "I was worried about you today. More than I knew I could be. And I knew—"

We both swore when the phone rang into the room.

Me, because that loud, shrill ring startled me. Dylan because when I startled I jumped and smacked him in the face with the back of my head.

Oh shit!

Even as I picked up the receiver I could see his bottom lip swelling up. I cringed and mouthed a 'sorry', but what exactly was I sorry for? Certainly for the growing boo-boo on his handsome face. But was I sorry the mood had been broken? Again? That the kiss had been, shot (or rather smacked) out of existence?

"Dix, Dix you there?"

"Oh … oh, sorry Mrs. P. You just caught me … caught me mid thought."

I gave Dylan the 'okay' sign and he headed to the bathroom. I heard the water running and a sucked in 'Ow!' as he put a cloth to his lip.

"Well," Mrs. P said. "I've got your supper ready. And Cal and Craig and I are just settling in for TV bingo. So if you want it hot and you want it before bingo rather than after—jackpot's twelve hundred—you better come and get it now."

"Will do Mrs. P."

"Supper?" Dylan asked coming out of the bathroom. His lip wasn't bleeding — anymore. But the little smooth bulge on the bottom of it would be there for a day or two. And as my eyes looked southward, that was the only thing bulging on Dylan Foreman now.

Way to break a mood, Dix. That's me, Dix Dodd, ball buster, lip buster extraordinaire.

"Yep. Supper's ready. I'll just go down and get —"

"Let me, Dix." His grin was self-mocking. "I could use a bit of a walk."

He hip checked open the door and backed/dipped his way out. That hidden door was a wonderful idea, but certainly not made with six-foot-four Dylan Foreman in mind.

I lay back on the bed when the door closed behind Dylan. The lights were still low but I threw one arm over my eyes anyway. I drew the other hand across the slightly rumpled sheets. What had just happened here? More importantly, what had almost just happened here? Saved by the bell?

Damn bell.

"Can you get the door, Dix?"

I jumped up when Dylan called and scooted across the room. He backed up when I shoved the door open. I stood in the dark hallway as with tray in hand Dylan moved around me.

"Leave it to Mrs. P." He gazed appreciatively down at the tray as he walked forward. "Shaved roast on whole wheat. Grapes. Three different kinds of cheese. And for dessert, cookies. Looks like chocolate chip oatmeal. And they're still warm."

I was watching Dylan's backside and Dylan apparently wasn't watching at all, because as he tried to step through the door, he cracked his forehead on the top of the frame.

With a loud crash, he and the tray hit the floor.

"Holy shit!" I leaned down over him. "Dylan, are you all right? Are you … quick," I said, remembering my first aid training from Girl Guides. "How many fingers am I holding up?" I held up a couple. He raised his head a little and squinted his eyes toward them.

"Dylan? Say something!"

He grinned, and put a hand to his forehead.

"Honey, I forgot to duck."

He was fine. Well not fine-fine (there was a fair-sized lump popping up dead-center on his forehead), but he wasn't seriously injured if he was cracking jokes, calling me honey quoting Reagan. I helped him to the bed.

"You sure you're all right?" I asked, picking up the wonderful supper

Mrs. P had made us. The sandwiches were a lost cause, but the main part — the cookies — were still good. "I can get Mrs. P to —"

"I'm fine, Dix."

The poor guy looked like he'd done battle with, well, me. Between the busted lip and the lump on his head, he was one sorry looking man.

Actually, we both were pretty sorry looking. Dylan with the lump on his head, me with ... well, me with the murder wrap hanging over my head.

I thought we'd hit pay dirt when I'd found Jennifer's journal. Clues had lain in there certainly, but answers? *The* answer?

I was missing something. It was niggling at me. Nagging. And it was right *there* — hanging just out of my reach. What was it? What was I missing here? I stood there with these thoughts twisting in my brain, staring unseeingly at Dylan.

"Is it bad, Dix?" He'd been studying my expression. And now raised a worried hand, and a careful one, to his forehead.

"Oh, sorry. I ... I was thinking about the case." Yes, I felt incredibly sheepish admitting that.

"But how bad's the lump on my head?" He patted some hair down over it, and in all seriousness asked. "Can you notice it?"

"Can I *notice* it? Dylan, it's a doozie." I laughed out loud.

"Geez, Dix, you're all sympathy!"

"Sorry. Sorry. It's *'oozie'* words. They get me every time. Always conjures up these weird mental pictures." And combine that with the lack of sleep and tension that needed breaking ... it's a wonder I wasn't rolling on the floor. "You know doozie ... oozie." I cracked up all over again.

He grinned. Okay, so he was lacking sleep and under tension himself. "Sounds like quite the affliction. For a moment there, I thought you'd been drinking. Thought you'd gotten all *boozie*."

Wow, that was bad. But yes, it sent thoughts of flying pink pigs crashing into skyscrapers in my head, and it sent another snort of laugher into the room.

"What? No comeback?"

Oh, so this was the challenge was it — *oozie* word sentences that made sense? We'd played dumber games.

"Not enough for you to get beaten at online *Jeopardy*, Mr. Foreman?" I asked. "Haven't had your ass handed to you often enough at trivia? Now I have to kick your butt at this, too."

Okay, I didn't always kick his butt at trivia. We were about 50/50 on that score. I suck at twenty questions (though I'd never admit to it under threat of torture!) And on the slow times when we did play online games, his little blue-shirted avatar was a wee bit more skilled than my pink-shirted avatar. But for the purposes of this current mindless competition, the trash talk was called for. Necessary, even.

He shrugged. "If you're not up for the challenge, you don't have to play. I mean, if you so *choose-ie*."

I snorted. "Just be prepared Dylan. You're about to *lose-ie*."

He rolled his eyes (a little heavy toward the top I noticed, no doubt trying to see if he could actually see the bump.) "*Lose-ie* isn't a word, Dix."

"It is now," I said. "And you should talk. *Choose-ie*?"

He said, "I think this case is getting to you. We need to find some *clues-ies*." For dramatic emphasis, Dylan picked up Jennifer's journal from the bed bedside him.

Not to be outdone, I grabbed the newspaper Mrs. P had delivered with breakfast. "Maybe I should look in here. You know, check out the *news-ie*."

Okay, I could see him mentally reaching on that one. He was desperately trying to think of something. Was I actually going to win this one? Was I —

"Why don't you read it to me?" He pointed to his forehead. "That smack on the head has left me kind of *woozy*."

I shook my head, and gently touched the goose egg growing on his forehead. "Dylan, you're more than a flirt. You're an out and out *floo* ...

A chill went along my spine and I held deathly still as it did. The feeling niggled itself up my shoulders. Nagged its way up my neck. Every fiber in me knew there was something here. Knew I'd hit upon something. My mind reached for it. My intuition grabbed for it. Goddamned well caught it!

"SON OF A BITCH!"

"Er, that doesn't rhyme with *oozie*, Dix."

"Oh my God!" I shrieked (and I'm not one to shriek). But I *had* it! *I freakin' well had it!* I jumped away from Dylan, bounded off the bed and cranked up the light Dylan had earlier dimmed.

"Jesus, Dix!" With both hands now, he felt along his forehead. "How bad is it?" He ran to the bathroom to check himself out in the mirror.

I raced around the room looking for my cell phone, finally having to call it from the motel phone in order to find it (I'd left it in the red blazer which I'd folded on the dresser — that blazer was just bad luck!). I grabbed my cell and raced back, already dialing as I jumped and landed cross-legged on the bed.

"It doesn't look that bad, does it?" Dylan came out of the bathroom still rubbing his forehead. "Like, you don't think it's permanent?"

"It's fine. Get your phone, Dylan. We've got some calls to make."

He blinked. "To whom?"

I nodded to the pictures strewn all over the bed. "The whole lot of them."

Genuinely perplexed now, Dylan shook his head. "What am I supposed to say?"

Before I could respond, the party I'd called answered the phone. I held a finger up to Dylan, signaling him to wait. I could tell his frustration was growing, but with any luck ...

"Hey, Dickhead," I said into the phone. "Where the hell have you been?"

He said something about the nude limbo videos Dylan had packed for him. Something colorful. (I took it he wasn't impressed.) Then he went into detail about how he personally was going to see to it that my ugly butt was in jail for —

I cut him off mid-rant. "Meet me at the Weatherby house tomorrow morning at 8 a.m. sharp. Don't be late."

"What the hell are you talking about, Dixieass?" he snarled. "You finally coming to your senses, gonna turn yourself in?"

I laughed. "Hell, no I'm not going to turn myself in. I'm going to do your job for you. Because I know who killed Jennifer Weatherby."

I hung up before he could scream at me anymore. And before he could trace the call.

Dylan stood dead still. He stared at me wide-eyed. "You know who killed Jennifer Weatherby? And who framed you?"

I nodded. I stood. I jumped on the bed. And jumped and jumped!

"I know, Dylan. Finally, it's all come together. There's only one person who could have killed Jennifer Weatherby."

I stopped jumping and filled Dylan in on what I knew.

As soon as he'd heard me out, Dylan picked up his own phone and started dialing. Both of us now were calling in the players. Calling them to the Weatherby house for 8 a.m. tomorrow morning. And each and every one of them would show up. They had a reason to. We gave it to them: *"Come to the Weatherby mansion at eight in the morning, because we know who killed Jennifer. And we know how you're involved."*

An hour later, calls made, Dylan left. We both aimed to get some sleep before we executed our plan. Excited, of course. Happy. But … there was something else there. He kissed me on the cheek as he left the motel room. Shoved his hands in his pocket, and hip checked the hidden door to exit the room via Mrs. Presley's secret entrance. This time, he remembered to duck.

I remade the bed my jumping had messed, stripped down and crawled between the sheets.

And of course, I dreamed of her — my Flashing Fashion Queen.

Still she tried to elude me. Still she was out of my grasp. Ah, but I didn't reach.

With her fancy, flouncy twists and turns, she managed to prevent me from getting a clear view of her face. But I didn't look so very hard this time.

Didn't have to.

And still, the bitch taunted me. Or rather, tried to.

"You're not going to do this successfully, Dix. You're going to fail. You'll never catch me. I'm just too smart for you. Haven't you learned that yet?"

And I chuckled as the Flashing Fashion Queen bounced away. "We'll see, Blondie," I called. "We'll see."

I slept wonderfully. Hands linked behind my head, I slept on my back, no doubt snoring like a sailor lulled by the waves of the ocean. And when I awoke well rested and ready a few short hours later, there was barely a wrinkle in the sheets.

Yep, it had been a perfect snoozie.

Chapter 19

MMMMMMMMMM ... HOMEMADE BREAKFAST. Mrs. Presley had made enough for two lumberjacks, which pleased Dylan to no end when he arrived. By the look of him, he'd not slept as well as I had, but I had no doubt he'd be ready, willing and able to handle what the day had in store for us. The swelling on the lip had gone down quite a bit. But the bump on his head had turned a lovely purple color.

"Geez, Dix," Mrs. P had offered upon seeing the worse-for-wear Dylan Foreman. "How wild did you two get in here? Playing cops and robbers? Or was it good cop, kinky cop? I bet I can guess which one you were, Dix. The kinky one, right? Next time I'll send down a set of fur-lined handcuffs."

Dylan just about choked on his toast.

I just about spewed my coffee.

Per usual, there was a single red rose on the breakfast tray. That and a pile of scrambled eggs, perfectly cooked sausage, and toasted homemade bread. Jam and peanut butter served in one of those fancy little silver things. She even had a little dish of mints. There was coffee, of course, and fresh squeezed orange juice. And speaking of squeezed ...

"I'll be back in a jiffy," Mrs. Presley had said, after the teasing was done and she'd watch Dylan and me both for a few minutes to make sure we were going to do justice to her breakfast. "Just gotta powder my nose, put on some lipstick, and then I'm ready."

"Ready?" I asked.

"Ready," she affirmed.

Dylan paused between forkfuls of egg. "You're coming, Mrs. P?"

"Are you kidding? I wouldn't miss it for the world."

My first impulse was to argue. For her sake, not mine. And in a weak effort, I did so. But Mrs. Presley wasn't about to budge. So we compromised, and Mrs. Presley agreed to travel with Dylan instead of me. A little less damning for her to turn up with him. And, as she reminded me, Dylan was a damn sight better looking that I was — lumps and all.

"We'll have to take my Harley, Mrs. P," Dylan said, in his best apologetic voice.

"I'll go get my helmet!" She clasped her hands together, beside herself with excitement. "And I'll hold on tight."

I bit down on the smile; I just bet she would.

One last time, I reminded Mrs. Presley that she had hidden a fugitive from the law. Though I had every confidence I was correct about who killed Jennifer, and who (grrrrrr) tried to frame me for it, there was no need for Mrs. P to expose herself as having harbored me. She just shrugged her shoulders. "By the end of the day, you'll not be a fugitive from the law, Dix. You'll be a hero." She stood in that way — shoulders back, hands on hips, feet firmly planted on the floor — that told me there was no sense in arguing with the woman.

But I really didn't want to.

I liked that she had faith in me. And for that alone, this petite little lady in her flowered shirt and granny glasses looked pretty much like a hero to me.

While Mrs. P went to make herself ready, Dylan and I ate the rest of our breakfast and planned. The players had all received a personal invitation, and I was sure each would be in attendance at the Weatherby mansion. (Of course, in Dickhead's case, he'd bring half of Marport City's police force along with him.) More specifically, I'd called the meeting for the very room where Jennifer had died — her study. And this time, I wouldn't be hiding under the desk.

At least I hoped I wouldn't be.

"One call and I can have you arrested on the spot, Ms. Dodd. And if you try to run, I'll make that call so fast you'll think you're running backwards." Judge Stephanopoulos held up her cell phone for emphasis.

"I understand, Judge. And I wouldn't dream of betraying your trust."

She huffed. "If it wasn't for Rochelle's faith in you ..."

I sent a quick 'thank-you-I-owe-you-big-time' look at my friend. Rochelle flashed back a 'you-can-bet-I'll-collect' acknowledgment. And I bet that she would.

I didn't like the formality with which Judge Stephanopoulos

addressed me this morning. But I couldn't blame her. *Technically*, she was helping someone wanted by the police. *Technically*, she could get in a bit of trouble here herself — the line she was walking was pretty thin. But, this was a woman made of some brass. And honor. She was also a woman who believed in justice, and I had a feeling she'd do whatever she could to see that it prevailed.

So when I had called Rochelle (to confirm some things I suspected and to ask for — okay, *beg for* — her help), she'd presented everything to Judge Stephanopoulos who, according to Rochelle, shook her head and reluctantly agreed to meet with me and hear me out. Under one condition — that after I'd had my say, I'd turn myself in whether my suspicions panned out or not. I had agreed. We met. She listened. And she — *yesss!* — agreed to help me.

We would go to the Weatherby home together, where I would turn myself over to the police. Judge Stephanopoulos was an officer of the court bringing in a fugitive. But she'd make sure I had a few minutes of say before Dickhead hauled me away. That's all I asked for. Yet if my theory was correct and I could pull this off, there would be no need for Dickhead to arrest me once this meeting was over.

Now, as we sat in the Judge's car, she glanced back at me again as she put her phone away. "All I can offer you is time and forum. But nothing beyond that."

"Of course, Your Honor."

We were simply driving around Marport City now as we waited for the meeting hour to approach. Having stopped at the local drive-through coffee shop, I was well and truly caffeinated. Dylan had gone over to the Weatherby house earlier, with instructions to call me on my cell once everyone had arrived.

Even though the Judge's windows were tinted and therefore I wasn't likely to be spotted, it was strange being out and about the town as 'me'. There were no disguises today. No hair dye, no tinted shades, no red blazer. Firstly, I didn't want Ned Weatherby or his parents to recognize me from the real estate agent fiasco, but also because I was through with running from the Flashing Fashion Queen. Through with disguises on this one. Through with hiding because of her.

"You know, Dix," Rochelle said, "Dylan Foreman could be in a bit of trouble here, too." She was sitting in the front passenger seat while Judge Stephanopoulos drove. "If you don't walk away from this scot free, Dylan doesn't either."

Judge Stephanopoulos nodded. "Rochelle's right, Ms. Dodd. Detective Head could well arrest Mr. Foreman for aiding and abetting."

I'd thought of that, of course.

I'd given Dylan the option of cutting and running from *mi vida loca* last night while he still could. As it stood, there was nothing that could concretely link him to me since I'd been on the lam. Sure, he'd helped me escape custody at the office, but that couldn't be proven. And Dylan was too smart to admit to anything, or be intimated under police questioning. He'd get a genuine chuckle if they pulled the good-cop, bad-cop shit with him. But once he entered that Weatherby house to set this up with me ... if my goose was cooked, his good-looking gander was hitting the BBQ too. I had made that perfectly clear to him.

Dylan hadn't blinked. Had not hesitated. He hadn't missed a heartbeat before he answered my offer with, "Forget it, Dix. We're in this together."

Those words echoed through my mind now, as we drove around Marport City.

Then my cell phone rang. Judge Stephanopoulos glanced at me via the rearview mirror. Rochelle turned once again in her seat to stare as I answered.

"We're ready, Dix. Everyone's here."

"Thank you, Dylan."

I snapped the phone shut. Drew a deep breath. "Judge Stephanopoulos, Rochelle, it's show time."

Judge Stephanopoulos nodded, then headed the car to Ashfield Drive. And though I knew what awaited me, she couldn't drive fast enough for my liking. But once the house was in view, my gulp was audible.

"Well, isn't that a proper welcoming committee," Rochelle muttered.

I'd expected cops, but good Lord! The street in front of the Weatherby mansion looked like a river of red and blue bar lights. Shit, there were enough police cars to escort President Obama through Kandahar.

My thoughts flashed back to Dylan. I'd instructed him to call me only when everyone was convened. Detective Head, on the other hand, would have been dead set against allowing this gathering to happen. He'd have used every threat and intimidation tactic at his disposal, including this display of police might, to make Dylan cave on that point. But Dylan hadn't blinked. *Thank you, Dylan.*

Everyone would be sitting in Jennifer's study right now, nervously awaiting my arrival. And Judge Stephanopoulos was my ticket in there.

I surely hoped.

I opened the door and climbed out of Judge Stephanopoulos's car.

"Dix Dodd, you're under arrest."

Detective Dickhead's gleeful words reached me at the same time as the reek of the stale cigarette smoke that clung to him.

"Back on the butts, Detective?"

"Yeah, and just see what it's done for my mood," he smiled. "Now, hands behind your back, Dodd."

He was in a better mood, all right. Hell, he was almost dancing as he pushed me up against the car and nodded to one of the female officers present. The officer — Officer H. Lapp according to her badge — frisked me quickly, then put the handcuffs on me. This I'd expected, given my last encounter with Dickhead when I'd taken off on him, leaving Blow-Up Betty in my place. He would make damn sure it wouldn't be happening again, and the female police officer was there to ensure that no pleas of feminine emergencies would throw things off.

But when Officer Lapp moved one hand to my head and another on the small of my back to prompt me into the police car, Judge Stephanopoulos, followed by Rochelle, stepped out from the Judge's car.

"Unhand Ms. Dodd," the judge said, quietly but with unmistakable authority.

The female officer glanced at Judge Stephanopoulos, then did a double take. "Oh, Your Honor."

Judge Stephanopoulos had presided over a great many criminal trials in Marport City, and most cops had testified before her at one time or another. She had a reputation for being intelligent and fair, for running a tight and efficient courtroom, and for being someone you just did not want to piss off. Officer Lapp looked to Dickhead for instructions. Yet she relaxed her hands enough to allow me to stand straight again.

"Judge Stephanopoulos," Dickhead said. "You're a little out of your jurisdiction aren't you?"

"I'm an officer of the court, Detective Head," Judge Stephanopoulos replied. "I'm making this my jurisdiction."

"Not from where I'm standing," he grated. "From where I'm standing, Dix Dodd is a dangerous fugitive on the run. I have to haul her in."

Okay, this is where it got tricky.

And I watched the two — Judge Stephanopoulos and Dickhead — my head snapping left to right, right to left with every volley of words. My money was on the judge. And, well, my *everything* was on the judge.

"This doesn't concern you at this point, Judge," Dickhead said. "This isn't your courtroom. This is *my* bailiwick."

"This may not be my courtroom, Detective. But I assure you it concerns me. According to Ms. Dodd, a crime has been committed."

"Yeah, by Ms. Dodd, and I'm —"

Judge Stephanopoulos raised her hand quickly, silencing him. "And, again according to Ms. Dodd, I'm directly involved."

He pinched the bridge of his nose, as though trying to summon patience. "Look, dear, if you've got information we should consider, I'll be happy to look into it. Right after we finish processing this prisoner."

Yeah, I caught it — *dear.*

And by the way Officer Lapp was biting her lip, she'd caught it too.

Rochelle jabbed me with her elbow. "Oh, man," she whispered, "the judge's gonna castrate him."

Castrate him? Why, was it Christmas already? I felt the excitement bubble up inside; I heard the carols playing in my head: *Deck the halls with Dickhead's balls, falalalala la la la la.*

Only when Rochelle elbowed me a second time — harder — did I realize I'd been humming.

Eyes narrowed, Judge Stephanopoulos regarded Detective Head. Like something out of a Clint Eastwood spaghetti western, she stood with her arms at her sides as if she was ready to whip out a six-shooter. He glared right back. And though I had little doubt before, I *really* had no doubt now as to who would be winning this exchange, because she smiled at him. It was not a sweet smile.

"Let me explain something to you, Detective," Judge Stephanopoulos began. "And I'll say it slowly so that hopefully you won't get hung up on the big words."

Dickhead blinked.

Another elbow in the ribs from Rochelle, and I bit back the *'you go girl!'* that threatened to erupt.

Judge Stephanopoulos continued, "Ms. Dodd is in no danger of fleeing at this point, Detective. You have her in handcuffs. You have her in custody in the pure definition of the law. You have many officers on the premises. On the other side of the coin, I have knowledge that an injustice has been done, and is continuing to be done. And I believe that this injustice will not be rectified until and unless Ms. Dodd addresses those gathered within that house, and gives the information to all, including yourself, that she has given to me. I am an officer of the court, acting in —"

"She can tell her lies downtown!" Dickhead interjected.

"She'll tell her *truths* here!" Judge Stephanopoulos's voice rang with authority.

Dickhead's struggle was written clearly on his face. For a moment, it looked as though he was going to concede. He ran his tongue over his lower lip quickly. He rocked on his heels. Just when I thought he was going to agree, his glance fell on me and his face hardened.

"No." He snapped. "Not going to happen. This is my show and what I say goes. And I say Dixielicks is going downtown."

"Then let me put it another way, Detective," Judge Stephanopoulos said. "Dix Dodd is going into that house right now. Rochelle and I are going with her. And if you try to stop us, you'll have to arrest me along with Ms. Dodd. And in that event, you'd better make damn sure that you keep me behind bars a good long while. Because I assure you, Detective, when I am no longer a guest of the county, and when Ms. Dodd has proven her innocence, I will make it my personal mission to have you busted down to picking up dog shit in the park. And if you don't believe me, Detective, then just try me."

It was the way she said 'try me' ... with the barely-there restraint in her voice. Almost as if she was daring him to call her on this. Almost as if she *wanted* him to do it.

Dickhead stared at the judge, hard. But not for long.

"Ah, hell!" He turned away and snarled in the general direction of Officer Lapp. "Well, what are you waiting for? Take Dodd into the house!"

Officer Lapp took me by the elbow, but not hard. Rather as a demonstration that I was indeed in custody.

Inside the Weatherby house, police lined the walls. Though no weapons were drawn, it was still intimidating walking the gauntlet. Obviously, they were serious about my not escaping custody this time.

And all eyes were on me as I entered the study.

"Dix!" Dylan had been sitting on a small sofa beside Mrs. Presley, but surged to his feet at the sight of Officer Lapp's grip on my obviously cuffed arm.

"Hey, Dylan." I smiled reassuringly. "Everything's cool."

Judge Stephanopoulos and Rochelle followed me into the room, and stood beside the door. And of course, Dickhead came to stand beside me, breathing down my neck.

I looked around the room.

Ned's lawyer, Jeremy Poole, sat beside a nervous-looking Elizabeth

Bee on a matching sofa placed on the other side of the room. She looked from Dylan to me, then back to Dylan again with a confused, questioning look on her face. A tall, portly man completely decked out in baker's whites stood between the two sofas. I knew this had to be Kenny Kent, the Weatherby's caterer. Billy Star was there, standing beside Jennifer's bookcase beside a rigid Luanne Laney. The latter had a steno pad and pen poised in her hands to take notes. Wow, that woman was efficient. Or psycho.

"Well, if it isn't Dix Dodd! I haven't seen you in ages," Mrs. Presley shouted into the room. "Why when Dylan picked me up this morning and told me about the party, I wouldn't have missed it for the world." Bless her little ass-covering heart. "And didn't I see your picture in the paper the other day? Something about ... some case you were working on or something?"

"Hello, Mrs. Presley," I said. "Good to see you again. And yes, that was me you saw in the paper."

She smiled and looked around the room. "You know, it's just like Old Home Week here — all these familiar faces." Half the men in the room averted their gazes — looking up, down, sideways and everywhere, *except* at Mrs. Presley.

Detective Head just looked angry. "Let's get this over with, shall we?"

I turned to expose my handcuffed wrists to him. "Can you remove these?" I had visions of dramatically pointing to the guilty party as I made my Sherlock Holmes-style speech.

"Not a chance," he sneered.

Damn.

"Damn."

"Please watch what you say, Ms. Dodd," Pastor Ravenspire said. He was standing between Ned and his father, and all three stood over the chair where Ned's mother sat behind Jennifer's desk. "I'm not used to such language. And frankly," he looked around the room — a little too quickly, a little too nervously. "I don't know why I'm here in the first place." He looked at his watch. "I ... I can't stay long."

Mr. Weatherby Senior took off his glasses, wiped them, and put them back on again. "You ... you look familiar," he said to me. He turned to his wife. "Doesn't she look familiar, dearest?"

"Yes," the old woman said slowly, thoughtfully. "Yes, she does. Give me a minute ... I'll place that face."

Oh great, that was all I needed for Dearest to recognize me. I'd have to do this quickly.

I drew a deep breath, expelled it, and began. "Each one of you has been called here today for a reason. Each one of you knew Jennifer Weatherby. Each one of you was close enough to murder Jennifer Weatherby. And one of you … one of you did just that."

I waited a moment for the hands-to-heart dramatic gasp, but obviously no one was as impressed as I was by my theatrics. I cleared my throat and continued. "A little over a week ago, someone disguised as Jennifer walked into my office. This person told me that her husband, Ned Weatherby, was having an affair and she wanted me to trail him for a week and keep a record of his activities."

Ned sputtered. "That's … that's preposterous! I wasn't having an affair. Jennifer was —"

He paled. He looked at his mother, his father, then quickly to the floor.

"What is it, Neddy?" his mother asked, turning in the chair to look up at her son. "Jennifer was what?"

Loyally, Ned remained silent.

So I finished for him. "Jennifer was having an affair herself, wasn't she, Ned?" I had no desire to bring this out into the open, but I had little choice in the matter. "She was having an affair, and you knew about it."

He let out a shuddering breath. "Yes, I knew. She and Billy Star had been involved for some time. But *was* is the operative word, Ms. Dodd. Jennifer ended it."

Billy *hmphed* loudly, but didn't say a word.

"Still, that must have angered you, Ned."

"Of course it angered me!" He looked at his hands and played a moment with the wide gold band he still wore. When he spoke again his voice was softer. "But I wasn't always the best husband in the world. Jennifer deserved … more. More attention. More affection. More everything. I was so concerned about making money, growing my business, sometimes Jennifer felt … forgotten. I know she did. That's why … that's why that damnable Billy Star was able to seduce her."

"Why didn't you fire Billy?

"I couldn't. When I bought him out —"

"— and you bought him just before stocks in the company skyrocketed, Ned?" I offered. Yes it was a dirty dig, but I wanted to gauge his reaction. I thought there might be a trace of guilt there, but Ned didn't skip a beat.

"That's right. When I bought the son of a bitch out, his continual employment was part of the agreement. I couldn't fire him for anything short or embezzlement. Certainly not for ... for having an affair with my wife."

"Still," I baited, "your wife turned to another man. That had to make you angry, and not only with Billy Star. But with Jennifer, too."

"Jennifer broke it off with Billy. She and I ... we were trying to work some things out."

"What kind of things?"

"Everything!" Ned swallowed hard and wet his lips. He appeared to be on the verge of tears. "We were renewing our vows on the weekend. And ... and we'd come to some understandings. She wanted to go visit her family in Toledo more, and I promised to go with her once or twice over the next few months. And she didn't want me going to Pastor Ravenspire's church so much. She didn't trust him." He glanced at Ravenspire, who himself squirmed in his chair. "Sorry, Pastor. That was a sore point between us. And Jennifer ... Jennifer promised to stop seeing Billy."

I'd glanced at Billy often through this exchange — his face grew redder, his fists clenched tighter. And now I redirected my questioning to him. "And did she stop seeing you, Billy?"

"She said ... she said she wanted to break it off," he admitted, "but ... but I *know* she didn't mean it. She couldn't have meant it." He began to cry. "I ... I loved her. And I know she would have loved me if it wasn't for Ned. Ned took everything from me with the business. I couldn't ... couldn't let him have Jennifer too."

"So you pursued things with her still?"

He nodded. "I did. Best I could. Quietly. But I would have shouted it from the rooftops if I could have. But, for Jennifer's sake, I didn't want anyone to find out. Not until I'd won her back."

"But," I continued, "Ned finding out was the least of your worries, wasn't it."

Billy's sideways glance confirmed what I had suspected.

"Luanne finding out was."

The pen stopped flying over the steno pad.

"Yes," Billy said. "She scares the hell out of me."

"That's enough, William," Luanne said crisply.

Apparently, Billy didn't think it was enough. He ignored her warning. "Luanne found some letters I had written to Jennifer. I was trying to win her back, but ... but Ned was doing everything he could to ruin that. Picking her flowers, wooing her. Working fewer hours so he could spend more time with her. So I wrote Jennifer, and told her how I felt. It wasn't about the money! About the business! Not anymore and I told Jennifer this. Somehow Luanne ended up with those letters. How she found them, I'll never know."

"I'm intuitive," Luanne said.

"No," I walked over to Dylan. He handed me Jennifer's journal. "You're *nosy*. Recognize this? If you were snooping through Jennifer's journal, then chances are you were snooping through her mail too. You've got your own key to the house. You had access to Ned's and Jennifer's itineraries. You knew when they were home and when they weren't."

Luanne paled, but she lifted her chin. "*Someone* had to protect Ned!"

"It's too bad no one protected Jennifer," I said. "You knew about this journal when no one else did."

"Luanne?" Ned said in disbelief. "You ... you spied on my wife?"

"I *had* to. Don't you see, Ned?" she implored. "I always knew that little tart would betray you. So I did what I did to protect you."

"How ... how much protecting did you do?" Ned asked, his voice trembling as if he was afraid of the answer. "You've never lied to me before, Luanne. Please don't start now."

Luanne's bottom lip quivered. But she squared her shoulders as she answered. "Over the years of your marriage, I've read all of her mail. Every letter she put in that desk drawer, I'd sneak in here and read it. And of course, I read her journal. Kept track of her activities. But I did it all to protect you, Ned!"

Billy glared at her. "You bitch! You killed her!"

In a flash, Billy was on Luanne; his hands wrapped around her throat. Almost as quickly Dylan and two male cops pulled him off of her.

"How could you kill her?" Billy shouted, straining in the grip of the two officers. "How could you do such a thing?"

"I didn't!" Luanne shifted her gaze from Billy to me. "Ms. Dodd, you've got to believe me. I didn't kill Jennifer."

I nodded slowly. "I know you didn't."

Chapter 20

Y OU KNOW, I don't normally enjoy being the center of attention. Ahahaha! That is so not true. I just love being the center of attention. Smack dab in the middle of it. Like right about now. No one in the room was entirely sure where I was going with this. Well, no one but me, Dylan, and possibly now the murderer.

After Luanne's denial of guilt and my attestation also to her innocence, the room was so quiet you could hear the proverbial pin drop. I mentally broke into a chorus of Queen's *We Are the Champions* but thought better of actually belting it out loud. Too cocky, even for me. And besides, I had a ways to go before I was home free on this.

But things were definitely moving along.

And every set of eyes in the room was on me. I felt them. Some more than others. Dickhead, of course, was glaring at me. But I have to give him credit; he'd been quiet while I had my say. He might not know where this was going, but he wasn't so stupid or vindictive as to stop me. Not when there was murder involved. Not even he would stoop so low as to let a killer go free just to bust my ass. And I could tell by the set of his jaw and the way he was listening to me, that he knew I was on to something.

As I stood taking a deep breath before continuing, I heard Ned's mother mumbling. "I don't know ... I know that face from somewhere. Somewhere recent ..."

Oh shit.

Jeremy Poole sat in the corner, so pale and still he could have been a wax statue. Elizabeth Bee sat perched on the edge of her chair, waiting to see what would happen next. Rochelle and Judge Stephanopoulos remained in the doorway, watching intently from the periphery, but not missing a thing.

Dylan was looking at me too, of course. I'd catch his eye every once in a while. I saw the encouraging nods. The hint of a smile. And I liked that. It felt good to be on top of my game while he watched. Strangely good. Weirdly good.

Cautiously good, Dix, I reminded myself. Cautiously good.

I let my gaze sweep again over the people assembled, each with their own agendas and fears and loves. Ah, yes, love. What a crazy thing it was. It could make us laugh or cry. It could scare the crap out of us or make us feel renewed. Make us feel stupid and brilliant all at once. It made old men pat their wives' hands and call them 'Dearest'. And as I knew all too well, love could break our hearts. It could turn us into romantic fools. And, yes, it could turn us into murderers.

"Well!" It was Mrs. Presley's voice that broke the silence. "If that don't beat all! I had the secretary pegged for sure." She nudged Dylan. "Just look at those beady eyes on her, will ya." She opened her purse, turned toward Kenny Kent the baker, and handed him twenty bucks. "You won that bet, Baker Boy," she said. "Double or nothing on Round Two?"

Swiftly pocketing the money, Kent replied, "I'll quit while I'm ahead."

Luanne wasn't my favorite person in the world, and Billy Star wasn't topping my warm and fuzzy list either. But neither of them had killed Jennifer. I was sure of it. Despite his initial reasons for wooing Jennifer, Billy had loved her too much to hurt her, and Luanne loved Ned too much to hurt him.

I began again. "You're all forgetting something here. Whoever killed Jennifer also did a damn good job of covering their tracks. Arranged for a mysterious Flashing Fashion Queen to come to my office disguised as Jennifer, and ask me to tail Ned Weatherby for the week. And I had to wonder why."

"To frame you!" an enthusiastic Mrs. P shouted.

"That's exactly what I thought at first, Mrs. Presley. But then I thought maybe it was more. Maybe it was so that Ned's whereabouts would be alibied very carefully. So that he couldn't be blamed for the murder of his wife."

Ned looked at me, clearly shocked. "Surely . . . surely you don't think *I* hired someone to pose as Jennifer, then killed her myself?"

"Actually, Ned," I said. "That very thought has crossed my mind."

"Ms. Dodd!" Jeremy Poole leapt to Ned's defense. "If you're going to accuse my client of murder, I'd make damn sure that you know just what you're getting yourself into here. With all the charges against you now criminally, I don't think you really wish to add a civil suit to your legal woes. As Mr. Weatherby's legal counsel I must advise him not to participate in any further discussions with you here today. In fact, I strongly suggest to Detective Head that this meeting is a sham, a travesty, and that this meeting should be over."

"Oh, I'm not accusing Ned Weatherby of murdering Jennifer Weatherby, Mr. Poole. Not at all. As I said the thought crossed my mind, then kept on walking." I turned and walked over to the lawyer. "I'm accusing you."

"Yes!" Elizabeth Bee hissed, pumping her arm in the air. She held her hand out flat and Mrs. Presley grumblingly pressed a twenty-dollar bill into it, which Elizabeth quickly secreted into her bra.

"What the hell are you talking about, Dix?" Dickhead said. But he didn't say it with quite so much of a snarl this time. He didn't say it with a *ha ha* belly roar of a laugh. He said it like a man who wanted to hear what I had to say. I had his attention.

Hell, I had everyone's attention.

Dylan handed me Jennifer's journal. Or rather tried to, but with my hands cuffed behind my back, that wasn't an easy task. I looked at Detective Head. "Things would go a lot easier from here detective if you'd let me out of these handcuffs."

He stared at me hard for a long minute, then moved to unlock the handcuffs.

"Don't make me regret this, Dix," he said as he removed the bracelets. "Because if I do, I guarantee you will too."

"Understood."

More out of reflex than because of any soreness, I rubbed my wrists quickly before I held up Jennifer's journal. I read from the homemade jacket of the book. "*The Secret Life of the Bombay Dung Beetle*, by Elizabeth Bee."

Loudly, Elizabeth *hmphed.*

"This is Jennifer's journal," I explained. "Her secret journal."

"I never knew she kept one," Ned said.

"No, she hid it well. But as we already established, *you* knew she kept it, didn't you, Luanne?"

"Once or twice a week I'd let myself in … when Ned and Jennifer were out of the house. Yes, I'd read it. I needed to know everything to protect Ned." Guilt free, she answered. "That's how I was able to inform Ned of the affair between Billy and Jennifer. Once I put all the notes and pieces together."

"But you didn't tell Ned how you came by that knowledge, did you?"

"No," she admitted.

"And," I continued, "usually you just read Jennifer's journal, said nothing, did nothing and put it back where you found it. Right?"

She sucked in a breath. "Yes. But the last time ... the last time Jennifer made an entry, I ... accidentally did something."

"Because the last entry Jennifer made angered you so greatly that you wrote a comment back. Didn't you, Luanne?"

"Yes!" she shouted. "I couldn't help myself." She looked around the room, as if seeking an ally for her behavior. "Jennifer wrote 'J cancelled caterer.' After all Ned was doing for her, she was canceling the caterer and thus I assumed she was canceling the renewal of the vows. That she was going to hurt Ned all over again. I just lost my temper. I just snapped! That's why I wrote what I did."

Kenny Kent, really interested now, shifted from foot to foot.

"The 'NO WAY IN HELL' written in the journal, Luanne?" I asked. "That was yours, wasn't it?"

"Yes." She lowered her eyes. "I know it was stupid! Very stupid! But I was just so angry!"

"This is ridiculous," Jeremy Poole said. "It proves nothing whatsoever about *my* guilt. If you ask me, it's Luanne Laney you should be pointing a finger at." He stretched his arm and shook a pointing finger himself for emphasis.

I pretended to mull that over. "Ummmmmmm ... no," I said. "You see it wasn't the person who wrote the NO WAY IN HELL that killed Jennifer. It was the person who cancelled the caterer."

"Oh for Heaven's sake!" Jeremy said. "It's Jennifer's journal. She cancelled the caterer. Obviously, her intention to renew with Ned was false. She was using him, again. Still."

"No, Jennifer didn't cancel the caterer. Jennifer always wrote in the future tense when she entered *her* plans; never what she'd done. Ever. This note was a done deal. This note wasn't on her to-do list. This note was something else. This 'J' wasn't for Jennifer."

"I took that canceling call myself, and I was surprised to receive it," Kenny spoke up nervously. "I always handle the Weatherby business personally." He smoothed a nervous hand over his baker's jacket. "Mr.

Weatherby had been planning this event for weeks. It meant a lot to him. We'd gone over the menu a half dozen times. We had the ice sculpture ordered; the Cornish hens set to be flown in. And all of a sudden, I get this call canceling from a woman claiming to be Jennifer Weatherby."

"And so you scrapped everything? Just like that?"

"Of course not! I called Mr. Weatherby's office — he was tied up in meetings. So I called Mrs. Weatherby back. I wanted to tell her that she'd still have to pay the bill. I mean, after all, we'd gone to a lot of expense and trouble for this event."

"And what did Jennifer say when you called her?"

Kenny ran a hand through his hair. "She assured me the job was still on. Assured me that it wasn't her who'd called. And she ... she also told me she knew damn well who'd called to cancel, pretending to be her. She was really, really angry."

"Do you remember the date, Mr. Kent?"

"Of course. It was the 30th of May. I remember precisely because that's the day I did inventory."

I held the journal up for everyone to see the date. "It was a week before Jennifer was killed. And I'm betting 'J' who cancelled the caterer killed her."

"That 'J' was for Jeremy. Not Jennifer." Ned spoke slowly, disbelievingly. "You killed my wife."

"Ned," he said. "You ... you have to understand. As your lawyer, I have to protect you. As your friend, I have a duty to not let you make such a big mistake as renewing your vows to that ... that —"

"She was my wife!"

Detective Head was getting antsy. "Canceling a caterer is hardly evidence of murder, Dodd," he said. "I suspect you have more."

I caught it as he said it — the subtle nod to two of his uniformed officers to advance in Jeremy's direction. Not so subtly, they did.

"Oh, do I ever have more. You see, someone tipped me off that the murderer was Jeremy Poole."

"Do tell, who was that Ms. Dodd?" Jeremy was trying to act cool — trying to remain calm. He failed miserably. "A little birdie?"

"Well as a matter of fact, *you* told me Jeremy. You tipped me off." I was smiling now. Okay, it was more like I was smirking in an I'm-so-smart kind of way. I held up the newspaper — the one that Mrs. P had provided the morning I went to break into the Weatherby house, the one with that horrible picture of me splashed all over the front page.

"I have here proof positive that it was Jeremy Poole that killed Jennifer and set me up. The interview he gave to the reporter. The one where he so gleefully trashed me."

"I read the interview," Detective Head said. "I read it a few times. There's nothing in there pointing to Poole as the murderer."

I looked at him as if he were an idiot. Mostly because I enjoyed looking at him as if he were an idiot. But also for the dramatics of the thing. "Wrong again, Detective. Jeremy Poole is a pretty smooth talker. Pretty good with the lawyer-ese. I'll give him that. But there's one word — one particular word that gives him away. He used it in this newspaper interview and he used in when he posed as Jennifer in my office."

"What would that be, Dodd?"

"The f word."

"Oh for f —" Detective Head stopped mid rant as he glanced toward the judge. "I don't think Jeremy Head is the only man to use that f word, Dix Dodd. If that's all you're going on, you're pretty much f'd yourself."

I shook my head. "That's not the f word I'm referencing."

"Tell him, Dix," Dylan said.

"Floozy," I blurted. It took every bit of restraint I had to bite down on an inappropriate laugh. "Jeremy used the word floozy when he was in my office posing as Jennifer Weatherby. And he used the word floozy again in the newspaper interview. Nobody uses the word 'floozy' anymore. Certainly not that much."

"So you have a coincidence, Dodd," Dickhead informed. "Nothing more."

"I do have more."

"I . . . I have to go to the bathroom," Jeremy said. Judging by how pale he now was, I believed him. He stood, wavered sideways, stood straight.

"Oh no you don't, Poole," Dickhead said. "I'm not falling for that one again."

An officer grabbed Jeremy by the arm and sat him down again.

"It was you who came into my office that day, wasn't it, Jeremy? You threw me off there for a while, dressed as a woman. You were very clever. But I should have known you were a man all along. No woman carries that many different tubes of lipstick. Nor that many different brands of tampons in her purse." I turned to Dickhead. "Do they, Detective? You were married, you know all about these things, don't you?"

His eyes narrowed. "Just keep going, Dixie."

I did. As if reading my mind, Dylan handed me the picture — the one with Jeremy and Ned coming out of the tennis court. The one where he was bent scratching his left leg under the white tube sock. "See this, Jeremy?"

Getting paler by the moment — so pale now I could see the stubble of beard on his white cheeks — he looked at the picture and nodded.

"This proves that you were posing as Jennifer."

"I hardly see —"

I smiled. "You shaved your legs before you put on that purple dress and came into my office. You had to have just shaved your legs for them to be this smooth. And for them to be this glaringly white, you'd have to have *not* shaved them before, or at least not in a hell of a long time."

"How ... how would you possibly know that?"

"I just *do*, okay!"

Jeremy Poole crossed the legs under discussion and set his hands over his knees. "This is craziness. You've proven nothing here."

Judge Stephanopoulos spoke up. "Well, maybe *I* can prove something here, Mr. Poole."

All eyes turned to the judge as, shoulders back, she strode into the center of room. "I have here a restraining order, Mr. Poole. One taken out against Ms. Dodd advising her to stay away from the Weatherby house and Weatherby Industries. Ms. Dodd was kind enough to provide it to me this morning."

Ned shot a look to Luanne, she shot one back at him. It was obvious that neither of them knew about this.

I didn't think it was possible, but Jeremy turned even whiter. I imagine those legs of his would have the potential to blind now if exposed to the light of day.

"And, Mr. Poole," the judge continued. "What most strikes my attention is the signature on this restraining order." Judge Stephanopoulos stood before him now, towering over him as he sat cowering in the chair. She snapped the restraining order open under his nose. "You spelled my name wrong."

"Oh shit."

"And I would wager, Jeremy," I said, "that when we manage to get a search warrant for the car and residence of a certain sweet little old lady —"

"I don't know any sweet little old ladies," he said.

He had me there.

"Okay, then if we manage to get a search warrant for the car of one cranky old woman with a broken ankle, a yappy dog and a sharp tongue, a.k.a. your aunt, we'll find evidence you've been a very bad boy."

Now it was Rochelle's turn to jump into action. "I just happen to have a search warrant right here, Dix. Typed up and everything." She turned to the Judge. "Your Honor?"

She pulled a pen from her purse. With a flare of pen to paper, Judge Stephanopoulos signed the order, and handed it to Detective Head.

"McGrath, Barnable." Two officers stood straight. "Get yourselves over to Mrs. Levana Fyffe's place."

"Er, what are we looking for, Detective?" Barnable asked.

I answered; Dickhead let me. "Check the car for fibers and fingerprints. And oh, check the house for some flashing fashion."

"Huh?"

"A purple dress that Jeremy here might have worn when he dressed up as Jennifer. Wide glasses. Fake boobs. Big floppy hat."

"Wait a minute," Detective Head said. "That still doesn't explain the gun. We found the gun that killed Jennifer in your possession, Dix."

Now it was Dylan's turn to act. "Let me take this one, Dix."

I smiled. "Go for it."

He cleared his throat. It looked like he enjoyed being the center of attention too. "I did some checking around myself, Detective. That gun you found on Dix was used by Talbot K. Washington in that double murder years ago. If you recall, during the trial, it was discovered to have gone missing."

"Holy hell, Foreman, tell me something I don't know."

"Okay, then I will. There was a young law student clerking at that firm when that gun went missing. He wasn't on the regular company payroll, only worked one afternoon a week for one of the senior lawyers who paid him under the table. I guess the old guy felt sorry for him."

"Let me guess," Detective Head said. "That would be our friend Mr. Poole who was clerking there."

Dylan nodded. "I went to law school with one of the lawyers who works there now. Apparently, Jeremy Poole was a poor, starving law student, but then quit working all of a sudden just after the Washington trial ended. Came into some fast cash somehow. And plenty of it."

"You bastard," Detective Head said. "You stole the gun didn't you? Or caused it to be stolen. Washington could have *walked* because of you."

"I . . . I think I need a lawyer." Jeremy wiped a hand across his brow.

Detective Head snarled, "I *know* you do. Get this . . ." — with a glance at the Judge, he adjusted his language — "... *gentleman* downtown. Let him call his lawyer, then leave him for me." The disgust in Dickhead's voice was evident. And for a moment, I almost felt sorry for him. Then I realized the disgust was probably over the fact that I wouldn't be going to jail after all.

"Why?" Ned croaked, his voice thick with emotion, eyes filling with tears. "Why did you do it, Jeremy?"

Out of courtesy, the two officers escorting Jeremy Poole from the room stopped long enough for the question to be answered.

Jeremy's bottom lip began to quiver, and his voice became that throaty voice he'd used in my office — his Jennifer voice. "Because ... I love you, Ned."

Collectively, we all did a double take.

"What'd he say?" Mr. Weatherby, Sr. asked.

"I think he said he loved him," Mrs. Weatherby answered.

"Loved Jim? Who's Jim?"

"No, not Jim. *Him.*"

Yeah, it was getting confusing. Not even I saw that one coming.

Unprompted now, Jeremy continued. "I've loved you for so long. When Jennifer got involved with Billy, I thought maybe ... maybe then you'd throw her out for good. But you didn't, you took her back."

"But why? Why'd you have to *kill* her?"

"She was livid when she found out that I'd cancelled the caterer. It was a stupid thing to do, I know, but I was jealous. And I didn't think Kenny Kent would call her about it. I thought he'd call you, and you'd finally, once and for all, just end it with Jennifer. I hoped. But it didn't work that way. And when Jennifer found out, she called me. I went over to apologize but she wouldn't hear anything of it. I begged her not to tell you, Ned. *Begged* her. And eventually she agreed."

"But that wasn't good enough for you, was it, Jeremy?" I said.

"I ... I couldn't take the chance. What if ... what if someday she changed her mind, and did tell him? Ned would turn against me. I ... I couldn't have that. So I posed as Jennifer, and went to Dodd's office. I was looking for a not-so-bright private detective, and given the dive she works out of, I thought I'd hit pay dirt. Dammit! All I wanted was for her to follow you around for a week! I did it to protect you, Ned."

"Protect me? Protect me from what? From *Jennifer*?"

"No," I answered. "He wanted to protect you from being blamed for Jennifer's murder. I provided a rock-solid alibi, all week, in fact, until

Jeremy had the opportunity to commit murder." I turned to Jeremy, "You were protecting Ned, weren't you?"

"Yes," Jeremy whispered. "Always."

"Then it was premeditated," Dickhead said.

Jeremy's mouth snapped shut so fast and hard I heard his teeth snap together. "I ... I think I need that lawyer now."

"Know any good ones?" Mrs. P shouted.

"Downtown, boys," Detective Head said.

Chapter 21

CERTAINLY, A CELEBRATION was in order. Not right away, of course. There were a lot of loose ends that had to be tied up before we could officially celebrate. But eventually, we did manage to get out on the town to yuk it up. Unfortunately, I made the mistake of letting Dylan make the arrangements. My bad. Okay, my very, very bad.

He picked the Six Shooter. Now, it's a decent enough bar, makes a wonderful Caesar, and the food is great. The problem? It's a karaoke bar, and Dylan is a horrific singer, a fact that is painfully obvious to everyone but Dylan. We're talking peel-the-paint-off-the-walls horrible. But what could I do? He really wanted to put this little soiree together. How could I say no?

But back to those loose ends. Like getting all the charges against me dropped. That wasn't the slam-dunk you might think. As you can imagine, the police get a little testy when people escape custody. Even innocent people. But thanks to Judge Stephanopoulos (and, yes, dammit, thanks to Detective Head also), the charges were soon dismissed. I didn't have to spend so much as a night in jail.

My being innocent of the charges — not to mention catching the real killer for the police — was certainly instrumental in getting those charges dropped. But I also suspect part of the reason for Dickhead's cooperation was the fact that he bagged not just one, but two criminals.

Thanks to me.

Well, thanks to Jennifer Weatherby, actually. And yeah, okay, thanks to Ned Weatherby's elderly mother. Mrs. Weatherby never did recognize me (thank you, Jesus!), but she did recognize Pastor Ravenspire. Or should I say Pastor Latray, of Richmond, Virginia? Pastor Slaunwhite of Toronto? Pastor Hanselpecker of Montreal? Well, then how about Pastor Ingles of Las Vegas, Nevada? (Turns out Ned's mother had not only a good eye for faces but also was a pretty fair card counter.) That man had warrants out for his arrest in a half dozen states and two provinces. It just so happened that Ned's mother was a huge fan of the blackjack tables in Vegas, and had seen Pastor Ingles's picture in the paper down there about five years ago. He had been wanted on fraud, embezzlement, and contributing to the delinquency of a minor.

While Ned's eagle-eyed mom had ID'd the Pastor, it was Jennifer, speaking from the grave, who'd allowed Dickhead to eventually haul Ravenspire's unholy ass away. A message that I'd delivered to Dickhead for her. (See? I can be generous when it suits my purposes.) Turns out the good pastor was the reason why Jennifer was socking away money. She realized early on that Ravenspire was a fraud, but her husband would listen to no ill about his beloved pastor. So until she could get enough on the charismatic preacher to convince Ned that he was corrupt, she was protecting what funds she could, fearing that Ravenspire would bleed her husband dry with his constant appeals for donations. Which was pretty astute of her. As it turned out, that had been his modus operandi in those other cases. He'd pretend to be building a shiny new church, then leave town with the building fund.

How did I know this? Mrs. Presley found a package zippered into the cushions of the sofa she'd been sitting on in Jennifer's study ("Something's scratching my butt, Dix."). The package had turned out to be stuffed with cash (nearly a hundred large!) and a note from Jennifer. The note had been tucked inside an envelope addressed to Ned. 'I'm writing this in case I get hit by a bus or car-jacked or something equally embarrassing,' it was prefaced. 'If you should find this, I needed you to know it was for US, not for ME. And after the thing with Billy . . . well, I just need you to know I wasn't squirreling this away to leave you.' She'd gone on to state her suspicions about the reverend and her hope that he would heed the warnings in death that he refused to hear in life. 'This is in case we need it to get back on our feet. We can do anything together.'

The tears had filled Ned's eyes as he held the note tightly in his hands.

I'd gotten a little teary-eyed, too. Mostly at the thought of a woman who'd been unable to outrun her past and the fear of sliding back into poverty that must have dogged her despite the poise and sophistication she'd acquired. If Jennifer had been thinking rationally, she'd have realized that no matter how much cash the reverend managed to weasel out of Ned, it probably wouldn't have made too sizeable a dent in his overall wealth, the vast majority of which would not have been liquid enough to be at risk. And the sum of $100,000 — so colossal to Jennifer — hell, to the rest of us — was pitifully small by Weatherby family standards. Not quite pocket money, but pretty close. To think of the contortions she'd gone through to amass it without alerting Ned and setting off jealous suspicions … all that buying and returning of merchandise … It was just so sad.

She'd loved him. Right to the end, she had loved her husband. Sure, she'd made a mistake with Billy Star, but so what? Life goes on. People make mistakes and then get up again and keep on going. I knew this. Jennifer knew this.

So yes, Detective Head's arrest of Jennifer Weatherby's murderer, as well as the infamous Pastor Take-Your-Pick, had made him less hell-bent to see me behind bars.

This time.

Last I heard, Dickhead was back on the toothpicks and just as irritable as ever. God help the criminal element of Marport City.

So it was that two weeks after my performance in the Weatherby study, we settled in for a celebration at the Six Shooter. My treat. Business was on the upswing. The publicity generated by the case kept me on the front pages of the newspaper (sans picture, thank you very much). I couldn't have paid for that kind of exposure. Clients were calling. Clients were signing. Heck, clients were even paying. And as I sat there waiting for the arrival of my guests, I was feeling pretty good. I wouldn't have to go back to the old firm. Ever. Jones's and Associates and the old boys club could amuse themselves all they wanted. They'd been wrong. Not only could I survive in their 'man's world', I could kick ass in it.

So, yes, a celebration was in order.

Dylan was late, but not by a great deal. Mrs. P caught me checking my watch and craning my neck to check the side door. For once, she didn't say a thing. Just smiled her knowing smile as she tipped up her third draft.

But before my neck developed a permanent kink, Dylan did arrive. His eyes caught mine as he walked in the door. And so did his smile. We were both on top of the world.

I couldn't help but notice the dropped jaws on half the female (and quite a few of the male) patrons of the Six Shooter as he strolled in. But Dylan didn't turn a glance toward any of them as he walked toward our table and pulled out the chair reserved for him to take, the one on my right.

"Hey, Dix. Sorry I'm late."

I looked from his sparkling eyes to his forehead. The lump was gone, not so much as a bruise left. That war wound was officially behind us.

He plunked two packages on the table, and with a bent knuckle, knocked on the smallest one — a small white box. "Had to pick these up."

Well, I knew what the smallest package contained. The business cards.

I'd let Dylan go ahead and order them. He told me he'd finally come up with the perfect slogan. So perfect, he was embarrassed he'd not thought of it before. He'd asked me to trust him.

And I realized — not without a little panic — that I did.

So I'd let Dylan order the business cards, slogan and all, without my sign off.

I moved a hand to open the white box.

And he placed his hand over mine. "Not yet."

Well, hell! I was dying of curiosity.

With a casual signal to the server, Dylan ordered a beer.

"You … you going to sing tonight, Dylan?" the male waiter asked.

"Oh, yeah."

The server walked away quickly, shaking his head all the way to the bar.

"Is it time for presents?" Elizabeth Bee looked quickly at the two packages Dylan had placed in front of me.

I was surprised she even had time to notice what was happening on the other side of the table. She seemed pretty happily occupied herself as she sat sandwiched between Cal and Craig Presley. Under the amused, watchful (and increasingly glassy) eyes of their mother, the two boys were each paying close attention to Elizabeth, and the young woman was soaking it up. Dylan had raised a questioning eyebrow when I'd announced I had invited Elizabeth to our little gathering. But I had a feeling about this young lady. She was smart, confident, and could lie like a rug — all qualities that came in handy in this business. And I just plain liked her. I wanted to keep her around.

"Sure, it's time for presents," Mrs. P answered for me.

I pretended to look surprised. Pretended not to have known that the gang gathered here tonight had been sneaking behind my back arranging for a cake (yes, provided by the one and only Kenny Kent, who'd also be joining us later) and presents for me. But hey, I'm a hotshot private detective. I'm smart as they come. I have intuition about these things.

Plus I'd overheard Dylan on the phone with his mother discussing the details.

Mrs. P handed me a parcel — small and flat, wrapped in brown paper. "This is from the boys and me."

"Thanks Mrs. P," I said. "Hmm, wonder what it could be?"

I unwrapped it, read the cover of the CD, and showed it around. It was a copy of *Jailhouse Rock* by Elvis Himself. But superimposed over the head of the dancing black leather clad Elvis, was a picture of me. Not just any old picture, but the horrible mug shot they'd used in the paper.

Mrs. Presley cackled. "I thought it was perfect for you, Dix, considering how close you came to singing it!"

"Er, perfect doesn't describe it, Mrs. P. Thank you very much."

"Me next, me next." Elizabeth jumped from her seat — left hip banging into Craig, right hip banging into Cal *(oh, she was good)* as she scooted around the table to me. She handed me a small, red envelope. The familiar Bombay Spa logo was a dead giveaway in the top left hand corner. "It's a gift certificate," she gushed even before I had it open. "For a free massage."

Dylan *pffted* a spray of beer onto his chin.

"It's signed by Mrs. Pipps and everything!" Elizabeth said. "It cost me a whole week's worth of tips. Oh, Dix, I hope you'll come."

I had to smile. First of all, there was no way in hell this was Ms. Pipp's signature — too flowery, too large and loopy for such a crisp, efficient woman. Secondly, there was no way in hell the young Ms. Bee would be spending a week's worth of tips on anyone but well, the young Ms. Bee. Thirdly, in faint print at the bottom of the certificate it read 'display sample only'. Okay, now I had to smile widely. There was no way I would be going back to the Bombay Spa unless I had to for a case some time. Certainly not as Dix Dodd. And Elizabeth knew it.

"Thank you, Elizabeth. That was very kind of you."

"Well," Elizabeth said modestly. "It's not much, but it's the thought that counts."

"Damn right," Cal said.

"Double damn right," echoed Craig.

Moving quicker than I'd ever seen these guys move, both reached to pull out Elizabeth's chair as she returned to her seat. She smiled, sweetly, at them both, then slowly sat her butt down.

"This is from the judge and me, Dix." Rather than rise, Rochelle handed the package to Dylan who handed it to me.

Rochelle was famous for her gifts. This had to be something spectacular. More Rolling Stones tickets? I knew they were touring again! It was a small package — hey maybe it was an iPod.

I tore open the package and held up — "Underwear?"

Rochelle and Mrs. P roared with laughter, smacking their hands dramatically on the table as I held the black, sequined thong thingie and clenched my butt cheeks tighter just thinking about it.

"Well, someone's been talking," I said, looking accusatorily at Mrs. P.

"Sorry, honey. Cat's out of the bag. I cleaned your room, remember? It's not green and tassely like that other stuff, but it's kind of . . . you."

"Does Judge Stephanopoulos know about this?" I asked, trying — and failing miserably — to sound severe.

"Hell, she picked them out."

Again, Mrs. P and Rochelle cracked up. Actually, now half the bar was laughing out loud, as I slowly lowered the underwear back into the package.

"Not in a million years can I imagine myself in this," I confessed.

"I can," Dylan said, waggling his eyebrows.

Eye waggle notwithstanding, he wasn't laughing like the others. Smiling? Oh, yeah. But not laughing. Suddenly, it seemed like he'd moved closer, even though he hadn't changed positions. I could feel the warmth radiating off his thigh, so close to mine. And even though it still kind of scared me, I let myself feel him close. And it felt pretty darn okay. He pushed his other parcel toward me.

Okay, I was getting the drift of this little gathering. Theme related — mementos of my tryst with the Flashing Fashion Queen. So when I examined Dylan's parcel, feeling along the square edges and sharp corners, I half knew what it was before I had even opened the framed picture.

"Dirty picture, Dylan?"

"Fine art, Dix."

It was the front page of the yellow legal pad that I'd been using the day that Jeremy Poole, decked out in drag as Jennifer Weatherby, had walked into my office. The tight little circles were there. The web-footed duck tracks I'd drawn as a subconscious reaction to the Flashing Fashion Queen's use of the word "floozy". (Hey, that's just how my brain works. But say it fast five times yourself and see if it doesn't sound like something that might come out of an inebriated Donald Duck). But now another part of that well-doodled legal pad caught my attention. The ladders.

My eyes stung as I realized these were not ladders to nowhere that I'd been drawing. No, these open ended steps were ladders to *anywhere*.

"Ladies, and gentlemen," the DJ, said, "Six Shooters karaoke night begins! Any brave souls willing to open the night with a ballad? Maybe one of the ladies?"

The DJ looked hopefully around the room. Hopefully, then desperately, anywhere except where Dylan Foreman sat beside me.

"Guess that's my cue," Dylan said. "My public awaits."

I cringed. He really had no clue how bad he was. "Dylan why don't you —"

He stood, kissed me on the cheek. "You can open the cards now, Dix." He straightened, then made his way to the waiting microphone and the increasingly unhappy looking DJ, walking with the easy, confident swagger of a rock star.

"Put on my usual, Charlie," Dylan said to the DJ.

This wouldn't be pretty.

I opened the business card box, pulled one out of the neat row, and held it up for inspection, not unaware that Dylan was watching me closely as I did.

I read:

> *Dix Dodd, Private Investigator.*
> *There's power in the truth. Let Dix Dodd empower you.*

I looked to Dylan who, with a nod and raised eyebrows, sought my reaction. I raised my drink in a toast to him.

"To the future, Dix," he said in the microphone.

"To the future, Dylan," I replied. Though of course he couldn't hear me over the din of the crowd. But he smiled, so I knew he'd read my lips.

I smiled back.

Oh boy.

Thank you for investing the most valuable commodity you have — your time — in reading our book.
We hope we managed to make you laugh!

Word of mouth is the most powerful promotion any book can receive. If you enjoyed this book, please consider spreading the word. You can do this by recommending it to your friends, posting a review wherever you bought it, or reviewing it at Goodreads or other such places where readers gather, and mentioning it in social media.

Again, thank you!

N.L. Wilson
(aka Norah Wilson and Heather Doherty)

Continue reading for an excerpt from FAMILY JEWELS, the next Dix Dodd Mystery.

Other Dix Dodd Mysteries
Family Jewels (Book 2)
Death by Cuddle Club (Book 3)
Covering Her Assets (Book 4) — coming late 2013

Other books by the writing team of Wilson/Doherty
Young Adult/New Adult
The Summoning (Book 1 in the Gatekeepers Series)
Ashlyn's Radio
Comes the Night (Casters Series, Book 1)
Enter the Night (Casters Series, Book 2) — coming February 2013
Embrace the Night (Casters Series, Book 3) — coming Summer 2013
Forever the Night (Casters Series, Book 4) — coming Fall 2013
Read about the Casters series at http://castersthebooks.com

Available from Norah Wilson:
Romantic Suspense
Every Breath She Takes
Guarding Suzannah, *Book 1 in the Serve and Protect Series*
Saving Grace, *Book 2 in the Serve and Protect Series*
Protecting Paige, *Book 3 in the Serve and Protect Series*
Needing Nita, *a free novella in the Serve and Protect Series*
Paranormal Romance
The Merzetti Effect — A Vampire Romance (Book 1)
Nightfall — A Vampire Romance (Book 2)

About the Authors

NORAH WILSON is a Kindle best-selling author of romantic suspense and paranormal romance. She lives in Fredericton, New Brunswick, Canada, with her husband, two adult children, beloved Rotti-Lab mix Chloe, and kitty-come-lately Ruckus Virtute. (Yes, she has two names.)

HEATHER DOHERTY fell completely in love with writing while taking creative writing courses with Athabasca University. Motivated by her university success, and a life-long dream of becoming a novelist, she later enrolled in the Humber School for Writers. Her first literary novel was published in 2006. While still writing dark literary (as well as not-so-dark children's lit), she is beyond thrilled to be writing the Dix Dodd cozy mysteries and paranormal/horror with Norah. Heather lives in Fredericton, New Brunswick with her family.

Connect with Norah Online:
Twitter: http://twitter.com/norah_wilson
Facebook: http://www.facebook.com/NorahWilsonWrites
Goodreads: http://www.goodreads.com/
author/show/1361508.Norah_Wilson
Norah's Website: http://www.norahwilsonwrites.com
Email: norahwilsonwrites@gmail.com

Connect with Heather Online:
Facebook: http://www.facebook.com/heather.doherty.5
Email: heatherjaned@hotmail.com

Family Jewels

A Dix Dodd Mystery

Description

Dix Dodd rides again! This time, to rescue her mother.

A resident of a Florida retirement community, Katt Dodd is a person of interest in not only a rash of jewel thefts, but in the disappearance of her boyfriend, Frankie Morell. Dix, the handsome-as-sin Dylan, and the irrepressible (okay, rude) Mrs. P head to Florida to solve the case of the Family Jewels before Dix's mother gets railroaded.

Of course, hilarious hijinx ensue when Dix goes into the Wildoh Retirement Complex (Motto: We provide the Wild, you supply the Oh!) undercover as Katt's erotica-writing daughter. Multiply the fun when Dylan gets himself hired as the Wildoh's newest employee, a slightly dim-witted security-cum-maintenance man.

Excerpt

THINGS WERE LOOKING up.

Since solving the case of the Flashing Fashion Queen, business had been booming for this PI. Though I'm not one to rest on my laurels, no matter how enticing laurel-resting may seem, every once in a while I just had to put my feet up on my desk, link my hands behind my head and lean back in my chair to savor the feeling. And I only fell over the first time. Damn chair.

The publicity generated from that infamous case had drawn so much business our way, Dylan Foreman (PI apprentice extraordinaire and hot as hell to boot) and I were extremely busy. Crazy busy. Stagette-with-a-host-bar busy.

True, most of our work still involved digging up dirt on cheating spouses, but we'd been handed some other work in the last few months. We'd found missing relatives and missing poodles. Deadbeat dads and surprised beneficiaries. We'd been hired a few times to do background checks on potential employees for big corporations. Oh, and I got one call from a B-list celebrity client who had us chasing all over Southern Ontario looking for his 19-year-old son who'd gone AWOL with his dad's credit cards. Naturally, the client had wanted the kid found yesterday, but he wanted it done on the QT. Dear old Dad hadn't wanted to involve the police, nor his estranged wife, or her new hubby, or the kid's current girlfriend or last girlfriend, and holy hell, not the last girlfriend's older brother, and especially not the media. So we had to track the son of celebrity down the old-fashioned way — knocking on doors, asking the right, carefully-put questions of the right people. And, of course, by tapping into my trusty intuition. (Okay, granted, when chasing a 19-year-old male, maybe hitting the strip clubs didn't exactly take a lot of intuition, but we still had to pick the right clubs.)

Also, Dylan and I had done a fair amount of business locating lost loves for those who still pined away for them. Apparently, in some cases, absence does make the heart grow fonder. Or stupider. Lost loves are lost for a reason, in my humble opinion.

"You're too cynical, Dix," Dylan would tell me whenever one of those lost sweetheart cases came our way and I voiced this sentiment.

Maybe he was right. Maybe I do have a little bit of a chip on my shoulder when it comes to men. Or a big bit of a chip. Or a great big chunk of firewood. But, once burned ...

Suffice it to say that while Dylan still had a streak of the hopeless romantic in him, I did not. Nada. And at the agency, I was still the bearer of bad news to the clients on the way in the door, and Dylan was still the sympathetic ear and shoulder to cry on on their way out. But that was one of the things that made us so perfect together.

I mean, so perfect working together.

And the best part of our growing business since the case of the Flashing Fashion Queen — we moved the Dix Dodd PI Agency! Nothing fancy, nothing too pricey — just a step up from the bottom-of-the-barrel rental we had before. Fewer broken bottles in the parking lot. And a few blocks closer to my mother's condo where I lived while she was in Florida. (I still didn't have a condo of my own; things weren't booming quite that well yet.) We were still in Marport City, of course, with no plans to relocate to a bigger center. There was enough under-the-covers action for undercover work in this burg. We were just doing it from a better address now.

We'd bought ourselves some new equipment and furniture. Cozier seats in the waiting room, and my personal favorite, a high-tech honey of a coffee machine. That puppy not only ground the coffee beans and delivered the coffee into an insulated carafe that kept it fresh and hot for hours, but — oh, bliss! — it also delivered frothed milk in 10 seconds flat.

Dylan's indulgence? A voice changer. We spent the better part of an afternoon working the kinks out of that machine — calling people up and saying "Luke, this is your father" in our best Darth Vader voices. But who knows? A voice changer might come in handy some day for more than just freaking out the guy at the comic shop (especially with the caller ID we spoofed!).

We also got newer phones and computer telephone call recording software, which we run on our newly upgraded computers. And I had to place a whole new order for business cards. The ones that read

Dix Dodd, Private Investigator.
There's power in the truth. Let Dix Dodd empower you.

The business card had been Dylan's design. Dylan's words. I still get a little choked up when I think of it. His pursuit of the perfect motto for the agency had, by turns, driven me crazy and kept me sane during the Flashing Fashion Queen case when it looked like my future might involve stamping out license plates in a federal correctional facility for women. But enough of that.

We also bought a fancy copier/printer/fax machine that sounded like a tweety-bird when a fax came in, replacing a slow-as-death desktop printer, a perpetually moody copier, and an ancient fax machine that squealed like a cat in its death throes. I hated that old fax machine, and no matter where I was in the former office (hell, if I was in the bathroom down the hall) that squealing sound would make me cringe. I'm talking nails-on-a-chalkboard cringe. This new machine was top of the line! It had all the bells and whistles — and a gigantic paper tray I wouldn't have to fill again for six months. Not to mention virtually unlimited fax capability. No more 50-page memory limit.

Not that I'd ever gotten a fax that long. But if such a monster did come in — hell, if ten of them came in — I was now ready for it.

So it was a bit of a thrill when the fax tweeted these days and started punching out the pages faster than the speed of ... well, the speed of my old fax machine.

Usually I got that little thrill. But not always.

And definitely not the day I got the fax from Sheriff's Deputy Noel Almond of the Pinellas County Sheriff's Office. I groaned. "What is it this time, Mother? Skinny-dipping in the seniors' pool again? Prank calls to the local radio station saying you're the original Bat Girl?" Probably not the latter; Mom had already done that twice. For Pete's sake, she was seventy-one! Couldn't she knit something? And would it kill her to sit in a rocking chair once in a freakin' while?

I leaned back in my chair, blowing out an exasperated sigh. But as I looked over the pages, I sucked that sigh right back in on a gasp.

My mother, Katt Dodd, was under suspicion in the matter of the theft of stolen jewels. Lots of them. Tens of thousands of dollars' worth. That was bad. But it wasn't the worst of it. That first paragraph was just the opening jab. The second paragraph of Deputy Noel Almond's letter delivered the punch: mother was a person of interest in a man's disappearance.

That was the second time I fell over in my chair.

Which is exactly where I was when Dylan walked into the office — flat on my back, shoes up in the air, eyes pointed toward the ceiling, head sunk to the ears in the plush carpeting.

"Trying a new yoga position, Dix?"

My gaze shifted from the ceiling to Dylan's grinning face.

"No," I said. "I'm trying to figure out just what we should pack for Florida."

I accepted a hand up from Dylan, righted my chair, and handed him the faxed pages I still clutched. And watched his laughing eyes go serious.

Thus began the first time I'd ever pressed my PI skills into service for family. And not just any relative. My mother. My MOTHER!

Of course, I dubbed it the Case of the Family Jewels.

"What's a seven-letter word for *fire-rising bird*?" Mrs. Presley asked from the back seat.

"Phoenix, Mrs. P." Dylan answered, not missing a beat.

But I could have gotten that one. Not that it was a competition between Dylan and me. Much. Not that we were keeping score. Out loud.

"OE or EO for phoenix?" asked Mrs. Presley.

"OE," I shouted. That should count for something.

Dylan gave me a grinning sideways glance.

I bit down on a grin of my own.

A few months ago when we worked the Weatherby case, we'd fallen into bed together, literally. Not that we'd had sex. Well, not *sex* sex. Still, there'd been a little tension between us for a while after that. We were getting back to normal now, though. Well, as normal as it got when your male apprentice-slash-assistant is smart, sexy, tall and handsome, incredibly good-smelling and funny. Oh, and young. Did I mention young? All of 29.

"And a six-letter word for *highest point*? Fourth letter's an M."

"*Climax*," I shouted, half turning in the seat and oh-so-proud of myself.

"No," she said. "No, starts with an S ..."

"No fair. You didn't say —"

"*Summit!*" Dylan didn't turn in the seat. Which was good considering he was driving at the moment. He did, however, cast me a wicked grin.

"But I like your word, too."

"Try this one." The seat squeaked as Mrs. P shifted her position.

I heard the tapping of the pencil on the seat behind us. This time, I'd be ready. Dylan tightened his hands on the steering wheel beside me.

"Eight letters. *Close and often passionate relationship . . .*"

"*Cybersex!*"

Dylan snorted a laugh. "Could it be *intimate*, Mrs. P?" he said.

She looked down at the paper. "Why, yes . . . yes it could be *intimate*. Thanks, kids. I think I'm good for now."

"Anytime, Mrs. P."

For the record, I liked my answer better.

I sank back in my seat. The moment silence prevailed again, my mind drifted right back to that fateful fax from Deputy Almond that started this odyssey.

The fax had come in late yesterday afternoon, and we'd left early this morning, grabbing a drive-thru breakfast and supersizing our coffees. We'd swung by the office and picked up all the fancy new PI equipment we might need. Then we'd picked up Mrs. Jane Presley.

Of course, driving wasn't my first choice. I'd wanted to jump on the first flight. But Dylan, in that damnable voice of reason of his, had persuaded me we'd be better off driving. Mother wasn't in custody, so we didn't have to be in a hair-on-fire hurry. Plus it would give me the chance to return my mother's BMW, or Bimmer, as she called it. And as I, too, quickly learned to call it. She refused to let me drive the thing until I stopped calling it a *Beemer*, which apparently is reserved for BMW motorcycles.

Not that I was aching for a chance to lose the luxury ride, which had fallen into my possession the last time mother had been to Marport City. She'd hooked up with Frankie Morrell and decided to return to Florida with him, leaving me the use of the car.

At this point I should say I never liked Frankie. And I liked him even less now. Because Frankie was the one who'd gone missing — the one the police suspected Mother of . . . um . . . disappearing. (The letter hadn't said murder, but I could read between the lines.)

Anyway, Dylan had pointed out that: a) we needed our equipment, which would be easier to transport by car; b) we'd need wheels in Florida anyway; and c) we needed the think time.

He'd been right, of course.

So how'd we gather up Mrs. P? All too easily.

I'd swung by the Underhill Motel to ask if Cal or Craig — Mrs. Presley's hulking sons who helped her run the motel — could stop by the condo while I was away, just to check on things. Not that there was a cat to feed or plants to water. Cats didn't like me and only the hardiest of plants could survive my inattention. Hardy being plastic. Preferably self-dusting. But there had been a couple break-ins lately in my neighborhood. Mrs. P was all too happy to offer up her sons to watch the place. Plus I knew that Cal was still seeing Elizabeth Bee, now that she'd broken up with Craig, and I thought maybe they could use some alone time.

"Gee, I've never been to Florida, Dix," Mrs. P had said. "And I haven't had a vacation in years." She pulled a pen from her shirt pocket and a small notepad from the pocket of her skirt, and began making a list.

Leave meat pies for the boys.

Tell Cal none of that spicy pepperoni till I get back.

Pack the sunscreen.

"Well, it's going to be pretty hectic, Mrs. P and —"

She kept writing.

Get new underwear.

Pack the summer pajamas — not the footies.

"I've always wanted to go, but never got the chance. But you know, I might get there someday. Someday someone might do me a favor. You know, like I do favors for other folks. Especially friends in trouble. Not that I'd ever expect anything in return, no matter how much jeopardy I'd put myself in for their sakes."

"Okay, okay," I said. "You had me at 'jeopardy'. Would you like to come to Florida, Mrs. P?"

"Why how nice of you to ask!"

"See you at seven a.m.," I'd said, backing out of the Underhill, pushing the door open with my ass as I did.

"Make it six, Dix. I'm a morning person, you know. I'll be ready."

"Six it is, Mrs. P."

"Oh, and Dix …"

I stopped with one butt cheek out the door. "Yeah?"

"I had you at 'Gee'."

When Dylan and I had pulled in the next morning at *quarter* to six, Mrs. Presley was standing outside the hotel, her long-faced sons at her side, red suitcase at her feet, and tasseled sombrero in hand. She had four big pillows with her, and a blanket — not a bad idea really. Mrs. P liked her comforts. She wore sunglasses that covered half her face, the very same Roberto Cavallis she'd loaned me once for a disguise. Bermuda shorts floated below her knees, and the wildest Hawaiian shirt I'd ever seen covered her top half. And in the front pocket of that shirt, tucked in a pocket protector — pencil-pen-pencil. She always wore that at the front desk of the hotel.

"Thinking of doing some work, Mrs. P?" I'd asked, nodding to the shirt pocket.

She pulled a rolled-up magazine from her armpit and waved it at me. "I love crossword puzzles, Dix. Don't you?"

Actually, I hated crossword puzzles.

Craig looked like he was going to cry as he opened the door for his mother. Cal wasn't far from snuffing back a few wet ones himself. I looked at him.

"Allergies," he said. "Damn lilacs."

"It's October, Craig." I said. "Lilacs are long gone."

"Goddamn *super* lilacs then ... they're the worst."

The boys were 28, but still very much their mother's sons. They were a close-knit family, and in its own way, I thought that was pretty cool.

"Now, you call as soon as you get there," Craig said.

"Yeah, collect," Cal added. "And it doesn't matter how late you get in. You know we'll be waiting up for you."

She kissed them both goodbye, and we loaded up the car.

"Now if either of you two need me to navigate," she offered. "Just say so. I never sleep in a car."

"You know I'm on business, eh, Mrs. Presley?" I'd said as we started on the highway. "Dylan and I are going to be pretty busy with my mother's ... er ... trouble."

"Ah, Dix, we all got troubles," she said. "But don't worry, you won't even know you've brought me along."

That had been a few hundred miles and a few dozen crossword clues back.

It turned quiet in the back seat, and when I looked back, sombrero over face, head on pillow and blanket pulled up to her chin, Mrs. Presley was sound asleep.

Good. I needed some time to talk this over with Dylan.

It was still Dylan's turn at the wheel, so I put the faxed pages before me to look things over one more time. Not that I needed to look them over again. Pretty hard *not* to commit the words 'a person of interest in the disappearance of one Francis Morell' to memory, and the whole stealing jewels things didn't exactly escape my mind either.

But no way. No way in hell would my mother do any such thing. Okay, she wasn't a model citizen. But any trouble she'd gotten into had been 'fun trouble' and usually dealt with by a not-so-stiff warning from some cop trying to hide a smile. No one could be all that stern with Mrs. Katt Dodd, 71-year-old resident of the Wildoh Retirement Village, Complex B.

Dylan glanced over at me. "So what do you think?"

"Well, for starters, what I *know* is that my mother is innocent of all charges."

"And you know this because …?"

"Because she's my mother!" I snapped.

"Good. That's out of the way." Dylan nodded to affirm. "Now, you know she's innocent because …?"

With anyone else, I might have been offended. But with Dylan, not a chance. I knew his legally trained mind was doing just what it should be. Helping me build my case, helping me order my facts.

I sighed. "Well, let's look at this piece by piece, starting with the thefts. Mother's not what you'd call rich, but she's comfortable enough. The condo in Marport City, the Bimmer, the condo in Florida — she owns it all outright."

"Right, and all in use. Would she sell if she had to?"

I thought so. Didn't I? Mother owned the condo I lived in. She insisted on keeping it, wanted me to live there, and wouldn't take a cent of rent. Would she tell me if she needed me to move out so she could sell it? *Dammit, Mother.*

I dug my fingernails into my palm. "If she was having money trouble, she would come to me or Peaches Marie."

"You sure?"

Was I? My sister, Peaches Marie, was currently vacationing in Europe with her college professor girlfriend. She was certainly closer to Mom. They lived closer to each other and they were more alike. Peaches was just as carefree as Mother, just as irresponsible. I was the steady one. The serious one. Peaches was well-educated, with that coveted PhD in Philosophy, but I was the one doing better in business. I was the take-charge older sister. Surely if Mom was having financial problems, she'd tell me. We weren't close, but were we really so far away?"

I must have drifted too long into my thoughts for when Dylan spoke again, he startled me from them.

"What did your mother do, Dix? For a living?"

I shrugged. "She was our mother. Things were different in my day." Yes, as soon as I said the words I caught myself self. *My day.* As if he needed a reminder of the age difference between us. As if *I* did. I pressed on, before he could dwell on that too much. "When my mother was in her mid-twenties, she married my father, Peter Dodd. He was a musician and toured North America. So she quit her own job and followed him. Until I came along, that is. And Peaches two years later. Then we all followed him on tours when we were very young. I can remember some of it — the lights, the instruments, the other musicians. Me and Peaches running around the tables and playing under them while the band set up in empty clubs, preparing to play gigs that we would never see. But that didn't last. Dad took sick. All those smoky nightclubs finally got to him, and he had to quit touring. But music was all he knew."

"Bummer. How'd your family survive?"

"Dad knew music, and ... well, music knew him. Peter Dodd was famous in the club scene in Ontario and parts of Quebec. So if he didn't have the lungs to sing the songs, he still had the mind to write them. Eventually, his work got some attention. I can remember the first time one of his songs played on the radio. Then the first time one topped the R&B charts. And I remember the first thing Dad did was call the jewelers and order my mother a honking big diamond ring. God, she loved that diamond. Not the most practical expenditure, but Dad always said it was worth it. He was in a wheelchair then, but looked ten feet tall as he put that rock on Mother's hand. Mom saw that too. She dubbed it our lucky diamond. She said that nothing bad would ever happen to us because of that rock. She said it was magic. Things got better then. More secure. More songs on the radio. Big-name stars calling the house. It was pretty wild. Before Dad died, he'd tucked a bit away I know. Probably thinking it would last our mother a lifetime."

"But times changed," Dylan said. "Age isn't what it used to be. Lifetime isn't what it once was."

"No, but I'm sure Mother is doing fine. But even if she were having difficulties, Katt Dodd would not steal." I bit my lip. Of course she wouldn't steal. Not in a million years.

"Dix?"

"Yeah?"

"What did your mother do before she married your dad?"

I looked half hopefully at the approaching sign indicating food, gas and lodging available at the next exit. A fresh coffee sure would be nice. Of course, if we stopped, Mrs. P would wake up and restart our crossword contest. It was a long drive to Florida. Abandoning the idea of coffee, I shifted in my seat. "Mom was an entertainer, too."

"A singer?"

"Ahhh, no. But she did spend a lot of time on stage."

"Oh, you mean she was a dancer. I guess that's where you got those great get-away sticks, huh? Dancer's legs."

Okay, that shut me up. Since when had Dylan Foreman been checking out my legs? And how? I wasn't exactly a high heel and miniskirt kind of girl, although there had been a few times undercover ...

I cleared my throat. "No, not quite that kind of an entertainer, either. Mom was more of a ... well ... more of a show girl, if you know what I mean." When Dylan still looked in the dark, I continued. "She went on stage ... skimpy costumes ... feather boas ... applauding gentlemen ..."

I could practically see the wheels spinning in Dylan's mind. Just about there ...

"Holy shit!" His eyes saucered wide. "She was a peeler!"

"Dylan!" I clapped a shocked hand to my chest. "That's my *mother* you're talking about."

"Oh, shit. I'm sorry. But you said —" He relaxed when he saw my 'gotcha' smile. "Okay, you got me. So, what was she?"

"Magician's assistant," I supplied. "And from what I've heard, a damn good one. She worked mainly with this Lazlo Von Hootzeberger fellow. I gather more than a few other magicians tried to lure her away, but she stuck it out with Lazlo. She toured with him all over Europe and North America before she met and married my father."

"Did she ever teach you and your sister any magic tricks?"

I shifted back in my seat. That was a tricky question. And I wanted to answer slowly and get this right. And I really didn't want to try to explain it again. "You have to understand my mother. She doesn't do tricks. She does magic. That's what she always told us."

"Like the Harry Potter stuff?"

"Not quite. But somewhere along the line, she convinced herself that she really had the ability to do magic and not just sleight of hand. Don't get me wrong: she's perfectly sane. But she's ..."

"Fun?"

I had to smile. If I ever had the privilege of picking out business cards for Dylan Foreman, they'd read *Dylan Foreman — Diplomat*.

"That's a nice way to put it," I said dryly. "Mother always told us she despised tricks. But she loved the *real* magic in the world. We believed her as kids. And you know, I think she believed it too." I shook my head.

In the back seat, Mrs. P snorted in her sleep. (Well, it was loud and ripping so we'll go with 'snort.' I rolled down the window.)

I looked at Dylan, and unfastened my seatbelt. "Now's my chance."

"Dix, what the —"

I turned, leaned over the back of the seat and gently took the magazine from Mrs. Presley's sleep-loosened grip. I plunked myself back down in the seat beside Dylan. "Let's copy all the answers from the back for the next few puzzles." I began flipping through the pages. "That way, when she asks for a clue we can — wait a minute!"

"What?" Dylan flicked a glance at the book on my lap, then back to the road.

"These aren't crosswords." I snapped it closed. "It's a circle-a-word book. Mrs. Presley was just trying to get us to talk dirty."

From the back seat I thought I heard another sound. I turned around quickly to see a sweetly-sleeping, angelic Mrs. Presley.

Made in United States
Cleveland, OH
06 December 2024